A SINGLE LIGHT

PATRICIA LESLIE

ODYSSEY
BOOKS

Published by Odyssey Books in 2016

www.odysseybooks.com.au

A Cataloguing-in-Publication entry is available from the National Library of Australia

ISBN: 978-1-922200-46-4 (pbk)
ISBN: 978-1-922200-47-1 (ebook)

A Single Light is dedicated to Craig, Cheyne, Kalin and Toni,
who travel alongside me on this journey;
exploring this world with adventurous spirits, stories and song.
I love you dearly.

From the Journal of Malaik

Blasted rock and charcoaled tree trunks covered the earth. Dazed people, nearly as grey as the desiccated forest that surrounded them, stood in scattered clumps, the only signs of life in any direction. Some swayed, pain hunching their backs with its weight, crevassing their faces into unrecognisable masks. Others remained motionless, too traumatised from the cataclysmic event to respond to the destruction that had ripped away their beautiful world and replaced it with … this.

I stood amid the ruin of our village. Despair curdled my stomach and my heart clenched with grief. Heat seared my eyes. I forced them to stay open, to witness the disaster this handful of people had survived. Half-bodies and parts lay scattered as if some ravenous monster had made a mess of his meal.

A stray breeze swept a thin layer of white dust into the air and I had to fight back the urge to vomit. A few short leagues away, pristine columns of energy shot from earth to a churning sky. Clouds seemed to sizzle as lightning flashed. At their base, ash-streaked dirt formed twisting clouds.

The breeze turned into wind and whipped the twisters higher, fanning it out into a great storm of sand and death.

I closed my eyes and waited for the storm to pass. The sting of sand flayed my body until I thought I could stand no more; that surely I had no more skin left to lose. A whimpering moan reached me and I knew I had no choice. It had been ripped from us all as surely as the life had been rent from our brothers and sisters. The whimpering was joined by another until the cries harmonised with the roar of the storm and gave it a horrible lucidity like no other storm before it.

Some voices faltered and faded; others sang on in misery and grew in strength. The wind dropped. Debris settled. The remains of the dead were blown away or covered and the land was clean again. Almost. I forced my head to turn with a grinding wrench of muscles and joints.

Dunes had started to form; their surface reflected the torture of the clouds overhead. An entire jungle had vanished in one day, a new desert formed. A river, deep and clear, had become a cracked and pitted gash in the earth.

Nothing would grow here for a long time; nothing would walk or hunt, play or dance in this arid expanse. I thought I might cry at the loss of what was and could have been, but tears evaporated as soon as they formed and I was left with nothing but the fist around my heart.

I breathed deeply and turned again, to face the columns. Many had died—Alffür, Ryrdri, animals and birds, plants—yet I stood on the banks of a once great river with the swell of hard fought victory prickling my soul, transforming my grief into the heavy realisation that the Alffür would go on, that nothing lasted forever, not even death.

Shuffling in the sand, the barest touch in my thoughts, I knew I no longer stood alone.

'We cannot survive such a holocaust again.' Uday, one of the artisans, stood beside me. I hoped that she was not the only one left. We would need all the Makers we had left to stand any chance of rebuilding. Tears tracked macabre lines across her cheeks.

'No,' I answered. 'We cannot.'

Others grouped behind us, reaching out for physical and mental comfort.

'Why must they destroy?' someone asked.

'It is their nature,' I answered. 'As it is ours to deny them.'

'And what of hope?'

I stared straight ahead. One by one, the columns flickered and extinguished. The sky too settled, steel-blue roiling clouds softened to grey and started to break apart. A gentler, cooler breeze washed over them. I could feel the healing start. My mouth relaxed from tight grimace into the beginnings of a smile. Cracked lips stung anew and then they too healed.

'Hope comes,' I told them and pointed across the carcass of the river.

Figures walked toward the opposite bank, their numbers growing as each column died. A paltry number. I couldn't tear my eyes away. Paltry, but strong. I could sense that much.

'*A buffer between those who would destroy and those who would not.*' My voice was losing its raspiness of a few moments earlier.

'Who are they?' Uday asked.

'Harbingers of future hope.'

The last of our people crowded closer, a mix of curiosity, fear, blind faith ... and yes, hope.

The first figure to reach the far bank halted and looked around, the hint of a question in the set of her naked shoulders. She looked at me cautiously. I nodded and opened my hand to welcome her to my side.

The air around her appeared to shimmer, reflecting light as ripples in water. She vanished behind it.

I felt her surge toward me, sensed the exact moment a tiny spark of energy lit in the palm of my hand, and met her dark gaze as it reappeared in front of me. Our hands clasped together to signify a new, eternal bond.

'Who are they?' Whispers slid around the small group.

Others joined us.

'They are the Hunters,' I answered. 'And they are here to protect us all.'

———◆◇◆———

*Alffür and Bledray are the
Children of Miaheyyu:
Twins born of the same Mother
divided like the fork in a tree.
Different yet from the same roots
dug deep into Earth.
One branch strives toward the knowledge and
understanding of Miaheyyu;
that all life is precious.
The other branch has forgotten their roots
and foregone salvation in the quest for
physical satisfaction.*

— Journal of Malaik

———◆◇◆———

1

Bellbird, a town partway between Sydney and Wollongong, separated from the cliffs and white sand beaches of the Australian coast by a ridge, a valley, and a thick belt of rainforest.

Jacarandas dropped petals and leaves with each swish of their long branches. Blue, green and rotting brown litter carpeted cracked footpaths and choked gutters. A week had strolled by since the last broom-wielding resident had attempted the task of clearing the seasonal debris. In 1988, Bellbird had reached the finals of the Bicentennial Tidy Town Challenge. A gleaming brass plaque hung behind the counter of the local post office-newsagent-general store commemorating the fact. Things had gone downhill from there.

Flo Winthorpe was the first to notice something was not quite right, sitting in the front parlour, windows open to catch any trace of breeze that might happen past. She dozed in her rocker with her walking stick resting on her lap and her floral-print dress unbuttoned to catch the humid air circulated by the fan beside her. Flo had drifted off to the creak of the fan as it rotated back and forth, not quite easing the heat but enough that she could pretend she was somewhere far cooler than another dripping summer in Bellbird. Dreams of younger days filled her head: splashing around at the beach, a winter honeymoon in Katoomba, a family trek down to the snow … aged lips smiled and she opened her eyes.

The curtains billowed around her, their edges gliding over her face, coming dangerously close to the old fan. She started up, panicked and not quite awake, to turn the switch on the fan.

Her hand didn't make it anywhere near the little side table or the fan; trapped like a frail bird in the grip of a hungry cat's mouth, it flexed, fingers clawing, then stilled to hang over the rocker's armrest. The stench of urine and blood and flesh whirled around her body, vanishing in a greedy groan of hunger and satisfaction. The chair rocked forward and the walking stick slid to the floor, fell back and Flo's head rolled to the side, her face pale and peaceful.

A shift in the light; shadows moving across the room, horrendous and distorted, and then settling into a more recognisable form as they reached the windows. The curtains dropped as the window closed. The back door opened with a creak and the shadows left. Only the fan kept moving, blowing warm air and a trail of dust around the room, back and forth, back and forth …

'Sweets for my sweet?' The man's cheeks were as rosy as the woman's. 'I've saved the last for you.'

'My darling, you are too good to me,' the woman purred. 'And such a pretty little thing.' She stroked the hair of the teenager between them, who was trembling in the grip that held her prisoner.

A whimper of fear gurgled in the girl's throat. 'Please let me go. I won't tell, I promise.'

'Hear that, Moriah? She won't tell.'

'Oh, honey-child.' Moriah's hand cupped the girl's face, long fingers caressing the tear-stained cheeks. 'You'd do that for us?'

The girl nodded. 'P … promise.'

Moriah smiled and the girl started to relax. Hope lit her eyes, the last of the day's sunshine reflecting gold in their sparkling depths.

The woman leaned down close, ruby lips brushing the girl's ear as she spoke. 'I believe you,' she said. 'But we don't care if you tell or not. Your promise holds no value.'

Wet sniffling sobs blubbered from the girl's mouth. 'Pleeeease.'

'What does hold value, my love,' Moriah continued, 'is the fact that you actually mean it. So honest, so true. I like that. Close your eyes, love, and sleep. Think happy thoughts. Everything will turn out just fine.'

Moriah straightened and fixed a hard glare on her partner. 'Hold her.'

He nodded, still grinning, and adjusted his grip under the girl's arms. Her head bobbed down as sleep took her. Her body sagged in the man's tight embrace. 'Are you considering her plea?'

The look he received in reply was enough to make his smile widen in terrible pleasure. 'I didn't think so.' He changed his stance and lowered himself to the ground, the dreaming girl on top of him. 'Whenever you're ready.'

Red hair glowed in the fading light, Moriah's face cast into shadows by its perfect frame. Jedidiah's body responded to her beauty and the hunger that leaked from every pore of her being. He was hungry too, famished, but Moriah would feed and then share, and Jedidiah needed the Sharing more than the limp body in his arms. Every nerve tingled with longing as he watched Moriah descend to lay, full-bodied, the girl sandwiched between them. Her mouth, so passionate and fiery, opened wide until it gaped, hovering over the girl's face, breathing in the scent of fear and happiness, revelling in the taste of what was to come. He felt her desire as if it were his own and strained to watch both their faces.

The girl twitched and an innocent smile turned her lips up, a soft sigh of satisfaction escaping to invade Moriah's senses, taunting the ever-present hunger that had led the couple to this isolated town. Moriah caressed the soft lips, teasing them open, then dropped to cover slack lips and nose with yawing mouth and pull in the human essence she needed to survive.

The girl bucked, her dreams suddenly not so pleasant, as her soul fought the attack. But there was no recompense, no way to stop the consummation. Moriah ran a hand over the girl's brow and the struggle was over; pale wisps of mist curled from mouth and nose as she was released, face peaceful in the end when most were not. Perfect in death.

Jedidiah moaned, hunger filling him as the last traces of the girl's soul left her body. He let go his grip and reached for Moriah.

'Time to Share,' he said, voice husky. The dried-out form of the girl between them began to crumble, powder into fine white dust, no essence remained to sustain her shape.

The couple writhed in ecstasy. Moriah opened her mouth for

Jedidiah to plunder, wrapping her dusty legs around him, mounting him, back arched, hands clinging. Their bodies entwined, shimmered, lost their human shape, vanishing into shadow as they reached the pinnacle of their Sharing. They rode their union into the dark of night, lust fuelled by the souls of Bellbird, all gone now, all theirs. Then they parted, took human shape once more and stood to dust themselves off.

'And now to finish the Alffürian Guardian?'

Taking an Alffürian by surprise was not easy, yet they had done it. He and Moriah, together, seeping into the landscape, had contained their hunger though starvation riddled their every thought, and laid the trap that enabled free reign over the human population in this one small town.

'Yes, my love, and now the Guardian. But we must hurry. I feel the ghost of another. She will be here soon.'

'We are strong …'

Moriah put her fingers to Jedidiah 's lips. 'This one is stronger. She is not yet near, but I can feel her presence.'

Jedidiah acquiesced, as he always did and opened his mouth to suck on the tips of the fingers that sought to still his words. He couldn't bear to lose Moriah.

The couple walked through the dead town, arms embraced. Past the blank storefronts with their useless notices and into an alley as dark as the night itself. Only a single light left on to guide their way.

Hunters travel through the worlds of shadow and light.
They know intimately the grey spaces that lay between.
They perceive the Way and
the Path through
sight, sound, touch,
and the shared wisdom
of the Alffür.

— *Journal of Malaik*

2

'Whole town packs up and hides come sunset, lass. You won't find anything open this time of night. That's for sure.'

'I'm expected.'

The truck driver scratched his balding head and sniffed. 'Yeah. So you said. Still, ain't the friendliest of places to be visiting, especially at night. Reckon you're better off going on through to the Gong and backtracking in the morning.'

'Thanks for the lift.' The passenger door creaked as it opened. Cabin temperature went from a cool twenty-two to an uncomfortable thirty-five degrees and rising before the hitchhiker could get one foot out the door. 'I'll be fine.'

'Yeah, right. Famous last words.' The driver shrugged. 'Your funeral. Hurry up and shut the bloody door. Hot as the devil's fucking boudoir out there. Good luck. You'll be needing it.'

The hitchhiker hooked her hand through the strap of her army surplus duffel bag and jumped to the ground. She closed the cab door without another word and waved as the air horn sounded and the truck took off in a cloud of dust and spitting gravel. Headlights washed over dark houses and deserted footpaths. Jacarandas loomed briefly, their blue flowers greyed by the night; feathery leaves, ghosts of their daytime fragility.

Branches twisted and bent as the truck passed, litter twirling in mad eddies in the wake of rushing air. The rumble of the diesel engine echoed around the town, softening with the hiss of airbrakes as it paused at the T-intersection that ended the main drag, indicated a left turn and revved back into urgent life. It left behind a quiet town, baking in the hot summer night.

Midnight in Bellbird and not a creature stirred. Except the hitchhiker. She pulled the strap over her shoulder and looked to the right. A side street, narrow and cobbled, gaped between two storefronts;

tattered posters from sales long sold out and community meetings long adjourned hung from the walls; forgotten litter nestled along the narrow gutters. Further down, a pinpoint in the pitch that was night in Bellbird, a light shone.

Scuffed boots made barely a sound as they crossed the black strip of bitumen road, silenced by the truck's echo and the oppressive heat. The hitchhiker walked across the road and down the centre of the lane. Shadows pulled at her jeans and stroked the dull cotton of her T-shirt. Hidden dust streaked her bare arms and billowed around her with each step. Ramshackle fences, a mess of rusted wire, chipped paint and petrified gates lined the worn cobbles. Homes were blinded and blank. She ignored them and walked on toward the wedge of light, stopping at the line it formed between the known and unknown. She took a deep breath and let it out slow, easing herself into the waiting radiance. At once her whole form relaxed, hair—neat and pulled back in the cab of the truck—escaped its bonds to caress her shoulders, bright eyes became tired and lined, tight lips softened into a tanned face well-used to travelling at the whim of a hooked thumb and a driver's caprice.

The figure drooped, slumped in her boots, but smiling.

A single light was on.

And Lael was expected.

⸻

One foot into the alley and Lael knew she was too late. She widened her senses and found no trace of human life. Nothing. She held back from probing ahead, not wanting to know too soon that she was too late also for the friend who expected her. Stones crunched underfoot, each step she made a lonely echo of the one before, until she reached the open front gate and stopped. Accusing light spilled from the window, backlit the open door, creased the night shadows in the empty hall. Lael forced herself forward, kept her Knowing to herself and confronted the guilt and blame leeching from every house brick.

'Malaik?' The call went unannounced, kept inside her head by the jangling warnings that assailed her. She took a step through the doorway and the warnings faded. Whoever had been here was gone now. Danger had gone with them. Only horror and grief remained. She kept moving, boots quiet on the thick runner lining the hall, and turned into the only lit room.

Malaik was dead. Caught like a strangled rat in a trap, barbed-wire wrapped around his body, circling his head, digging into his throat, twisted around his wrists and waist, between his legs—tight against his groin—and down his legs. Lael sniffed the air, blood and pain and the faint scent of morning glory flowers, and … Lael sniffed again, belladonna. A lethal combination.

Lael stepped closer. Blood, black and thick, oozed from the cuts on Malaik's head. Still fresh. Lael clenched her fist. She'd been so close. Not more than an hour from finding her friend alive instead of dead. 'Your timing stinks, Lael.'

Malaik's face was dusted with the herbal concoction that would have made him vulnerable to attack, easy prey for the Bledray Ghouls that haunted the earth and eased their hunger on the essence of humanity. With the Guardian so weakened, the town had no chance—a veritable feast just waiting to be eaten.

Lael turned away from her friend's tortured face and wondered how the Ghouls could get so close as to kill a Guardian in his own home. It was unheard of. Out in the open, yes, definitely possible depending on the strength and hunger of the Ghoul. But not here, the very centre of his strength.

The light came from a desk lamp, its halogen globe sending streaks of whiteness across the room. Papers, disturbed and spread across desk, chair and floor, waited like tombstones for someone to read them. Lael moved the few steps to the desk, her boot treading on something hard that cracked under her weight. She shifted her foot and bent down.

Malaik's pen. Lael picked it up and gathered the papers, keen now to see what he had been writing when he was attacked. In some sort of reasonable order, some of the pages were numbered. Lael sat down and read. One page was a letter to someone in town, personal, not relevant. Another was the start of a journal.

Lael and the others, siblings born of fire and light, are our saviours. The First Hunters an extension of the Alffür born to fight our foe so that we can protect the fledgling race of Ryrdri …

He had sensed trouble was coming. Nothing tangible, an inkling, enough to be worried and that was all. The last page was addressed to Lael, though only the letter L at the top indicated to whom it was intended. Short and to the point, opposite to the florid turn of phrase he used in his journal. Lael read and re-read the words and frowned.

'Oh Malaik,' she said. She screwed the page into a ball and held it to her chest. Her friend's final words etched into memory.

The Bledray are gathering.

The Alffür and Bledray were decimated by the last full gathering.
The Rydri came close to extinction.
In the devastation of old civilisations, new arise.
The culture of Alffür
cannot be rebuilt,
but it can live on
in hidden ways within the culture of the Rydri.
We cannot,
we will not,
let them fall to our enemy.

— *Journal of Malaik*

3

Rick Hendry stared at himself in the mirror. He had a serious case of bedhead and frothy toothpaste dripping down his chin. Add the sleep-stained bloodshot eyes and the sallow skin and Rick reckoned he'd fit right in with the extras on Fright Night. He leaned over, spat into the sink and washed his hands and face. He grabbed the comb he kept next to the sink and by the time he was standing straight again he had managed to partially tame his matted hair. His eyes remained the same.

'I need sleep,' he told his reflection. 'Lots of it.' He threw the comb back down and walked out of the small bathroom. The corridor was still dark. Outside, daylight had been waiting for action a good two hours. Insomnia followed by hours of restless half-sleep and finally deep sleep, only minutes before his alarm clock rang, made him late. Bare feet padded on the polished wood floor, ankles cracked; in the kitchen the sound of the electric kettle boiling reached a crescendo then clicked into silence.

Rick walked in and, without bothering with any more light than the window provided, made coffee. A heaped spoonful of instant, a generous slurp of milk, mix together, pour in water, have a mouthful, go to the living room, get dressed—underwear, pants, socks, shoes and shirt—coffee, out the front door, tour of front yard—pick up the paper if it's there—finish coffee, back inside, dump the mug and paper on the table, and then back to the bathroom.

He was so bored with the whole routine he called his life, the stupid predictability, the numbness of his current existence. But he couldn't change, even though his doctor said he should. Couldn't even break the old habit of dressing in the living room so he didn't disturb anyone else. Anyone else had long since departed. He could dress and undress anywhere he damn well pleased, but every night it was the same. The next day's clothes laid out on the lounge, a ball of socks tucked into shoes, kettle left full and waiting to be switched on, clean mug sitting beside it. Predictable. Numb.

A car horn sounded and Rick hustled back out into the living room, grabbed his briefcase and coat, and rushed out the front door.

There was a time when he'd have had lunch made for him, fresh sandwiches or leftover lamb roast and some cake. But that was gone. Lunch would be whatever the nearest café was offering on special.

The door slammed as the horn blared again and Rick frowned at the driver. A headache was already starting in the crease between his eyes and for a moment he contemplated staying home, lounging in front of the television, going back to bed. The moment passed before he reached the car. The door opened and Gabriela Salek, sitting straight-backed in her seat, grinned at him. Her long hair was pulled back in its usual spiky bun and her smile gleamed with her everyday enthusiasm. Rick threw his briefcase and coat into the back of the beat-up sedan, and folded himself into the passenger seat already sweating in the heat of the morning.

'Morning, Rick. There's coffee and a muffin there for you. Don't knock it over.' Gabriela nodded at the cardboard tray perched on the console between the bucket seats.

Rick grunted and pulled the door shut. 'Hot enough to roast a dinner for fifty in here. Mind if I open a window?'

'Still not sleeping, huh?'

'Told you why,' Rick replied. He reached for the foam cup. The coffee smelled bitter and strong. *Probably no milk …* Rick peeled off the plastic lid and sighed. No milk. 'You got something against cows, Salek?'

Gabriela laughed, put the car into gear and pulled out into the dead street. Rick's house was one of few that shared the last road between the town and the bush, a narrow, gravelly track that had once been tamed with bitumen, now slowly succumbing to neglect. Each bump, each pothole was a reminder to Rick that it was probably time to let go and move on. Just like his neighbours and their falling down houses, the creviced footpaths, the dammed gutters. Nearly the whole street had packed up and moved on. Yet Rick stayed, alone with his memories and habits, and the other diehards of Everlene Street.

The car dropped into the biggest pothole in the road with a bang and screech of rubber and metal. Coffee sloshed over Rick's fingers and he swore. His headache started to pound. Soon as his own car was back on the road, he was driving himself and not picking anyone up. Gabriela leaned forward to adjust the radio volume from plain loud to blaring. *And no fucking radio either!*

Rick took the muffin out of its greasy paper bag and bit into it. Sugar stuck to his lips, hot and sweet. He licked his lips and washed the sticky flakes caught in his teeth down with coffee. 'That was good,' he said, looking around the car for the rest. Gabriela never bought just one. 'Any more?'

Gabriela reached behind the passenger seat and pulled out a family-size bag of baked goods. Their aroma filled the car. 'You know, breakfast's the most important meal of the day. Save some for me.'

Rick grunted in acquiescence as he shoved another muffin in his mouth and slurped the coffee. Another day, another artery-hardening breakfast. Rick could hardly wait to get to work.

Rick hung up on his wife with pleasure. He didn't know why she persisted on ringing him at the office, but once a month, regular as his morning routine, she rang to say hallo, remind him of his shortcomings, tell him she missed him and would he please ring her parents. They still liked him even though she did not and she was getting tired of answering their questions as to his wellbeing. Just as regular, he promised he would. Both knew he wouldn't, though really he should get it over with and then maybe she'd stop ringing. After all, who divorced whom here?

He pushed away from his desk with the horrible premonition she was going to ring back, and went to the kitchen for coffee. Bad coffee, but enough caffeine to get him over this hate thing he had going with his computer, and more than enough bitterness to take his mind off his ex-wife.

Rick perched his mug on the corner of his desk, sat down and stared at the computer. A print message beeped its failure at him.

Rick picked up his desk phone on the first ring, ex-wife forgotten and still swearing at the computer screen in front of him that now insisted his latest story was corrupted, could not be recovered, and the machine would need to reboot. What the fuck?

'What?'

'Is this Richard Hendry?'

'Who's this?'

'No names, please, Mr Hendry.'

'Yes, fuck you …' Hendry moved his mouse and clicked 'Yes'. The screen wavered as if in thought and went blue.

'I assure you this is a serious matter, sir. My career would be in considerable danger if it was known I was even making this call.'

'I was talking to my computer, not you. So why are you?'

'Pardon me?'

'Making this call. Why are you making this call?' Rick hit the side of the monitor. The screen was still blue. He really didn't have time for this. No time at all.

'It's in relation to a missing person …'

'I don't do missing persons. Ring the police.' Rick was about to hang up. The computer blinked at him, considering whether to reboot or crash altogether. He'd have to call IT and get them to go through the back-up tapes for him. It would take hours. His deadline was 3pm. He glanced at his watch. Shit! 2:45. No time. There was a frustrated sigh on the other end of the phone line and Rick paused. He didn't have to be a complete shit every minute of the day, did he?

'Look,' he said, tucking the receiver back under his chin. 'I can give you the phone number. But I really can't help you more than that. I'm a reporter, not …'

'I know that, Mr Hendry.' The sigh again and then silence.

'You still there?' Rick looked at his watch. 2:46. Fuck!

'Yes, Mr Hendry. I'm still here. I can't call the police … I am the police. And there's not just one missing person, there's at least eight.'

Rick froze mid-action, his hand a centimetre from slapping the monitor one more time. He diverted it to his top drawer and his mobile phone. 'Give me a number. I'll call you back.' Rick pressed the numbers on his mobile as they were spoken. 'Give me ten.' He hung up, pushed his chair back and left the office. On his desk, the computer screen came back to life, the document file had automatically recovered after all and awaited his attention. Click on 'Yes' to recover or 'Cancel' to open a new file. It stayed that way well past 3pm.

⁂

'So, what's going on?' Gabriela popped open a bottle of beer and walked from the drab kitchen into the drab living room. 'Rick? First you miss the deadline and then you disappear without telling anyone where you're going. Harry nearly had a fit. I swear I've never seen so many shades of purple on one man's face.' She sank into the typist's chair by Rick's vintage computer, sipped her beer and started going through the papers and old floppy disks that littered the table.

'This is a hunka junk, Hendry,' she called, picking up a 5-inch floppy and waving it in the air. 'These old things aren't good for anything but coasters. Rick?'

Gabriela lifted the beer bottle to her lips and spun around in the chair. What was the silly bastard up to? Far as Gabriela knew, Rick never used his wife's old computer, hated all computers with a passion. But here it was, all set up, connected to the Internet and printer spitting out pages faster than was healthy for a dot matrix machine that should have been retired at least ten years ago. She stopped spinning to lean over the printer and lift the paper. 'What the hell?'

'Gabriela?'

Beer sloshed from the bottle as Gabriela jumped in surprise.

'I didn't hear you come in. Help yourself to a beer …'

Gabriela gave the bottle a little shake and laughed. 'Yeah, already did. I … ah, knocked. What are you up to? I wouldn't have thought this computer would hook up to a modem.'

Rick shrugged. 'It does, though barely. I've got a lead on a new story. Nothing much.'

'Enough to blow off your deadline on the Fitzgerald story? Harry fired your arse … again. So are you going to let me in on this …' Gabriela turned back to the ream of paper folding in on itself behind the printer and scanned the top page, '… fairy story?'

'No.'

She flicked an incredulous expression at Rick and sat down on the chair to inspect the browser windows Rick had left open. 'Legends from the Crypt? The Undead in Georgia? X-files and the Real Truth? What are you into? Share with your partner.'

'Not ready to share yet, Gabi. I'll let you know when I am.' Rick stepped forward and closed the windows down. 'Staying for dinner? I usually get Chinese on Thursdays.'

Gabriela leaned back in the seat, swinging from side to side, eyes narrowed. Her lips thinned for a moment as she contemplated Rick's most recent abnormal behaviour. 'You're the original sceptic, Rick. What is it about ghosts and ghouls that's got you all worked up?'

'And you're the original sticky beak.'

'What can I say? I'm a reporter too. Comes with the job.'

'Dinner, or do you have to get home?'

'How could I resist?' Gabriela sighed and gave in. Rick could be tight as a clam when he wanted to be and pumping him for information wasn't the only reason she had decided to visit. Her old friend and mentor looked like shit. His job at the paper was on thinner ice than usual and, as far as Gabriela could tell, he had no life. The time had come to offer Rick Hendry a little guidance, even if she had to force-feed it to him.

Rick walked across to the telephone, flicked through the various letters, bills and other bits of paper tucked between it and the wall, and pulled out the home delivery menu for his favourite Chinese restaurant. 'Laksa sound good to you? And some beef chow mein?'

'Throw in some fried rice and I'm yours for life.'

'Bestill my beating heart,' Rick replied, picking up the receiver, and dialled the restaurant number. He placed the order, nodding and giving monosyllabic answers as it was read back to him. 'How long? Right, thanks.' And hung up.

'Forty minutes,' he told Gabriela. 'Another beer?'

'You bet. I'll get them.' Gabriela finished off what was left in her bottle as she walked into the kitchen to restock. She could hear Rick in the next room as he sat down on the wheelie chair and started typing. The printer had stopped while Rick had been placing the take-out order. Ghosts and ghouls! Gabriela shook her head. 'Who would have thought it?' She took two more beers from the refrigerator and turned to deposit her empty in the sink.

The bottle of sleeping pills sat in the same place they'd been last time she'd dropped in. Gabriela put down the beers and picked up the small jar to read the prescription. She remembered when Rick had finally gone to the doctor a month ago after putting up with stomach cramps and heartburn for most of the past year. Stress, the doctor had diagnosed. No big surprise there. Rick and stress had been bed partners for years. More than she could say for Rick and that wife of his. For a while there, the two had deserved each other. Rick's only saving grace in the union was that he didn't find solace in someone else's bed, whereas ex-wife, Meg, had done the rounds as fast as she could. Gabriela shuddered. *What a bitch!* She rattled the jar and read the label. The doctor had prescribed pills and several relaxation techniques, all of which Rick ignored. *Typical ...*

'Take two with food.' She ran her thumb around the sealed cap. 'Better not risk it.' The computer pinged, chair wheels scraped on the wooden floor. Gabriela put the pills back in their spot as the kitchen door swung open.

'You get lost?' Rick asked, walking in to open cupboard doors and pull out plates, drawers for knives and forks. 'Man could die of thirst waiting for those beers.'

Gabriela chuffed with laughter and removed the caps from both bottles. 'Just admiring the stunning view from the window.' She pointed a bottle toward the backyard. Leaves, dead twigs and lumps of rotting mulch covered the patchy lawn. A branch had fallen from one of the trees onto the tin roof of the garden shed in the back corner. The panel had dented, collected rain at some point, and now sported a thick coating of dried out lichen. Strings of the dead plant hung from the roof like a trail of tears. 'What do you call that? Rustic dereliction?'

Rick moved to stand beside Gabriela at the sink. 'More like the "winter of my discontent". You like it?'

'Yeah, it's got a kind of abandoned appeal. Bet it will look great underneath a few more layers of fungus.'

'Looks even better from the living room with the blinds drawn. You going to give me one of those?' Rick nudged a bottle.

'Sure. Sorry.' Gabriela turned away from the window. 'Did I tell you Annie's got a new job?'

'Didn't know she'd left the old one.'

'Well she has now. Onward and upward, you know. Managing some big fancy event in Canberra.'

Gabriela regaled Rick with the details while they waited for dinner, and then in between mouthfuls of the best Chinese food this side of Sydney. He started nodding off after the third beer and fell asleep after the fourth, head; fighting all the way to dreamland. She pulled off his shoes and covered him over with a blanket. The big talk would have to wait. Rick needed sleep more than lectures.

'Sweet dreams, Rick,' she said, turning off the lights. 'You need them.'

———◦◦◦———

I do recall our villages:
homes of wood and thatch that burned as easily as
everything else.
We had artisans who created all that we needed,
but no books and no technology.
Our history was in
our song and our crafts.

— *Journal of Malaik*

———◦◦◦———

4

Orange blobs of light spluttered in a dotted circle, tendrils of smoke lifted from the forest floor to mix together in a blueish haze of eucalyptus-scented dawn mist. Embers burst upward in mini explosions of heat and light dancing with the night before dropping down to extinguish on the dusty ground. Occasionally one landed on a stray piece of summer-dried grass and sizzle into life. Tiny spot fires were stomped out, their remains ground into the cleared earth even as a low voice beckoned the flames skyward in spirit if not in all their deadly glory.

Lael had released Malaik's body from its crude prison and dragged it through the house, out the back door, and deep into the forest that encroached on the unfenced backyard.

She'd climbed as high as she could in the hilly bushland, bent over nearly double to balance the weight of her friend with the slope of the hill, until the rainforest thinned and the cloudless sky was visible through the canopy of half-stripped eucalypts, tree ferns and giant flame lilies. Lael thought it a strange mix, like a twisted memory of what rainforests were meant to be like. At the top of the hill was a broad stand of Christmas bush, their bright red flowers black without the sun to light their flames. She found Malaik's circle here, in the middle, marked out with bushrock in the centre one flat, fire-darkened rock. She dropped to one knee and carefully laid out the body beside it, shifting it a little so Malaik took up the centre place then lifting it to rest on his chest.

Lael paused to catch her breath. Her friend was not heavy, even in death, but the walk had been long and grief-ridden. Long life did not make death any easier. A well of black despair stirred deep inside her and she choked back a broken sob. Long life made death harder, grief more painful. Lael pulled away from the body and walked back into the trees. She needed to fashion a broom to clear the ground of the highly flammable debris that covered it and collect leaves to light Malaik's way from this existence to the next. Lael was sweating hard by the time the circle had been prepared and dawn wasn't too far off. She had to hurry before the sun arrived and the secret pathways vanished with the night.

Squatting to light each bunch of leaves with a match, Lael started a verse that hadn't passed her lips in many years; an Alffür chant to the dead. 'Fire of the heart, water of life, air of the senses, earth of the bone …'

With the last pile lit, she gathered the bushrocks and used them to build a cairn around the fire rock on Malaik's chest.

'You have been called from the place of your dwelling …'

A final handful of leaves were left on the firerock, a last match lit.

'May blessed soul-friends guide you …'

The match flared to life, dropped from Lael's hand and set the cairn afire.

'May the Gatherer of Souls call you …'

Lael sat down, face smeared with dirt and tears, hair ragged, shirt stained with sweat, and she crossed her legs at Malaik's head. His white face, eyes open to see the Way, was blotched with black flakes of blood and torn in places where the barbed-wire had scored deep gouges in the dead flesh. The iron of the wire had finished off what the poison had started and prevented any hope of rebirth.

Malaik was lost to her forever and the pain that loss caused scalded every muscle and fibre, every molecule of Lael's being. She closed her eyes as the heat from the cairn reached her. Flames burst into the sky, burning brighter as they fed on first leaves, then rock. Lael spread her hands out, palms down. White light radiated downward, cleaned the blood and gore from Malaik's face, and spread along neck to shoulders, down arms, over chest and on to feet. His whole body glowed.

'May the homeward path rise under your feet …'

Lael leaned forward to press her lips on Malaik's forehead in final farewell.

'And lead you gladly home.'

Lael raised her hands skyward and released the power she held into the night. The fire snapped and stretched, a sliver of moonlight reaching to the heavens and beyond. Thunder boomed, a shower of leaves rained over the circle as rushing wind roared its way through the forest and up the hill, catching the light and the fire, twisting and twirling until both were gone, carried on their way to eternity in the Land of the Living. The last tail of wind swished around the clearing, cold and sharp, swept away the leaves and doused the last struggling flame.

Lael dropped her arms, chilled to the bone, though her eyes still felt the fire and her hands tingled. She lowered her head and her body shimmered, caught for a moment between shadow and light, hard reality and formless void. Before her, only the fire rock remained, fully blackened now and cracked down the middle sitting at the centre of a perfect circle of scorched earth. The cairn was gone. Malaik was gone. Lael clenched her fingers into hard fists, her body solid once more, hunched over and shaking with the force of her anguish.

She cried until she ached all over and her head throbbed, then she lay down in the dirt, pulled her knees up to her chest and slept.

⁘

Rick thought he'd been here once before, though he wasn't sure where *here* was. Last time it was daytime and he could see for miles, a dark blue ocean and white waves, grey cliffs overhung with stunted bushes that smelled vaguely of his mother's medicine cabinet. Yellow blossoms tumbling through valleys of red rock, beautiful birdcalls cut through with raucous laughter, blue sky, bigger than he'd ever seen. All that was lost in the dark, but he knew it was the same place. He looked down and saw hands moving, picking up leaves and twigs, placing them beside glistening slabs of stone, weaving them into strange shapes. He could feel the hands work, the muscles stretch and contract, the fingertips scraping over ground. The leaves felt brittle and cracked easily, the smell of eucalyptus wafted up to his nose.

But they weren't his hands. And the brief glimpses of legs and booted feet, that felt like his legs and feet, weren't his either. He'd never owned boots so scuffed or worn jeans so faded and thin. There was no ring on his left hand, no watch on his wrist. The sections of arm he could see were tanned darker than he'd ever been, even after a two-week honeymoon spent lounging and fucking on a Caribbean beach. These hands were rough, the nails short and dirty from digging and collecting leaves. 'And feminine', if the long natural elegance of the fingers was anything to go by.

These hands had pulled a corpse down from a wall, unwrapped wire from a tortured body. They'd dragged the body through an unfamiliar hall, out into an unfamiliar yard and then gently lifted and carried the body into thick bush. Rick had stared at the path ahead, felt loose rocks shift beneath his feet, the sting of low hanging branches whip his face. He hadn't recognised a single tree or landmark, but he knew where he was going, to the circle.

Rick didn't want to watch anymore, yet he couldn't turn away. The hands that weren't his spread out and tingled with electricity that came from within. Rick knew there was not a socket or circuit for miles. He clenched against himself as the current travelled along nerve cells, his ears buzzed, his tongue stuck to the roof of his mouth. It built into a fireball held in only by will. Words muttered. Rick's lips moved with the sounds, not understanding the strange utterings but feeling the pain behind them, feeling the cold press of dead flesh against live.

Then everything burst into white light. Rick flinched, eyes burning and chest heaving. He hurt inside and out. Vertigo assailed him and Rick could see stars, glittering jewels in a vast black sky. Threads of gold and silver wavered in the breeze, wrapping around his arms and legs, lines that held him like a balloon given its freedom. He wanted to fly, to embrace the stars that swept through and around him. He was love, he was harmony, and he was free. Threads of light became an apparition with long hair and sleeping eyes; a face with soft lips that mumbled a name. His name, he thought, though he couldn't be sure.

The eyes opened, blue stars shone out and suddenly he could see his own face, stunned, gaunt … transparent. He saw his lips move, whisper a word; saw his hand reach out, looked down and saw the stranger's hand take his. The grasp was warm, comfortable, but barely there, and then he was fading and the stranger was fading. Stars rushed by, the contact was lost and Rick felt bereft. He landed with a thud, every bone in his body rattling.

He opened his eyes and saw a broken rock.

'About time,' he heard.

'Who are you?' Was he talking to himself?

'You'll know soon enough.'

'I'm dreaming.'

'Are you? I'll be home soon.'

'Where's home?'

There was no answer for some time and Rick thought that perhaps the dream was over. Yet he could still feel the hard ground beneath him, dirt crunched against the skin of his cheeks. A stone or a stick dug into his hip and he squirmed to dislodge it. His chest filled with air and slowly released. A hand reached out and touched his shoulder.

'Wherever you are.'

Rick woke with a shock, those last words echoing in his ears, sounding loud in the quiet room. He looked around, half-expecting to see the stranger in the room, confused that he was on the lounge and not lying in the dirt in the middle of the bush. He twisted and stretched out the kinks in his neck and back. What the fuck was he doing on the lounge? He swung his legs over the edge of the cushions and sat up. His mouth felt dry and furry, his skin hot and itchy.

'Water.' Rick got up and walked out to the kitchen. Cupping his hand under the cold water tap, he drank deeply, splashing his face when finished and wiping his wet hands down his neck. He pushed his messy hair from his face, slicking it back with water. Mind groggy and dream already fading, Rick decided he needed a shower more than anything else. Ten minutes later, with a towel wrapped around his waist, he walked out to the living room. No clothes. He scratched his head and moved on to the kitchen. Rick blinked and covered his eyes with his hand when he flicked the light switch in the dark room. Squinting against the brightness, he reached for the kettle. Empty. And no cup waiting.

'What the hell?' Then he noticed the number of empty beer bottles and Chinese food containers in the sink. Gabi had helped him get pleasantly buzzed and talked him into insensibility. The last thing Rick remembered was listening to her recount, yet again, the scene in the boss's office the day before and something about her partner moving interstate. Funny arrangement, that relationship, but still better than his had ever been by a long shot. He'd been tireder than usual, he was always tired, but he never slept. When he did he went to that place that felt like home and scared the hell out of him at the same time. It hurt to go there and it hurt to leave.

Of course there would be no clothes out or water in the kettle. He'd slept on the lounge. He filled the kettle and put it on to boil, pulled a clean cup from the cupboard and slammed the door closed. 'Bloody pain in the neck. My whole day'll go to shit now!' He stormed back to his bedroom to find clothes and get dressed.

Miaheyyu is the breath of life.
Without her kiss,
life cannot exist.
She is that which hides
deep within us;
the compulsion to create,
the inner eye that recognises true beauty and wonder,
the part of us all that searches for meaning in the mundane.
For all life is mundane.
We do what we need to survive, individually and as a community.
Without and within,
our Selves crave connection with Miaheyyu,
some acknowledge this yearning and follow its path.
Most do not.

— Journal of Malaik

5

Anthony Baglio wasn't sure what to do and it scared the shit out of him. He, who always knew exactly where he was going to place his next step, what he was doing from one day to another, one year to another, had no idea what each new moment might bring. He liked everything organised in neat, tidy compartments, planned and listed; it was what made him a good agent, it was who he was. Flexibility was acceptable, and even the occasional bout of spontaneity—he planned for inconsequentials. But lately it seemed that his days were filled with big jumbles of unplanned inconsequentials, and he hated it.

The latest had him on a plane from Sydney to Perth following up on yet another figment of information. Halfway through the flight and intent on forgetting the turmoil of his life for even a short time, Anthony had picked up the folded newspaper left tucked behind the vomit bag and the glossy *Inflight* magazine by a previous traveller. He'd read with bored interest until he came to page five and the exposé written by Richard Hendry. The reporter had given the local police a harsh dressing down after investigations had revealed the mismanaged and vaguely corrupt handling of a suspect kidnapping case.

Anthony caught the by-line in much the same way one might catch mud in the eye—unexpected and hard to miss. Details were insignificant and Anthony had forgotten most of the article by the time he'd disembarked from the plane, turned on his mobile phone and dialled the number for the *Sydney Tribunal* ... and received his first taste of Hendry temper.

The man was an arsehole all right, but an arsehole who might be just what he needed.

The second taste came as they dawdled along the corridors of the Australian Museum in College Street, Sydney. Their combined interest apparently engrossed in the displays yet punctuated by fierce whispers. Hendry accused Baglio of being a plant to obtain the names of his sources inside the police force. Baglio accused Hendry of being a pain in the arse stubborn prick who had no idea what was going on in the big world outside of the *Sydney Tribunal's* limited print run.

'Right … we've got that all sorted out,' Hendry had said, red-faced, scowling and hunched over to address his words to Baglio and no one else. 'Now cut to the chase and tell me why you're dragging my butt all over the museum?'

So, beneath the upraised trunk of a hairy mammoth trumpeting fury and pain at the dire wolf that nipped at its feet, Anthony had cut. 'As near as I can tell, it started a month ago …'

And he was pretty sure he'd done the right thing, but he couldn't be one hundred per cent certain. Anthony reached for the bottle of pure malt resting on his bedside table and refilled his glass. He caught a distorted reflection of himself in the glass and frowned.

'Life's a gamble, my friends,' he told both bottle and glass, raising them to the dark sky outside his hotel window. The window threw back the image of mussed black hair going grey at the temples and in need of a cut, and a gaunt face behind the day's growth of beard; too many hours in front of his laptop and reading obscure texts, too many flights from one side of the country to another. His fellow officers stuck to their theories of runaway lovers, adventure-addicted young men and bored housewives, and had begun to call him 'The Spook'. Anthony knew better. Day after day of 'Mulder moments' told him so. There was something out there taking people from their homes and leaving almost no clues or recognisable evidence, and he planned to find out who or what that something was.

Anthony swung his feet from the bed, took a sip of the expensive Scotch whisky, and stood up. Rest time was over. In the morning he would visit the residence of the latest person to mysteriously disappear, Miss Elizabeth Barton, a housebound invalid from Sydney's south. Right now he had databases to comb and reports to download. By the time he drove his rental vehicle past the muddy wetlands and oil refineries of Kurnell and pulled up at Miss Barton's empty home, he would have a list of all reported missing persons in the state of New South Wales for the past two weeks.

Anthony walked across the small room to the narrow desk and his laptop. He would also have an update on any supernatural and just plain weird occurrences in the Sydney area courtesy of the online forum he had started two weeks ago in Candle Bay, Western Australia.

All the friends and families of the missing people he was investigating mentioned ghosts. It seemed to be what the human mind returned to, ghosts and magic. Anthony had paid it scant attention, until Candle Bay, and the way the family of three brothers, who'd been missing a week, rolled their eyes and crossed the breasts.

'Spirits,' they'd moaned. 'The spirits are hungry.' They told whispered stories of beasts that fed off humans like vampires, beasts that could only be defeated by calling on more of their kind.

'They kill each other,' he'd been told. Then they'd stood in a circle, hands joined and started to sing in a language Anthony had never heard, while the mother of the three knelt in the centre, softly weeping as she nicked her wrist with a knife and fed her blood to the earth.

⎯⎯⎯◦◦◦⎯⎯⎯

The two-storey house sat forlorn and quiet in the crook of Bentley Place, a short street filled with similar houses and similar yards. Anthony could hardly contain himself. He actually had a lead. Miss Barton hadn't walked without aid in over ten years. Six years ago, neighbours had helped her convert the downstairs area of her home into suitable, if cramped, living space. Her whole life was contained in three small rooms. Anthony had walked through them, nose itching at the layers of dust that coated the old-fashioned bric-a-brac laden furniture, looking at family photos, lifting throw-rugs with his pen, inspecting the details of one woman's lifetime.

'Wasn't usually this dusty,' the neighbour had stated. 'Lizzy had a regular cleaning service around once a week, twice if she was expecting visitors.

A day-bed in the corner sat neatly made, unslept in; chair beside it, half-pushed out from a side-table, as if someone had been sitting there and stood without pushing it back under. On the table, a book, open and upside down, pages spread wide and waiting; a teacup mostly full, the dark brown liquid coated with a layer of dust slowly turning to slime.

They went upstairs to the empty rooms.

'Her boy's room,' the neighbour offered as Anthony walked into the first. 'His name was Peter. Died in the same car crash that crippled his mother. Horrible it was. They started fixing that stretch of road after that, what good it did poor Peter …'

Anthony nodded and left dead Peter's room to enter what was once the main bedroom. A mirrored built-in wardrobe lined one wall. Indentations from a large, heavy bed marked the carpet.

'Lizzy had one of those four-poster beds.' The neighbour it seemed was a font of information about Miss Barton.

'Was there ever a Mr Barton?'

'Lizzy and her husband divorced when Peter was still a toddler. Barton's her maiden name. His name was "that bastard, Frank". I never met him, thank God.' The neighbour chuckled. Then she'd given Anthony the first piece of clear evidence that a second party was involved with the disappearances. Looking at the open blinds of the bedroom window, she said, 'You know she never comes up here anymore, could barely make her way around downstairs, let alone haul herself up here, but Joe—that's my husband—said he'd seen a light on. Just the one, this one. He was taking the dog out for its evening business before we all went to bed. Silly dog's scared of the night and sleeps inside. Or he wouldn't have noticed. Told me straight off and I came out to look but it was off by then.'

'Miss Barton …?' Anthony had started to say, but was silenced by the neighbour's scowl. 'Don't be an idiot,' that look told him and Anthony closed his mouth. Then he looked down and noticed that right where the bed and six years of dust should have been, was a patch of clean carpet. 'Did you tell the police about this, Mrs McFarlane?'

'Nope, forgot all about it until just then. And it was the next day they reckon she up and ghosted out of here.'

Anthony looked at the chatty Mrs McFarlane. 'Ghosted?'

'Sure, how else could she have gone anywhere without anyone knowing? We mind each other in this street, you know. One big family on Bentley.'

The local police didn't know as much as Mrs McFarlane. APBs had gone out; hospitals, CityRail, bus and taxi companies notified; grainy photographs published in all the newspapers; and missing person bulletins tacked on to radio and television broadcasts. But Elizabeth Barton had been gone a week and already the reports had dropped in importance, shuffled behind wars and famines, bizarre events in other countries, and a grisly murder that had half the southern Sydney area scared to open their front doors at night.

Anthony accepted a mug of hot tea and pushed the McFarlane's amorous dog away from his leg one more time. He stole a surreptitious glance at the clock above the fireplace mantel and hid a grimace from his effusive hostess. Odd place for a clock but the face was painted with a lakeside scene while wooden ducks ticked away the seconds. An immeasurable gap between what Mrs McFarlane considered art and what Anthony Baglio would even let past the front door. Rick Hendry was due any minute and, while he would prefer to be sitting in his car, Anthony had been drawn into listening to Mrs McFarlane's chatter.

'… And you probably didn't notice that funny smell. Stronger than usual and Lizzy's a stickler for getting rid of smells. She would have sprayed the room before she'd leave it smelling like that, liked lavender the best, sometimes gardenia. Takes all the right precautions, ever so careful about cleaning up after herself. Not that there was anything to clean up as such, I checked, but she'd never leave a smell around.' Mrs McFarlane scooped the dog up in a firm grip and sat down opposite Anthony, scratching her pet's head and playing with its ears. 'Leave poor Mr Baglio alone now Pooky. Daddy catches you doing that stuff and it'll be a trip to the vets for fixing'

'Smell?' Anthony hadn't noticed anything in particular. A faint odour perhaps but homes often had kept the smells of their owners and each one was different. A touch of mustiness was to be expected; it had been closed up for a number of days. He lifted the mug to his lips and blew at the steam pouring off the hot liquid.

Mrs McFarlane caught the grimace this time and smiled, amused at her guest's trace of discomfit. 'Urine, pee, wee wee … piss!' She nuzzled her nose against Pooky's ear and made a low crooning sound. 'And a trace of shit too, but nothing there but the smell.'

Anthony braved a sip of the tea. Peppermint and steam wafted up his nose, scalded his tongue and throat. He coughed and put the mug down before he could burn himself further.

'Lizzy got me onto that peppermint tea. Good for the digestion and sinuses. The oil itself will rip whatever's clogging up your system right out.'

Anthony's head was buzzing, eyes watering, and he wondered if he'd ever be able to taste anything again. Was that the sound of a car pulling up outside? Anthony peered out the front window in time to see a blue Suzuki idling past. He stood quickly, determined to leave whether the blue was Hendry or not.

'I believe my associate has just arrived, Mrs McFarlane. Time for me to get back to work. Thank you for your help, and the tea, delightful.' He buttoned his jacket, ignored the layer of white dog hair on his trouser leg and retrieved his briefcase from the hardback chair near the front door.

'You're welcome, Mr Baglio. It's always nice having visitors, nicer to know someone's still taking Lizzy's vanishing serious too. Joe will be home about five if you want to talk to him yourself. You and your friend are welcome to stay for tea as well. We eat at six before our shows start. Gives us time to sneak in a bowl of ice-cream before bedtime too.'

'I'm afraid if we want to get moving on this case we'll have to decline your offer. Not much time for socialising at the moment, but I will indeed contact your husband if I have any further questions.' Anthony stepped out the doorway, with Mrs McFarlane right behind him. 'Thank you once again.'

Mrs McFarlane put Pooky down on the path, disappointed that her visitor failed to pat the dog goodbye. The pampered pooch sniffed Anthony's shoes and pressed himself against his leg. 'Look at that. Pooky wants you to stay. Isn't that sweet?'

Anthony turned away and began walking down the path and directly across the road where Rick Hendry was unfolding himself from the front seat of a brilliant blue Hyundai Getz. He hooked a camera over his shoulder and straightened with a groan, obviously glad to be out of the too-small car. Anthony let his gaze travel along the car's perfect finish and back to Hendry.

'It's a loaner. Belongs to one of the interns at the paper. Mine's at the garage.' Rick was embarrassed. His Land Rover could squash the Hyundai like a bug, if it was working. No one at the office was prepared to lend him a vehicle, except the intern, new and star struck.

'Pretty blue … and compact.' Anthony grinned at the reporter's embarrassment. Pooky barked from inside his owner's house and the grin dropped. 'Let's get inside before that damned dog comes back outside. It has an unhealthy infatuation with Armani and Italian leather. My social life might be non-existent but I'm not that hard up for company.'

Rick's turn to grin now and he did, right up until he walked into Mrs Barton's front room and Anthony told him about the smell and the dust, and the upstairs bedroom. Rick had paled at that point, eyes watering, but took photos wherever Anthony pointed and then some. Anthony pulled out a mini-digital camera from his pocket to take some as well. They collected samples of the dust, 'borrowed' the cushion from the chair Mrs Barton had been sitting on to drink her tea and tossed about several theories on what the frail old lady might have done to make herself so thoroughly disappear.

Not a single theory was correct.

6

Jamie Morell looked from the slide under her microscope to her computer screen to the pages of scrawled notes that covered the remaining spaces of her workbench. And frowned. She hadn't seen such convincing evidence of irregular blood type since … well, since ever. Others had reported the anomaly and named it, but this was the only time she'd come across it herself.

'T' type blood was virtually unknown across the majority of the world's medical practitioners and biological scientists, and pretty much laughed off as someone's idea of a joke. If she hadn't seen the anomaly for herself and started asking questions, the mystery would have remained unknown. And if the blood hadn't come from a brutally murdered woman then even those initial questions would have been unasked. Jamie jotted down a few extra notes and reached for her mobile phone. This was right up Ben's alley and, if the scant information available was any sign, her old friend was probably the only one who might know where to look next, somewhere outside the world of scientific research and into the realm of superstition and legend.

'Ben? It's Jamie … yeah, good. Listen, I've got something you might be interested in … new case … hot as the dev … can't talk about it over the phone … definitely … no sooner? Okay, come in the back door … see you then.'

Jamie disconnected the call and dropped her phone into her lab coat pocket. Ben wouldn't be here today. In the meantime, she'd follow up on what the other lab techs had. Right now she just had time to duck next door and get copies of the autopsy report and any photos. Ben would want to view the body too. That might be harder to swing. Jamie put on her best serious face, tucked a stray hair behind her ear, picked up a clipboard and some folders, and walked out of the lab. She'd need to check if anyone had claimed the body. Maybe she could get Ben in as a concerned uncle. Kelly in reception owed her a few favours; she'd get her to arrange the sign-in papers.

Jamie ignored the techies she passed, most not paying her any attention either, used to her distracted air and tendency to move about while her mind was lost deep in thought. She walked straight into the autopsy room and over to the files, sorting through them as she always did, matching up her pathology reports with case numbers and clipping the papers together in neat bundles. The coroner walked in and out, mumbling a greeting. A secretary came in and left a bundle of transcription papers and tapes on the bench next to the files. She left without a word. Jamie finished filing, signed a worksheet stating that the blood work for cases 53095AA3-1 and 53095AA-7 were completed, and pulled those sheets from her clipboard to give to the coroner's secretary. Leaving the filing cabinet drawer open, Jamie copied her worksheets and several other papers on the photocopier in the corner. She returned the papers to the cabinet, closed the drawer and left, via the secretary, to return to the privacy of her own lab to eat lunch and read the autopsy report on the Jane Doe with the mysterious blood type 'T'.

'What do you think?' Jamie crossed her bare feet on the edge of the coffee table in her living room and yawned. Ben had woken her with an apologetic phone call at 5.30am and knocked on her door five minutes after that.

'Haven't seen anything quite like it.' Ben stared at picture after picture, his greying head bent low over the photographs. He stopped at one portrait of a face as white as stone, dark eyes lifeless beneath a crown of twisted wire. 'She have a name yet?'

'She came in with no identity. No missing person reports. Police put a composite picture of her on the six o'clock news last night and not a bite.'

'What about where she was found? Anything on that?'

Jamie shook her head. 'Scuff marks around her body but no

footprints and the only out of the ordinary evidence found, beside the wire corset, was a fine white powder. I'm waiting on the chemical analysis for that, but it's not why I called you.'

Ben dropped the photos on the laminate tabletop and took the slim file Jamie pushed across to him. 'What's this?'

'Blood test results. They're done as a matter of course to determine type and possible genotypes.'

'This says inconclusive.' Ben frowned and looked at Jamie. 'How is that possible?'

'Turn the page … I repeated the tests five times and came up with the same result for each. It's not possible. So I hit the Internet and did a search on abnormalities …'

'And? This printout is on animal blood types. You're not going to tell me she's a werewolf, are you?' Ben's lips curled in a smirk.

'Keep reading. I was about to give up and run the tests again when I noticed that link down the bottom: non-human. It took me to a page on …' Jamie lifted her shoulders and hands up in an embarrassed shrug, '… shape shifters and the like. I skimmed through it. Most of it was pure rot, but there was something on blood so I followed the lead and ended up on a newsgroup posting talking about "T" type blood. It's not an official designation, but apparently it has no genotypes and no trace of human alleles. Read the descriptor. Exactly the same as Jane Doe's, from the dark colouring to the "inconclusive" markers.'

'Non-human?'

'Well …'

Ben flipped back to the start of the report and read it again. Jamie waited for him to finish and when Ben looked back up, continued on.

'There's probably some other answer, but every path I take comes back to this.' She flicked the paper with his finger. 'Non-human. Not werewolf or werecat, or any other type of mythical monster, but non-human. Apparently rare, non-dominant, if it mixes with human at all, and possibly long-lived. No reports on who they are or where they came from. Just whispers and rumours, phantoms slipped into the end of fairytales. Except that body lying in the morgue is no fairytale.'

'DNA testing?'

'Underway. As well as genome sequencing. Skin patch tests came back unusual but within the boundaries of human variable. Organs appear reasonably normal, usual number of fingers and toes …'

'I want to see her.'

'It's all organised for this morning. There's a change of shift at 7am. Go in after that. Tell the receptionist you're there to identify the Jane Doe that came in on the fifteenth. She'll take you right to her.'

Ben nodded and reached for the mug of coffee Jamie had set down on the table a half-hour before. He sipped and winced. Cold. Then drank it anyway. 'Who else knows about the blood?'

'The usual staff, but only the inconclusive results, I've kept the extra research to myself. The general consensus is that there's some contaminant involved. There's a techie working on it. She's good but she hasn't come up with anything so far.' Jamie took both Ben's mug and her own, and rinsed them out in the sink. 'We've got time to eat if you're hungry. I could whip up an omelette easy enough.'

'Thanks, Mel.' Ben's stomach rumbled as he spoke and he patted its widening girth with a grin. 'My stomach will love you forever.'

'And the rest of you?' Jamie lifted an apron from its hook in the kitchen and slipped it over her head to protect her pyjamas from food splatter.

'The rest of me has been all yours for years.'

Jamie laughed and opened the refrigerator. 'How about a grilled tomato and some mushrooms with that?'

Ben's stomach rumbled loud and long. Jamie took that as a yes.

While Anthony Baglio inspected Lizzy Barton's home for evidence of foul play, Drs Jamie Morell and Ben Sokolof stood opposite sides of the current Jane Doe in residence at the City Morgue.

The coroner stood at her head, holding back the white sheet that covered her body. 'And what do you do, Dr Sokolof?'

'I'm an archaeologist. Work mostly in the Territory. Just down in

Sydney for some seminars at the university and a bit of fundraising.' *Some of it's true, anyway …*

The coroner's expression appeared sympathetic, fundraising a common necessity in the medical world as well. 'Do you recognise her, Dr Sokolof?'

Ben frowned and hoped the coroner would take that as some uncertainty on his part. 'I'm not exactly sure. It's been a long time, years, since I've seen my niece. I don't often get back to this side of the country.'

'I understand,' the coroner said. 'My wife's brother is an archaeologist in southern Turkey. We hardly ever see him. Not that that's a bad thing, though don't tell my wife I said that.'

Jamie remained unmoving while Ben nodded and pretended. Normally she wouldn't be included in this part of the identification process, but she'd 'just happened' to walk in with the archaeologist and agreed to Sokolof's request for help in dealing with this unfamiliar situation.

'I recall there was a mark behind one of her knees. A scar from a fall ice-skating one winter. She couldn't have been more than ten at the time …'

'Excuse me if you will. I don't have anything in my report, but it doesn't hurt to check these things.' The coroner squeezed between Ben and the drawer holding the body to uncover the legs. He lifted one side of the body and peered underneath. With a little help from Jamie the sheet slid away and exposed the woman's entire length. 'Sorry about that. Grab that will you, Dr Morell?' He let the body down and leaned over to pull her up on the other side. 'Just take a look under that knee will you, Jamie? Any scarring that you can see?'

Jamie bent until her face was level with the drawer. There was no mark. She knew that already, but she frowned and looked anyway. 'Maybe …?' She said, unsure, glancing at Ben.

Ben walked around to Jamie to look for himself, memorising as many of the Jane Doe's features as he could, the pattern of cuts and gouges on her body, the complexion of her skin. He squatted beside Jamie, looked and shook his head.

'No,' Jamie said. 'Just shadows and some bruising.'

'I don't think it's her,' Ben said, lifting the leg higher when he noticed a faint line running from her knee, down her calf and encircling her ankle. 'I wish I could be sure.'

'Well, if there's no mark. Are you in contact with any other family members?'

'Not really. I'm something of a black sheep—we both are.' He touched the woman's cold face with his fingertips, rubbing them together when he brought them away. 'But I'll make a few calls. See what I can do. I think her brother lives out west.'

Jamie started covering the body. The coroner gestured for Ben to join him in the hall. 'Because of the situation involving her death, we'll be keeping her here a while longer. Let us know one way or the other once you've talked to the rest of the family. I'm sure the police will be interested in finding out who she is … or isn't.'

The two men shook hands. 'Thank you. I appreciate your help, and Dr Morell's.' Ben turned to Jamie as she came up behind them and took her hand, pumping it with gratitude.

'I'll show you out,' Jamie said. The coroner nodded and left to return to his caseload.

'Interesting. Busy man.'

'Extremely, but still has time for the Does of this world.' Jamie made a show of helping Ben to the exits, stopping at the glass entrance doors to shake his hand. 'Will you still be around for some lunch?'

Ben looked out into the street. People hustled past, faces buried in private thoughts, barely taking the time to look around. It promised to be another warm day out, but nowhere near as warm as he was used to. 'I think I will,' he said. The electronic door slid open as he stepped in front of it. 'In fact, I think I'll be around for quite a few lunches.'

'Meet you at the café down the street at one, then?'

'I'll find it. We'll talk about what else I think as well.' Ben joined the flow of pedestrian traffic. 'Find out as much as you can, Jamie. A chemical analysis of that residue on her face would be good. There's something about her, I just don't know what.'

'Will do.' Jamie stepped back from the door and let it close behind Ben. She had time to work her way through a few more cases and have a nice long chat with the tech working the Jane Doe case, and there was a slim possibility that DNA results might be in. So much to do and the day not getting any longer.

I find it difficult, swallowing the depth of our failures.
Most days start dark and end darker.
Once our kindred, now our enemy, the Bledray,
scour the face of this earth with insatiate hunger.
To think of all that has been lost fills me with blackness.

— *Journal of Malaik*

7

Waves undulated across the green-blue waters of the bay. Wind flicked sprays of white foam into the air, catching droplets of salt water and scattering them high and far. Boats cut paths through the waves, opening wounds that closed, scarred and faded away within seconds, leaving nothing behind but the heavy waters and the sour stink of their exhaust.

The bay marked the southernmost seaward reach of Sydney; a line drawn between bush and urban crawl that came under threat each weekend from tourists, bushwalkers and an array of boats.

'If it wasn't for all the boats, this'd be a real peaceful place. Almost like paradise, sea and bush and lots of sky. And close to the city.'

'The boats bring the people, my love.' Moriah raised her face to feel the salty air on her skin. The sun was warm, but still weeks from being summer hot. The water in turn was weeks from being summer cold. 'And we want the people.'

'Of course, I know that. I don't mind them.' Still full from the last feeding, Jedidiah was more worried about encroaching on the city's Protectorate, especially with the scent of the Hunter haunting them. 'But it's risky, Moriah. We haven't been this far north before …'

'We haven't killed a Guardian before either and now we're stronger for it. Already I feel the first stirrings of hunger tighten my belly. What is risk when we are so close to everything we desire?' Moriah's tongue traced a glistening path over her lips. Perfect white teeth flashed a moment between them.

'Moriah, you're teasing me,' Jedidiah growled.

'Take the risk with me,' Moriah said. Her eyes opened and stared fire across his skin. Objections and worries were consumed in the flames.

'I'll risk anything for you, Moriah.'

They stood on the pontoons of a ferry wharf that serviced a small community clinging to bushland and civilisation in equal amounts. Behind them waited the homes of two thousand people.

Ahead lay four million more.

———◦•◦———

Loneliness drives the Hunter
to connect with Rydri.
It is their common ground;
the need to touch is more than sustenance of physical being.
It also assuages the emotional
and existential aspects.
Alffür seek
wisdom and understanding.
Bledray seek only
physical satisfaction

— *Journal of Malaik*

———◦•◦———

8

They were near. She could smell them. A faint trace of decay under-
lay everything, sharp and burning, not quite enough to make the
eyes water, but not far off.

He was near too, but that was more of a feeling in the bones type
of thing, a hot flush in the nether regions that came from too long
without physical contact.

Both targets would have to wait a little longer. She needed to
clean up and get some rest. It'd been a long walk from Bellbird back
out to the main highway to find a ride north. And Bellbird had been
no holiday.

Lael turned away from the motel room door. As far as motel
rooms went, it wasn't bad. Neat, if a little cramped. Decent size
bath. She ignored the dull walls and carpet and sat on the bed to
pull off her shoes and socks. The bath was all she cared about at the
moment, warm, clean water, maybe some bubbles … She reached
for the radio by the bed and fiddled with the dials until she found
some slow music. Turned it loud enough to drown out road noise
and headed into the bathroom.

The tiled floor cooled her hot feet and for a moment she considered foregoing the bath awhile longer to strip and lay naked on the
white squares. She turned the taps on and dropped the plug into the
drain before she could take the fleeting thought seriously.

'What a mess!' Lael wiped steam from the mirror and inspected
every layer reflected in the tarnished glass. Her clothes had seen
better days, surely, but would clean up okay, and the motel had
a laundry she could use. She pulled her shirt over her head and
dropped it on the floor. Her jeans sagged under the belt that held
them up, having passed the 'so stiff they could stand on their own'
phase sometime the day before. She unclasped the belt and let
them drop, and then, because she couldn't even bear to look at her

underwear and bra she removed them as well, and kicked the lot into the corner.

She'd forgotten the bubbles.

'Damn! What's a bath without some bubbles in it?' She took the sample size bottle from the sink, checked the label, and emptied half into the crystal clear lake of her waiting bath. 'Field of Wildflowers here I come.' The aroma, a not quite accurate guess of natural flora, rose in a cloud of steam vapour and filled the room.

Lael started to relax for the first time in over a week, since the first Guardian died and sent her trailing northward for the perpetrators. She stepped into the bath and knelt down. The heat of the water burned her skin, but it was a scouring she'd been looking forward to, needed. She rocked back on her feet and sat, gasping as the burn hit the more delicate areas, and sighing as she laid back and let the water lap over her tired, dirty body. Water still cascaded from the taps, whirlpooling at her feet, building mountains of white bubbles that formed growing islands, an archipelago that swirled around her knees and along her thighs.

The first Guardian … she lay her head back and closed her eyes. There hadn't been time to digest all the impossibilities that had taken place since that single, equally impossible event had occurred. In thousands of years, the Ghouls they protected against had never overcome the Guardians. And now, two within a week, one of them Malaik, and Lael's senses had failed to detect yet another. A third Guardian gone?

A paragraph from Malaik's journal came to mind: *Only the promise of Lael seems able to break through my dismal barrier of doubt and despair. If we are to win this bloody game, it will be due to our service and her sacrifice.*

Oh, Malaik. They'd been friends forever, teacher and student before that. The world would not be the same without his steady presence to guide her. She missed him already, wanted to talk to him, ask what it was she was supposed to do now.

This was becoming too much for her to handle alone. Of course, she wouldn't have to. Already avenues were opening. Help would be at hand when she needed it. Whether it would be enough or not was the tough question, and with the Guardians sitting tight in their protected areas unable to leave, Lael had the burden to shoulder. She could only hope her shoulders were strong enough.

Water sloshed over the side of the bath with a noisy splash.

'Shit, the taps.' Lael sat up to turn the forgotten taps off and sent a tidal wave of water across the floor. 'Fuck!' The floor glistened with bubbly puddles. The thin bathmat and her clothes were sodden. She looked at them through hooded eyes. They needed washing anyway …

Lael lay back down in the deep water, let her arms and legs float, and her thoughts drift away from the flooded bathroom to the avenues she would soon be walking.

*Alffür and Bledray
have no magic
save the elements of
Earth and Sky.
They brim with life that most
cannot see.
Their essence vibrates
with energy.*

— Journal of Malaik

9

Quin watched the girl for an hour before he made his move, sidling alongside her as she stood knee-deep in the surf. She didn't appear to notice him, staring out at the yellowing horizon instead, not blinking, barely breathing, long black hair floating away from her face. Her skin was perfect, pale without venturing into Gothic, a hint of freckles across her cheeks. Tiny gold hoops hooked her earlobes, a tiny gold stud glinted in her nose. Generally speaking, body-piercing did absolutely nothing for him. Ears, fine, but anything else gave him the creeps. Yet somehow, that touch of gold on the side of her nose beckoned him closer. He wanted to touch, to kiss, to lick.

The girl turned her face toward him and, for the first time, he could see her eyes: black almond-shaped jewels. Oh, God, he wanted to touch.

'Hi.'

Even her voice was perfect, soft and gentle.

'Hi.' *Smooth, Quin, real smooth.* 'Are you a friend of Ethan's or Theresa?' He was a friend of Ethan's. They'd gone to school together and kept in touch after, mostly at the regular beach parties Ethan hosted. It helped a person's popularity enormously to live behind Wanda Beach, with its white gold sand and roaring surf, and always ensured full attendance at beach parties.

She smiled and Quin felt a hot flush start in his toes despite the cold water that washed around them.

'Theresa's,' she said.

'I haven't seen you around before. You one of her uni friends?'

The girl nodded, still smiling. He was in love.

'My name's Quin. You thinking of going in?' He pointed to the waves and felt his knees turn to mush when she laughed and shook her head. Hair curled around her face, danced in front of her, brushed against his arm. He reached up to push the hair back from her face just as she turned toward him. His fingers grazed her lips instead. The hot mushy feeling in his legs zapped northward like an electric charge.

'My name is Carena,' was all she said, watching him now as he tucked the stray hair behind her ear and let his fingers drag down its extraordinarily silky length. 'I prefer not to swim.'

Quin figured that. This was as close as she'd come to the waves in the hour since he'd first seen her.

'Would you like to go for a walk?'

'Yes.'

He didn't take her hand, though he wanted to. Didn't steer her in any particular direction either, but they ended up on the edge of the sand hills anyway.

'There's so many people down there,' Carena said. The breeze was a little stiffer on top of the dunes and her hair whipped around her. She ignored it. Quin wanted to wrap himself in it; let its wildness bind him to her.

'Quiet up here,' he said, though the breeze could be heard snaking its way through the dunes and the sand squelched beneath their feet. 'Come in a little further. We can pretend we're the only people around for miles once we're at the bottom.'

Carena took his hand and ran down the slope. 'Still too close,' she called out, laughing, and kept running, winding a way through the sand hills until the breeze had dropped and the sand was threaded through with a thick mat of grass. 'This is better.' She dropped, panting, and lay on the ground.

Quin looked around. They were in deep enough for it to be creepy, for faded parental warnings to echo in the still air.

'Quin.'

The sound of his name from her lips banished childhood misgivings and he fell to his knees, leaning over her with what he hoped was a trustworthy smile and not a lusty leer on his face.

'Come here, Quin.' He nearly did. On the spot. And hoped for more forbearance than that if he was reading her expression right.

She reached up and pulled him down on top of her, his legs

sliding out from beneath him as if they'd turned to jelly. She tasted sweet and hot, and he tingled all over just from the touch of her lips on his.

They rolled. She rubbed herself against him. A hand found its way to his crotch. He burned and would have yelled for the sheer pleasure of it, but her lips silenced him. Her mouth engulfed him. He arched his back, tangled his fingers in her hair, came quickly after all.

And died.

⸻⸻⊹⸻⸻

Carena walked out of the dunes, collected her towel, hat and sun-screen, and left the party, satiated for now and in no hurry. The temptation to gorge filled her with every gust of breeze that brought the scent of people to her.

Several young men and one woman stood nearby, leaning on the rail that separated path from vegetation. Wet-suited to varying degrees, they watched her every movement. Their hair was salt-crusted back on their heads, shoulders brown and layered with more sea-salt. Not long out of the water, Carena surmised. Just long enough to dry.

'So very, very tempting.' She turned away and followed the path past beach and crowded units. Left it to cross sandy grass, and stopped in the centre of a circle of stones.

'How appropriate.' Outside the circle, trees loomed, guardians to the stones and the people that picnicked around them. 'But there's no Guardian here.'

Carena was so happy she felt like laughing out loud and dancing through the stones. She made a mental note to return to the park at night. Late, after the noisy hotel across the road had closed. Or maybe sooner and give in to the need to gorge after all.

*The Alffür and Bledray exist between the planes of
astral and earth—
ethereal and physical.
Each form adds to our experience of Life.
Each form is equally valuable and, before the holocaust,
was equally lived.
Survival depended on solidity.
We needed to anchor ourselves more fully to the earth;
tie ourselves to the Rydri in ways we had not done before.
We entered their communities and kept our secrets.
Moving on when the need came as we are long-lives.
Protecting and subtly guiding where we could.
We had no wish to take over,
no desire to lead.*

— *Journal of Malaik*

10

'Is there anything that connects any of these cases?' Rick downed a glass of Anthony's Scotch and sifted through the papers. 'Anything at all?'

'Does complete randomness count?' Anthony sent a listing of names, places and dates to his portable printer and leaned back in the uncomfortable hotel chair. 'Take a look at these names, note the dates. There's been a steady, if slow, case of mysterious vanishings for as long as records have been kept. I've narrowed down my search parameters to exclude the more obvious runaways and deluded souls, and to include all people with plausible reasons why they wouldn't willingly vanish.'

'Like Elizabeth Barton …' Rick pulled the list from the printer. It was long, but not so long that any pattern was apparent, and not so close together in time that suspicion had been aroused. Until now.

'Exactly like Elizabeth Barton. Look at the first name, William James Pederson, Singleton, 1889. Last seen on his porch smoking a pipe and wearing his Sunday-best after attending a local dance. Mr Pederson became engaged to marry at that dance. He was planning a trip into town the next day to buy a ring. His pipe, hat and dinner jacket were found the next morning by his young sister. He was never seen again. No explanation. No evidence of foul play. We can't even put it down to primitive investigation techniques. The same result was found for the last eight disappearances.'

'There's the dust …'

'Not present at all crime scenes.' Anthony reached for the bottle.

Next on the list, 1892—Mary Clarke had gone missing from her aunt's house in Albury on the New South Wales–Victorian border.

'Smell?' Rick scanned the two pages quickly, shaking his head 'no' to Anthony's offer of another drink. The smell at the Barton house had been pretty strong, bordering on rank, surely someone somewhere had noted such a phenomenon.

'Only Mrs McFarlane reported an odd smell. I barely noticed it and certainly did not notice any smells at the other scenes.'

'You barely noticed it? It was all I could do not to walk out.' Maybe it was just him. He'd always had a sensitive smeller. Could pick up the scent of his ex-wife's lover at a hundred paces, could detect the scent of her lies from across the room. Still, he'd never smelled anything quite like Lizzy Barton's front room. He gave himself a mental shrug and tried not to think about it. 'Would have dissipated fairly quickly anyway, I suppose. Strange, isn't it?'

Anthony filled his glass and emptied it. 'Strange doesn't begin to describe …'

The laptop, half-buried under a growing pile of documentation, beeped for attention. Anthony shifted the papers and stared at the flashing orange light in the task bar. He moved the mouse until the cursor covered the bright icon and clicked.

'What is it?'

'I've had a hit on one of my newsgroup queries … it's not really related.'

Rick watched as Anthony read through the message. Not related maybe, but nothing much was in this case. Anthony frowned, keyed in a few instructions and continued reading.

'Are you going to share sometime soon?'

'It's odd, but, the query is in relation to unusual blood groupings, which in turn appears to be connected to current weird and wonderful happenings. The username is random alphanumeric at a webmail address.' Anthony paused and tilted his head to the side. His frown deepened. 'What do you think that the chances of a mysterious appearance could possibly be connected to our mysterious disappearances?'

'What makes you think they might?'

'The date and the fact it appears completely unexplained. Also, the username. Most of these contacts go out of their way to create imaginative names. This one doesn't.'

Rick stood and walked across the room, the list of missing still in his hand. He peered over Anthony's shoulder to read the screen. 'That's the same date Miss Barton went missing. Coincidence?'

'Could be, could be, but with all the loose ends we've got trailing after us, a little coincidence could be a good thing.' Anthony clicked on reply and started typing, asking for particulars, place, names, anything else odd beside the blood.

'Ask them about smell too, and dust while you're at it.'

Anthony looked up with a question in his eyes.

Rick couldn't explain his sudden hunch so he answered with a shrug. 'Couldn't hurt.'

'No, I suppose it couldn't.' Anthony finished typing and hit send. 'Now we just have to wait.

As far as hunches went, asking about smell and dust was only the tip of it. The dream had come back to Rick in a flash of smells. The one from Elizabeth Barton's house, yes, but a host of others as well: eucalypt, earth, burning, a few he couldn't interpret and another he could only describe as an acrid stench he'd rather not smell again. And then those hands, work-rough and strong, but warm, he was sure of it. Warm and trusting. Could the dream also be connected?

He left Anthony's room without mentioning either the dream or the smells, and drove home thinking of nothing else.

Until he walked through the front door to the sound of the telephone ringing itself hoarse and the answering machine blinking a total of ten messages demanding attention. He answered the phone first.

'Where the hell've you been?'

'Gabs? What's up?'

'Don't call me that! I've been callin' you for hours and you ask what's up? Where've you been? Do you ever check your fuckin' voicemail? We've got a story about to bust wide open and Harry'll skin us alive if we aren't the ones busting it! I'm sick of covering for you, Rick. You've got to get in here, now.'

'Gabriela, shut up for a minute and let me talk. I'm not coming into the office now. It's late and I'm tired. Been working on another story, you know that ...'

'Forget that story, Rick. It's a fairytale. This one's better, bigger. You've got to get down here ... oh, fuck it! Stay there, I'll come to you.'

The phone went dead and Rick dropped it onto the lounge as he walked passed. 'Great. Visitors.'

He didn't want to talk to anyone, let alone to Gabriela about some new story. He had a feeling that his fairytale was bigger than anyone could imagine. Tomorrow, he and Anthony would head down to the south coast. A week ago, a newlywed couple had vanished while honeymooning at Ulladulla. The police report, while remaining inconclusive, suggested that a shark attack was likely. The couple had hired a boat and some dive gear, asked about local diving spots and headed out into the sunrise. Their boat had been found anchored at a spot close to shore, dive gear intact and apparently unused, honeymooning couple gone. Police were also looking into the possibility of faked deaths.

Anthony had thought that last implausible. If you were going to fake your death on a dive boat, why leave the dive gear behind? Why have the boat anchored? Why leave no evidence of accident or foul play? Why, in fact, would a newly married couple, with no apparent connections to crime, or careers that might tempt crime want to fake their deaths?

After reading through all the reports in Anthony's possession, Rick agreed.

Where to go next with this though? Rick dug his fingers into the back of his neck and stretched. Anthony wanted to go to Ulladulla. Rick didn't mind. He liked it down there, but would the trip uncover anything more than they'd already discovered? Any more than Anthony had found in Perth or, before that, in Victoria? He'd give this story a couple of days and then he'd move on.

Rick opened the refrigerator and waited for divine inspiration in the form of dinner to reveal itself. It was a little early, but he was hungry. Somewhere along the line, he'd forgotten to eat and breakfast was a long time ago. He groaned at the offerings. Half a head of old lettuce, some cheese, numerous jars, cans and bottles and some Lebanese bread. Nothing took his fancy, though he supposed some homemade pizza would be doable. He took out the bread, cheese, a tin of pineapple and the tomato sauce.

'Basically all the food groups anyway.' He flicked the oven on and started fixing some dinner. 'Might even get to eat before Gabi gets here.'

Rick was taking his first bite when she arrived, banging on the door then opening and walking in. Gabriela hated waiting.

'Of all the days to go missing, Rick, dammit! I told Harry you were after another story. He said to tell you to drop whatever it was and get onto this.' She slapped a manila file onto the table. Some photos and a few typed pages slipped out.

'Since when've you needed your hand held?' Rick took another bite of his pizza. He would have preferred some ham on it, but the pineapple was sweet and the melted cheese comforting. He didn't offer any to Gabriela.

'I don't, smart arse. Harry thinks it's too big for either one of us on our own. Wants us to watch out for each other while we're digging dirt. He has a hunch about this one, Rick, and you know Harry and his hunches.'

That made Rick think about the feeling that had plagued him all the way home. That his dream was no dream and that coincidences were anything but. A whiff of decaying odour wafted past the melted cheese and he nearly gagged. He coughed instead and happened to glance down at the photos, and for a second stopped breathing at all. A dead face, skin scored by a strand of barbed-wire, stared out of the glossy black and white print. If this face had been male and the hair lighter, he'd swear it was straight out of his dream. Yet that face had gone, obliterated in some weird kind of funeral pyre.

'Who's that?' Rick swallowed, gulped for air and spoke all in one awkward action.

'No one knows. She was found a few days ago.'

Gabriela pulled the photographs clear of the folder and spread them over the table. They were pixelated, poor quality, but there was no doubting how similar they were to the face in his dream. Judging by the marks on the body, the woman had been wrapped in barbed-wire like some kind of sacrificial offering. Her wrists and ankles were cut deeply, black circles that gaped, bloodless. Her throat, chest and breasts were patterned with puncture wounds, one nipple destroyed, the pattern leading down her stomach and disappearing in a thatch of blonde pubic hair.

'She was found a few days ago in Sutherland. South of here.'

Rick nodded. He knew where Sutherland was. He and Anthony would be driving right through it in the morning.

'Apparently she'd been dead a day or so before that. The coroner's put it at occurring sometime on the fifteenth, but he's still not sure.'

'I remember hearing about it.'

'These photos were emailed to Harry this morning from a so far untraceable account.' Gabriela put his hand up to hold off any questions. 'Before you ask, no we're not one hundred per cent sure that it isn't some elaborate hoax, which is why we're keeping it hush-hush, for now. That's where we come in. I've got a few bits of information. The email told us where to find the body. It also suggested that the dead woman was something of a mystery, even if she weren't dead. A few biological issues that don't quite add up to being human …'

Gabriela stopped talking. Rick looked up to see what the problem was and followed Gabriela's gaze to the printouts of the day before.

'Something about blood,' Gabriela said, shaking her head as if her thoughts were leading too far off the track.

Rick sat. Blood. Again. And then the date burst into neon lights in his memory. The fifteenth. Five days ago. One day before the disappearance of Elizabeth Barton. More coincidences? This had to be the same query Anthony had received.

'Rick? What story are you working on?'

Gabriela looked at him with a strange 'I absolutely don't believe I'm even thinking about this' look, chewing on her top lip, eyebrows joined in a deep V. Rick didn't know how much he should share. Didn't want to tell Gabriela everything only to have her laugh in his face.

Instead, he pulled his mobile phone from his pocket and pressed redial.

'Don't go to bed,' he said into the phone when it answered. 'I'll be back there in half an hour with something new and a visitor. Make sure there's some Scotch left in that bottle.'

He disconnected the call and met Gabriela's increasingly concerned face.

'I'll tell you on the way.'

'Tell me what on the way?'

Rick grabbed another piece of the cooling pizza. 'A fairytale,' was all he'd say.

Gabriela collected the file and started to follow Rick out. 'Not a bedtime story, I hope.'

'Nope. I'm beginning to think it's more the stuff of urban legend.' Rick ushered Gabriela ahead of him, flicked the lights out and closed the door. 'We'll take your car.'

<hr>

It took less than thirty minutes to get back to Anthony's hotel. Gabriela could hardly believe what Rick was telling her. She remembered when spontaneous combustion was the latest fad of the weird and weirder. This sounded just like that. Spontaneous missing persons. She laughed and gave Rick her typically cynical, 'Yeah, right,' which Rick didn't appear to appreciate in the least. Shit, he was dead serious. Well, she'd never doubted Rick's instincts before, she'd at least hear him out.

'And who's this other guy? Are you sure about him?' Gabriela switched lanes to avoid a slow driver. 'Keep to the left, you idiot!'

'Sure as I can be, but I never leave myself completely open, you know that. Who can ever know a person anyway?'

You got that right. Less than a week ago, Rick was as cynical as they come. He scoffed along with the best of them at anything that hinted at the supernatural or New Age mumbo jumbo.

'I'm just having a little trouble picturing you chasing down some quack story …'

'That's just it,' Rick said. 'At first glance, I wouldn't touch it, but there's compelling evidence to suggest it might all be true. Little clues here and there that, on their own, mean nothing. Put them together though and look at the big picture, suspend belief for just a little and it's there. The biggest story of our careers ...'

'Or the biggest hoax.'

'Yeah, so we keep it quiet till we know for sure.' Rick slumped back in his seat, massaging his temples.

Man needs more sleep, no two ways about it.

'So what makes you think the two stories are connected? More of those little clues?'

'Yes, more of those. Baglio can fill you in more. This is his pet project. His hotel is on Jamison Street.'

Gabriela slowed as she reached Jamison and squeezed her car into the only available parking space near the hotel Rick indicated. Nice.

The façade of the hotel was as far removed from their current assignments as it was possible to get. Gabriela looked up at the randomly lit windows and the flickering lights above the main entrance and felt an unexpected shiver of apprehension. Or was it?

She sure as hell hoped so.

***

Gabriela still didn't look convinced. Rick had to admit that their leads were tenuous at best, but they were connected. He could feel it. He looked out the window of the cafe, at the shadowed faces of the people rushing past. Dusk provided neither enough light to see clearly or enough dark for artificial lighting to yet make a difference. The gloaming, he thought—a sliver of time between day and night, light and dark, one world and the next.

He should tell Gabriela and Anthony about the dream, but he couldn't bring himself to do it just yet. Not while it all felt so personal and unfinished.

A steady stream of people came into the café in search of a

caffeine fix on their way home from work. Each of them carried the same faint look of relief as they entered the light, and relaxed as they joined the queue and read through the specials board. A few skimmed through newspapers to avoid looking at anyone, others smiled and made small talk. Good atmosphere, Rick realised. He was glad they'd decided to take a break from the hotel room.

'So what makes you think this blood thing is related to your missing persons? Seems to me, after everything's said and done, that you're walking a pretty fine line.' Gabriela burned her lips on coffee and nearly spilled it in her lap. 'Shit, that's hot.'

'Gut instinct, I suppose. I don't know.' Anthony shrugged. 'I've never been a fan of the great coincidence excuse. Your case, on the other hand, appears to be the work of a serial killer. Ritualistic laying out of the body, quasi-religious overtones. Textbook, really. On the other hand, my "blood thing" certainly seems connected to your corpse.'

Gabriela blew on her coffee to cool it down. 'Too many bloody hands is what it is. We've got a possibility on the blood, possibility on dates, and even on region. And let me tell you this, the shire just doesn't get that many ritualistic murders. Murder–suicides and a few drug-relateds maybe, but serial killers? Hardly ever. They do get their share of missing persons though. Lots of sand dunes, bush, and sea to get lost in.'

'There's more out there.' Rick knew it as sure as he knew too much coffee gave him serious indigestion. 'We haven't found them yet, but there's more.' He looked up to see Anthony nodding and Gabriela shaking her head.

'I sure as hell hope not,' Gabriela said, taking a mouthful of the coffee and squeezing her eyes closed against the heat.

'I'll go to Ulladulla tomorrow as planned,' Anthony said. 'It seems like backtracking, but anything we find at this point has the potential to be big.' He added more sugar to his cappuccino. 'You two go look at this mystery body and visit the crime scene. See what else you can unearth.'

Rick stared into his cup, steam plumed off its surface. He wanted to drink it in one gulp, let it burn all the way down to his gut, bring some reality back to his feelings. He'd be tasting it all night, regretting all night, but right now he wanted the bitter liquid inside him more than anything else.

He brought the cup to his lips, inhaled the strong aroma, and drank. Screw the indigestion!

*While the ability to hunt the Bledray seems to be
innate in our 'children',
guidance is needed
in fine-tuning strategy, communication and relationship.
The Bledray hunger for Ryrdri.
The Children of Alffür hunger for connection.*

— *Journal of Malaik*

11

Lael unfolded her legs and stood stiffly. The Guardian for this area was definitely dead. She would have to find her body, somehow, and perform the traditional rites or there would be no release from her torment. She wiped away a tear and reached for her clothes. The circle of Guardians were aware now that the Bledray Ghouls had risen, that they had found a means to break free from the shackles the Guardians imposed, but they still could not leave the protected areas. Help would come from them on a less physical realm. Lael would prefer a bit more muscle by her side.

The burning scent of the Ghoul had strengthened in the short time Lael had taken to clean up and communicate. Not the same as Bellbird, a shade weaker. A single Ghoul then, Lael decided. Also unusual, but easier to dispose of.

She pulled on her spare jeans and shirt, her socks and boots, and grabbed her jacket. The days were hot, but the nights still cool this close to the sea. She tucked her room key in the breast pocket of the jacket and buttoned it. Checked her wallet for money and left.

The ocean breeze blew in as soon as she opened the door, cool yet fresh, the salty tang doing little to disguise the foul stink of her quarry. She shut the door behind her and strolled down the steps.

Hunting in town was done best at a stroll. She'd take the time to look in all the shop windows and all the faces that passed by, blend in, assimilate the smells and colours. Use the human life around her as a cloak of invisibility. Five minutes to the main street from her hotel would give her time to collect her thoughts and plan some sort of strategy. She'd been doing this so long though, that strategy had become second nature.

Northy's Hotel—trendy, by the sea, popular and loud.

Lael ordered a drink and let her senses sink in to her surroundings. Listening to the different levels of talk: friendly gusto, slick and not so slick come-ons, shy introductions, drunken singing and the ever-present hum of alcoholic slurring. Music played so loud that most people were forced to yell to be heard. Lael hated it; too many bodies, too much noise, too little fresh air. She took her drink when it came and walked out the front.

Across the road, a park, plaza and group of restaurants were nearly as crowded as the pub. People roamed all over, down to the beach, into the poorly lit park, along the foreshore. It looked much more inviting.

Lael squinted. The shadows in the park were long, made dark by the artificial lighting at the edge of the plaza and the trees that no doubt sheltered families by day. A haze of light, barely noticeable, shimmered under one of the trees, and the smell of the crowd and sea faded under the onslaught of rancid Ghoul.

The smell enveloped her like smog around the city and she had to swallow back the urge to vomit. She would prefer to turn around and walk to the bar, get herself another drink. Instead, she removed her jacket, closed her eyes and let the smell in, reading it like a book, a biography of who, what and when. She didn't like what she read.

When had they found this much power? When did they get this daring?

She didn't doubt her own abilities, but as the taint of her prey prickled her skin, she knew she would need to be stronger. She would have to feed.

A hand rested on her shoulder and she smiled. A crowded pub was the perfect place. Who would notice a touch or two when everyone stood shoulder to shoulder anyway? She turned to look at the hand and the face hovering behind it.

'You look like you could use another drink.'

'I might,' Lael answered and leaned into the hand, encouraging the touch.

The man, somewhere in his twenties she judged, grinned. His

eyes lit up at her positive response. His hand slipped across to Lael's other shoulder as he rested the full length of his arm across her back. She shivered at the warmth of his skin on hers and felt a wave of desire as his spirit touched hers.

Absolutely perfect. Lael broadened her smile and shook her glass enough to make the ice cubes clink.

'Well, then. Let me be of service. What'll you have? I'll see to it in an instant.'

Lael liked his voice and his manner of speaking, a cross between gentleman and rogue. If she didn't have work to do, she could stand listening to him a while longer.

'Lemon, lime and bitters.' She held his hand in place as he made to move. 'With a drop extra bitters.'

'Wait for me here?'

'Don't be long.' She released his hand with a slow tracing of fingers.

'I'll be right back.' The man vanished into the crowd and Lael turned to see who else was close by.

A young couple, faces almost locked together, mouth to ear, so they could hear each other speak, were closest. She straightened, left her glass on the base of a huge palm, and brushed by them. The back of her hand touching the woman, her fingertips the man. A fleeting stroke of less than a few seconds. Any longer and the couple would notice, both her intrusiveness and her feeding.

She wheeled away, through the open doorway, into the thick of the crowd, grabbing elbows, touching backs, caressing a backside here and there, even shaking hands with whoever was drunk enough not to care about her forwardness. She reciprocated the process as she went, until the people crowded in on her, brushing against her as she passed, reaching out to touch without realising why, many unaware of their actions. Lael was careful not to let it get out of control, releasing the endorphin her feeding caused in slow moving wisps. She neither wanted the drinkers to get overly excited or her prey to sense her coming.

The abundance of humans in such close contact made her dizzy, but, as always, her lust was severely curtailed. Iron control was the main difference between the Guardians and the Ghouls, and the saving grace of humanity.

The young man with her drink pushed away from the bar and wove a path through the increasingly rowdy clientele.

Time to leave.

Lael followed the man, a few paces behind. Paused, as he did, when he realised she hadn't waited for him and then, as his shoulders slumped and then shrugged, nudged his arm.

'I nearly gave up on you.' Lael took the drink and returned his relieved smile. 'Thanks. It's so crowded in there.'

'Are you with anyone?' He glanced around, but seemed satisfied that he'd found some willing company. His hand cupped her elbow.

'No.'

'Would you like to be?' He leaned in close enough for Lael to feel his breath on her cheek.

She breathed it in, sweet from the ginger ale mix in his drink, minty with toothpaste. She liked it, wanted more, and stopped herself with a resolve that grew shakier every minute she stayed immersed in the crowd.

'I would …' She had to say no, but that didn't mean she had to enjoy it.

'But?' His expression resigned to her knock back. 'No, don't worry. Maybe some other time.'

'Maybe later tonight.' Lael held up the glass. 'Thanks for the drink.'

'Yeah, sure thing.'

He left her alone and she turned away, her attention back on the park and the slicks of shadow under the trees. The odour had abated, drifting in the air currents, soured to the flat stagnation of a Ghoul full, but still on the prowl.

Time to cross the road.

Lael took her drink with her.

Music played out across the square, louder in front of the open restaurant doors, softer in the narrow gaps between, each song different to the last yet similar enough in style that it didn't lose itself in a jangle of noise. A sculptured fountain dribbled water from its spigot, collected it in a pool at its base and, according to the sign, recycled it to the top of a concrete whale. She wandered past, drink still in hand, following the sandstone brick wall to its end, and then the grass line to the concrete path that divided the park from the beach.

The Ghoul was close. Over her left shoulder somewhere, lurking beneath the trees. The shadows weren't so dark up close, but spaces still existed, pockets of near-absolute black, where the Ghoul could claim her victims. Lael felt sure it was female, not that it mattered much. It certainly didn't to the Ghouls. All touch was a sensual gift that they took and gave according to their own whim and hunger. With no Guardian to restrict them, reduce their pleasures, many more people would succumb to their avarice.

Lael let her cognisance reach out in tendrils of airborne sensory detectors.

There.

A flash of electricity jolted up her spine as she felt the wrapt presence of the Ghoul. *Satiated yet still feeding. Better for me, not so good for the people wandering through the park.* Lael wished the weather would change, send them all home, but no such salvation came, nor would it.

Lael strolled the path, let her senses widen and diminish until they were undetectable. She concentrated on the people, who talked to one another, who thought of the mundane, letting them all slip by. Lust, desire, greed, wanton cravings she sought, the pheromones of those about to die at a Ghoul's touch.

Wind blew through the heavy tree branches, rubbing them against each other, forcing them to bend and twist. The Norfolk Pines surrounded a circle of rocks like sentinels, silent witnesses to the hidden deaths taking place beneath their wide reach. Close to the circle, and near a low brick building on the other side, stood the pine tree the Ghoul had chosen as her feeding ground. A splash of darkness ringed it, a trick of building lights, park lights and the moon.

Lael watched as a man entered, walking as if drunk, led by a slim woman with long black hair. The woman looked innocent; a slash of red silk covered her body loosening into a swaying skirt low on her waist, feet bare. A laugh, tinkling like an out of tune piano, punctuated enticing words that flowed from the woman's red lips. The power to enthral glowed from the woman in a curtain of starlight, invisible to all but her own species. Lael could see it left behind in every footstep, see traces of it glittering from tree trunks and the squared rocks of the circle. Pretty, she supposed, in a snail slime trail kind of way, and telling. *Very telling.* The Ghoul was feeding indiscriminately. *Shit!*

A group of people chased each other in and out of the rock circle. One ran straight past the Ghoul and her victim, stepping into the shadow and nearly stumbling at the edge. Some prescience warned him away and he grabbed his girlfriend's hand and dragged her in the opposite direction. Game over, judging by the look on his face. The moment of distraction gave the victim enough wit to turn away from his destiny. Lael saw his boot heels edge toward the light. But it wasn't enough. He vanished again into the dark, his hesitation replaced by fervour. Lael had witnessed the taking enough times to understand the process.

Lael circled the park, staying on the other side of the line of trees, until she came up behind the Ghoul and its victim. Their voices softened, mumbling love words, his growling deep in his throat. A hitch in the sounds they made signalled his coming end. Lael stood beneath the branches. Limited space narrowed her choice of attack. The fight would be dirty and fierce. Height would be her advantage tonight. She blinked in the darkness, stared upward and let her form coalesce into the night air.

The Ghoul, intent on ravishing the man, noticed nothing.

Lael looked down on their joined outline.

Dirty and fierce …

She reached down, her hand materialising enough to grab a fist-ful of the man's hair and yanked him into the tree.

'Stay there,' she hissed as she dumped him on a low branch. 'Don't let go.'

The man looked dazed, confused, but he'd get no chance at further instruction. On the ground below came a stunned gasp and then a shriek of insulted rage. The beautiful woman in the red dress evaporated into a blur of befouled mist and shot straight up, ruining leaves and tree-limbs with her hot touch.

She chased Lael to the uppermost boughs where they ducked and swirled. Lael shrunk into a tight ball, her hand once more immaterial, allowing the Ghoul to surround her, waited less than the second it took for the Ghoul to sense victory and then exploded outward in a blistering display of heat and pure power. The Ghoul started to reform, falling as she did so, her dress ripping on twigs. Lael dove after her, an arrow piercing anything in its path, reaching her just above the still stunned man, and wrapping solid fingers around her throat.

'Your name?' Lael's voice came sibilant from within the mist.

The Ghoul twisted in the Hunter's grip, a screech from between clenched teeth her only reply.

The hand tightened, the arm it sprang from appearing as a corded length of muscle, skin emerging from the muscle and spreading upward showing shoulder, torso and finally the Hunter's determined face.

'Name?' Lael repeated, this time her lips forcing the demand. She planted her feet in the crooks of two branches and came closer, pinning the Ghoul hard to the tree with her knee.

'Carena!'

Lael felt sick with satisfied knowledge and once again started to shimmer.

'Wait,' Carena pleaded. 'I can help you.'

But Lael had no desire to talk to a Ghoul. Unless …

Lael's transformation halted.

'How did you kill the Guardians?'

Carena renewed her struggling.

'Tell me now or join your brethren in the void.'

'Tricks, bait. Easy. Lure them in. They all but kill themselves.'

'How?' Lael's fingers dug deep into the Ghoul's throat.

The struggling stopped. Carena looked directly into Lael's eyes. Emotion oozed from every pore of the Ghoul's skin, trapped innocence reflected in her eyes. She glowed with the intensity of the force outlaid. Lael blinked and almost relaxed her hold.

'I can't help what I am,' Carena said. 'My hunger consumes me. I have to feed or go insane. I know no other way. We're all brothers and sisters, the same. Yet the Guardians don't share their knowledge. Won't help us.' Her voice was sweet, a slight lisp added to the innocence she projected. 'We want help. I want help. I hate being this way …'

What the Ghoul said made sense. *Is this all it takes? A plea for help?* Lael's fingers were starting to ache. Doubt crept into her thinking. *What if they could be helped? What if …*

'Easy, easy, easy,' the Ghoul whispered.

Lael's fingers tingled now. The Ghoul's lips stretched across a toothy, demented smile.

'So, so easy. Even you.' And the Ghoul changed from solid form to glittering mist, and left the cover of the tree.

Lael followed her, shimmering and shifting, attuned to the vaporous form and the scent trail it left behind. Lael went for height, flattened herself above the Ghoul and waited, following but not attacking, letting the Ghoul gain the taste of escape and freedom. Through the park, across the beach and along the shoreline, skipping over waves until the Ghoul reformed and a beautiful young woman walked ankle-deep through the water.

Lael attacked, wrapping herself around the Ghoul's head, smothering her body and contracting until she had forced herself inside the Ghoul's form.

The Ghoul stumbled, walked haltingly a few more steps, all grace of limb gone. Lael continued to contract her being, concentrating only on the centre of her power and then exploded, reforming even as the Ghoul splintered into a billion glittering stars and faded into nothingness.

'I'm not quite that easy,' Lael said. The water was cold, but she liked it, and the fresh wind helped take the taint of Ghoul from her senses. She still had an awful taste in her mouth. *Could use a drink …*

'Shit, I left my jacket at the pub.'

We have remained hidden from the Rydri, humans, for Millennia.
We are no fools.
Those that we love and protect are also our nemesis.
Their destructive path through time threatens us all,
yet their potential for greatness travels with them.
Miaheyyu hides deep within their psyche.

— *Journal of Malaik*

12

Jamie Morell buried her hands deep into her jacket pockets and with shoulders hunched, paced her living room. Ben counted each slap of her bare feet on the timber flooring. Five steps, turn, six steps, turn again.

'I'm going to lose my job,' she said over again, followed by, 'I can't believe you did that. I'm going to lose my job for sure.'

'I'm making tea, want some?' Ben waited for a reply and then went into the kitchen anyway and put the kettle on.

Five steps, turn …

'Nice hot cuppa is what she needs. Strong and black, that'll calm her down.'

Six steps …

Ben knew he'd done the right thing. When you came against a brick wall in this kind of research the best thing to do was shake a few trees and see what fell out. And as far as he and the Jane Doe lying in the morgue were concerned, trees needed shaking. Probably lots of them.

Jamie's newsgroup query hadn't drawn much, a few jokers, a few more scammers and one response that wanted more information. That email had sounded authentic enough, but Jamie was loathe to give away too much. Her reply had been circumspect and had elicited no further response as yet.

Test results, including DNA and a second look at the blood, had been labelled inconclusive and ignored. The woman remained nameless. The police kept their investigations to themselves. No one appeared particularly interested in the abnormalities the woman presented and the clues to something larger than her own death.

The kettle whistled and Ben pulled two mugs from the cupboard. Teabags and sugar were already on the bench. Ben liked Jamie's kitchen. Small and neat, utensils kept to a minimum and easy to find. Orderly. Ben liked that about Jamie too.

Pouring the water into the mugs, he thought a little more about Dr Morell. They'd been friends for a while, passing acquaintances a while longer than that, usually meeting up at seminars and conferences, he on the fringe of the scientific community, Jamie right in the middle of it.

Funny how that for all their differences in opinion and differing methods of approach, their basic core beliefs were the same: that things were not always as they seemed and that answers were sometimes found outside the box of current scientific thinking.

They'd spent a whole weekend talking about it once, in between seminars at a conference in New Zealand. *Revolutionary ideas of the past are generally accepted today …* Ben would have preferred ditching the seminars and listening to her the whole time.

'I am going to lose my job. You are aware of that, aren't you?'

Ben's reminiscence shattered and he looked at her with what he hoped was an apologetic expression. *If she doesn't see that it's time for her to move on anyway, she will soon.*

'Maybe not. I didn't use your name. There are several other possible sources for the leak. The police, for instance.' He offered her one of the mugs and she took it, eyeing him with annoyance and, he noticed with relief, a lot less anger.

'And the photographs of the body on the steel table, half-covered with sheets labelled City Morgue? Don't you think they'll notice any of that?'

'I know Harry Stanton. He'll want a full investigation before he puts his poker in the fire. Believe me. He'll get one of his boys to do some snooping first. He told me himself. They'll start with the police investigation and just ease on around to anything else that seems suspicious.'

'Who?' Jamie's eyes were hard as steel when she was annoyed, her expression uncompromising.

'Who what?' Ben cringed. Hard as steel and icy too.

'Who will be doing the snooping? Who should I expect or look out for?'

'Gabriela Salek. She's a good reporter, good investigator. I gave her my mobile number. She doesn't know anything at all about you.'

'You're staying at my flat. You visit me at the morgue. It's only a matter of time before they figure out who the source is.' Jamie turned and walked back into the living room. She stood staring out the window.

Ben left his tea on the bench. He really hadn't thought Jamie would be this upset. He stopped behind her and rested his hands on her shoulders.

'They might eventually, yes. I won't try to say otherwise. But they won't today. Today everything's fine and this afternoon I'll book into a motel and I'll stay away from you and the morgue. No one there knows who I am. Everything will be all right, I …'

'Don't make promises you can't keep, Ben.' Jamie turned into Ben's arms and he could see that the annoyance had faded to resignation. 'I knew I was taking a risk when I rang you. I'll take whatever comes, just … no more surprises. Okay? Next time you want to stir things up let me know first.'

'That I can promise you.' Ben's hands slipped from her shoulders to her waist. He pulled her gently against him, the hot mug in her hands warming his chest, steam from the tea warming his face. He breathed in deep. 'The tea smells good.'

He dipped his head down to nuzzle her neck and hair, lifted it to give her a quick kiss on the lips. 'You smell good too.'

'I don't have to start till late today. Let's go back to bed.' Jamie sipped the tea, smiling.

Ben took the mug from her hands, left it on the windowsill and guided her toward the bedroom. 'Let the world wait. Let it hang on a wish and a prayer while we dance our dances and sing our songs, and make heavenly love in the sweet air of our dreams.'

'Has anyone ever told you how incredibly aggravating you are, Dr Sokoloff?'

'All the time, Dr Morell. All the time.'

*It is not known what triggers
a Gathering.
A sudden weakness in
Alffür Guardianship?
A sudden burgeoning desire
to devour?
To the Bledray,
Rydri life essence is both
food and drug.*

— *Journal of Malaik*

<h1 style="text-align:center">13</h1>

'What the hell is that smell?' Rick shoved his digital camera in his coat pocket and retrieved his handkerchief to hold over his nose and mouth. Blue and white police tape fluttered from the open doorway. More tape inside indicated where the crime had taken place.

The house, the street, the whole neighbourhood was deep in suburban Sutherland, a sterling example of post-World War II architecture after a 1970's renovation invasion. Azaleas and roses grew side by side in a thorny abundance of winter growth. The houses either side of the dead woman's home displayed well cared for gardens, knee-high brick fences, gnomes, and carefully clipped and swept driveways of matching faux sandstone pavers.

'What smell?' Gabriela walked in behind Rick, apparently unconcerned by the stench that lingered in the stale air of the house. 'Probably just needs a little airing.'

'Needs more than a little.' Rick peered around corners and opened doors, identified the lounge room—old television and stereo, a listing bookcase and a blanket-covered lounge; a bedroom—single bed made, no extra furniture; and stopped at the plastic tape that barred entry to a sunroom.

Sunshine filtered through large windows in hot streaks, all the light the room needed. Outside the windows, a jungle of rainforest plants filled the small backyard. Inside, a collection of potted plants blurred the glass division between yard and house. Here too, the furnishings were minimal. A white cane sofa with white cloth covered cushions, a matching chair and a low table with a single drawer, partially open; no prints on the walls; no vases of flowers or decoration. A plain archway connected the sunroom to the kitchen.

Gabriela walked through the archway wrinkling her nose. 'Kitchen connects to the lounge room. It's a bit whiffy in here.'

Rick thought it more than a bit whiffy. The stink was enough to make him gag, almost as if …

'You don't think there's another body here, do you?'

'Nope. Doesn't smell that bad.' She looked at Rick with a frown, clearly thinking the man exaggerating, and walked across to the wide glass doors. 'I'll open these and let some fresh air in.'

Rick kept the handkerchief over his face and looked about for stray corpses.

'So what does your secret report say happened again?' Rick's voice was muffled behind the covering, but Gabriela appeared to understand as she opened the file of information she'd brought in.

'The victim was tied and wrapped with barbed-wire and hung on the wall.'

They looked at the only wall space large enough to take a body. Blood smeared the white paint in several places. Fingerprint dust had left black swirls that vaguely outlined the position of the body. Two nails, both crooked, one loose, projected from the wall in grue-some fashion, all too easy to imagine a body hanging there. Rick forgot about the smell and remembered the camera. He pulled it free of his pocket and started taking photos.

'What else?'

Gabriela jerked away from the wall and continued reading. 'No identity. Police found no letters, no wallet or drivers licence, no bills, nothing. The place had been gone over though and they're assuming it was all stolen. Neighbours reported that she hadn't lived here that long and, I quote, "She appeared friendly, but no one had actually talked to her as yet." End quote.'

'Strange. Her own house and no ID. Did she own a car? Did she rent? Someone must know who she is.'

'Well, this isn't the full police report. Just what I've managed to scrape together. But my contact can't or won't divulge the house owner's name and there is no car.'

Rick moved closer to the wall, touched the area under the nails with one finger and frowned. A white powdery dust adhered to his skin. He sniffed it, frowned again and dragged his finger across the other still-white areas of wall. More of the powder coated his finger.

'Do you have any idea what this stuff on the wall is?'

Gabriela, who was going through drawers and pulling at cushions, looked up and came closer.

'What's it feel like?' Gabriela touched the wall with her index finger, then rubbed the finger against her thumb. 'Kind of a silky feel, don't you think?' She sniffed. 'Doesn't smell much like the fingerprint dust and that's black anyway.'

'It smells like a cross between flowers and old socks.'

Gabriela pulled some plastic sandwich bags from one pocket and keys from another. 'Let's take a sample. It might be leftovers from the Forensic Science Guys and it might not.' She scraped some of the dusty film from the wall into the bag and sealed it. 'At least now we know why the room smells the way it does. I'm going to look in some of the other rooms. See if this woman left behind any clues about herself at all.'

Rick let her go without a word, still thinking about the smell of the house. Now he'd had time to become used to it, he realised it smelled familiar. More like the rotting corpse smell he'd suspected than flowers and old socks, and yet he hadn't been near any dead people recently, only Elizabeth Barton's place, and this was different somehow. Less stale, more fresh … *What is it?* He closed his eyes and concentrated on breathing the scent in, trying to remember and ending up rushing to the open door, eyes streaming and throat constricting. Now it smelled like shit, fresh, ripe faecal matter. He could almost hear the flies buzzing greedily around it.

Outside and the smell faded to a distant unpleasantness, which he immediately recognised as an odour he'd been smelling on and off for the last couple of weeks. *Maybe it's me?* He lifted his arms and sniffed, but no, the odour was definitely not emanating from his armpits and Gabriela would have said something, loudly, before now if it had been. He turned, taking in the lushness of the plants, the depth of their greenery and something else, further back in the shadows. The leaves sparkled as if a child had gone on an art and craft-fed rampage with a jar of glitter. His feet sunk into the long grass, dark shoes disappearing in the foliage.

'There better not be any bloody snakes back here.' He took heavier steps and started to whistle in order not to take any cold-blooded residents by painful surprise. His brother, senior by eighteen months, and full of tall stories, had taken him bushwalking regularly as they grew up. Each walk started with the story that snakes, spiders and other creepy crawlies in the bush were scared of whistling giants and that as long as you were whistling and thudding along the path, they would think you were a whistling giant and you'd be safe from attack.

Rick had stopped believing the story somewhere in his mid-teens, but the habit had set in and right now, about to step into dark, glittery shadows, he felt it only too prudent to announce his arrival. His whistling faded, however, when he noticed that the glitter decreased as he drew closer, and the smell from the house—the rotting, dying, dead dog in the sun type of smell—grew stronger.

God, it's here.

A bird flew off from the tree branch overhead and Rick jumped, his heart thudding, louder than any giant. Something rustled an overgrown daisy bush and he whistled a dry tune, desperate to get sound out and only managing a stuttering exhalation of air.

'Looking for dead bodies?'

'Holy fuck, Gabriela!' Rick nearly fell over and for a brief moment wondered if he should check his pants. 'You scared the shit out of me.'

Gabriela's smile looked plastered across her face. Rick glared at her and turned back to the garden when the rustling sound came again.

'Did you hear that?'

'Hear what, Rick? Hell, it's an overgrown garden, doesn't look like anyone's touched it in years, probably full of rats and snakes. Maybe lizards. Maybe …' She pointed to the fence dividing this yard from the next and the kitten that stood there staring at them with twitching whiskers. 'Maybe it was the neighbour's cat.'

'Yeah, maybe.' Rick felt his face flush.

'Maybe the cat chasing a rat.'

'Yeah, okay.'

'Maybe a snake munching on blue-tongue burgers and …'

Rick walked away, keeping his back to her laughter, the twinkling garden, and the graveyard smell. By the time he reached the back door, he'd decided to go wait in Gabriela's car. When he got to the front door, his mobile rang.

'Tony? You in Ulladulla already? That was a quick trip?'

'No.' Anthony Baglio's voice crackled with static intensity, solid sounds cut through with a silent knife.

'I can't hear you, you're breaking up.'

Gabriela walked out the front door, shaking her head and still laughing. Rick waved for her to keep quiet.

'Say again.'

'Can you hear me now? I said there's been a change of plans. How soon can you get to Bellbird? It's about a half-hour or so south of Sydney.'

'Well, I suppose I can get there in half an hour or so. We're just leaving the house …'

'Have you got pictures of the crime scene?'

'Sure, I took a few.'

'Good. Bring Gabriela and the pictures with you. You aren't going to believe …'

'Believe what? You're breaking up again.'

'Just get here as fast as you can … the whole town …' The phone went dead.

'What is it?' Gabriela waited for Rick to fill her in, one hand on her hip, the other holding the manila file.

'That was Baglio. He wants us to meet him.' Rick took his camera out, turned it on and started reviewing the images of the crime scene, thankful that he'd taken enough and didn't need to go back into the house.

Gabriela started walking around the car to the driver's door, her back hunched as she sorted the key for the car from the rest on the keyring. 'Where?'

'Bellbird.'

*The hunter is always on guard. The time and place of battle
with the Bledray cannot be known in advance.
Therefore, any time, any place holds the potential for
victory or defeat.*

— *Journal of Malaik*

14

Sun warmed the near empty streets of Bellbird with a sullenness that weighed in the air. Anthony ran a sweaty hand through his sweaty hair. It pained him, really, to finally be taken seriously at the cost of so many lives. The investigators who had descended on Bellbird like a plague of flies were neatly, and concisely, still avoiding the truth, the death of Bellbird. Some blind fools suggested that the disappearance of the entire population was probably due to a slow, and therefore hitherto unnoticed, desertion of the town for better climes, better attractions.

Shove your fucking hithertos where the sun don't shine, shithead. Anthony had to bite down on the words to prevent them becoming a permanent stain on his record.

One witless fool had the audacity to suggest alien abduction, albeit with a shrug and a disbelieving look on his face.

Fools. It was much worse than that. And Anthony believed it. Without knowing why or how or who, whatever was taking these people, whatever had taken a whole town, was something much worse than abduction or seasonal migration.

A whole fucking town for chrissakes! They were taking him seriously, but not seriously enough.

Anthony had left the other investigators in the shade of the post office portico to stand in the middle of the street with the sun beating on his head like a sledgehammer. He peered in both directions, hand forming its own portico over his eyes, looking for the reporters. He doubted they'd be driving up from Wollongong considering he'd left them in Sydney and they were in Sutherland when he rang, but checked that direction anyway.

Nothing but straggling houses and an avenue of beautifully blue jacaranda trees. A stray puff of wind pushed its way through the petal litter on the street, sending the fresh and decaying blossoms upward to meet the sun before the heat slammed them back down.

So far, he'd been in ten houses of an estimated two hundred, politely knocking on each door, identifying himself to the shadows and walking into silence and sour heat. Each house had smelled the same, traces of urine and rotting food, a waft or two of something dead, but not a single blood spot or sign of struggle.

Just the smell and the dust, which had been at Miss Barton's, and already discarded as nothing unusual. Anthony had taken samples anyway, his pockets were full of them, and he noticed, as he waited in the street, that the unpleasant smell was now his smell too.

A quick look at his watch told him that no way would the reporters be arriving for at least another twenty minutes. He had to get out of the heat before his brains fried.

A lane leading away from the main street remained uninvaded as yet by the sun; a monstrosity of trees growing from front yards and back blocked the still rising day. Uniformed police officers wandered in and out of the few businesses, taking photographs and notes. Plain-clothed officers spread a widening net throughout the town. Yet this one street stayed immune to demanding knocks and desperate pleas.

Anthony decided to walk the lane alone.

Miaheyyu is the meaning of life,
the ribbon of soul
that runs through us all.
She is the mirror through which we may see our inner selves of
thought and knowledge.
Miaheyyu is the mystery of everything.

— *Journal of Malaik*

15

Lael had never felt more alone than this moment, standing, unseen, in the shadows of the City Morgue. The day had started hot, even for summer, the weather reporters had stated; an early summer on the back of a dry winter and an ominous start to bushfire season. Lael remembered hotter summers, drier winters. She wasn't particularly concerned, but then the rising danger they all faced wouldn't come from bushfires or heatstroke.

More Guardians had perished in the space of one night. More Ghouls had rejoiced in their never-ending hunger. The crux was now, this day, this moment, before too many more could die. She could feel it building around her, tightening her skin, cramping her legs and feet until she was sure her blood would stop flowing, heart cease beating.

Endurance had been learned so long ago that she could put the pain and despair aside and keep moving. Around her, people walked and talked, cars drove by, buses lumbered along. Lael ignored them all for the sake of the Guardian currently entombed inside the morgue. This would be the last chance she would have to put her sister at rest. The last Guardian, perhaps, that would find rest for some time.

Lael left the shadows and entered the building through the front door. Not a soul noticed her passing.

⁓◦◦◦⁓

'Come on, Ben. Pick up.' Jamie paced again, this time outside the café down the street and around the corner from the morgue. The same one where she'd met Ben for lunch a few days previously. 'Pick up, dammit!'

'Your tea's ready, miss!'

Jamie whirled around, hand digging in her purse for money, and strode up to the counter.

'Thanks,' she said as she dropped four dollars into the woman's hand. 'Keep the change.' She took the tea and strode out. Ben still hadn't answered.

'What's the point in having a damn mobile if you don't turn it on?' She pressed redial, sipped her tea and walked along the street in the opposite direction of the morgue.

Traffic sounds grew louder as she approached Parramatta Road and she hastily turned down a narrow laneway. *Too quiet, too quiet. Someone'll hear.* Jamie retraced her steps to the café and prepared to redial, yet again, when Ben answered the phone.

'What took so long? I've been ringing for ages. Where are you?'

'Just driving around. Sorry. Didn't hear the phone. Has that reporter shown up yet? She was talking about trying to view the body this afternoon ...'

Jamie's laugh sounded as cold and scared as she felt.

'Well, she won't be doing that. The body's gone.' Her voice scratched in her throat, sounding false and shaky as it passed her lips.

'What?'

'Gone? As in vanished. As in missing. The police are there now, cornering everyone, asking questions. They know about you. Pretty soon, they'll know about me.' *I'm gone for sure. Passing on information. Letting in unauthorised personnel. Doing unauthorised tests. Goddamnfuckitalltohell!*

'Where are you now?' Ben, she was glad to hear, was nearly as scared as she was.

'At the café getting coffee.' Jamie smiled at a face she vaguely recognised. Another regular at the café, she figured, and turned away.

'Go back.'

'How can I go back? I can't lie to the police. Even if I wanted to, I'm the worst damn liar in the world. They'll ask me one question and I'll tell them everything. They'll know my favourite colour and the name of the first boy I kissed by the time I'm through. Are you laughing?' *If he wasn't the most aggravating man ...*

The face she'd just turned away from tugged at her memory and she looked around to see who the woman was. Recognition hovered on the edge somewhere between losing her job and being thrown in gaol.

Ben wasn't laughing outright, but he was close to it. She could hear it in his voice.

'Stop laughing and tell me what to do.' She broke off as she saw the woman at the counter taking a mug of coffee and walking between the tables to the rear of the café.

'I'm not laughing, Jamie, not really. Answer every question they ask you with the truth. You don't have to lie, just hold off on any extra information. If they ask about me then go back to our original story, that I'd shown up to identify the body, but it turned out I was mistaken.'

Jamie paused in the doorway of the café, looking after the woman, who now sat in the corner leafing through a newspaper. No good, she couldn't place her, and she didn't look like anyone who worked at the morgue. Too casual, in jeans and a light T-shirt, thick hair not tamed with an assortment of slides and bands, and definitely too tanned.

'Jamie, you still there? I'm sorry, really. I didn't mean to laugh at your expense. Jamie?'

'You know that's weird … I thought I saw …'

'What's weird? Are we still having the same conversation?'

Jamie bumped into a chair and nearly dropped her cup. 'Shit!'

'Jamie, you okay?'

'No, no, I mean, yeah, fine. Just spilled my tea. I thought I saw … No, I don't know what I saw. I'm having a shit of a day, Ben, and it's all your fault. I'll try not to reveal my childhood sexual deviancy and, if they ask, I'll tell them I haven't seen you for a while. So you'd better stay away for a couple of days.' Jamie kept her voice low, but the general hubbub of the café, she hoped, prevented anyone from hearing what she was saying anyway.

'Do you know how it happened? Did any real relatives come in?'

'As far as we all know, she was there one minute and gone the next. I suppose they'll check security tape and all that.'

'I'll ring you tonight, late, to find out what happened, but if you need me or something else happens, ring me straightaway. I'm going down to …'

'Tell me later. No lies, remember. I've got to go. They'll be looking for me soon. Be careful, Ben.'

'I will. Bye.'

Jamie disconnected the call and looked for the woman, but a man in a suit now sat in the corner, ensconced as if he'd been there all day with coffee, cake and the newspaper spread over the table like Mother's-best tablecloth. The woman had vanished.

The experience of time is different for those that are
both ethereal and solid.
The rules of solidity govern and
we are all bonded to time.
Ethereality escapes those bonds.
In the astral plane,
the passage of time is to be observed but not experienced.
We cannot travel forward or back in time,
but we can … Hover.
Observing life change as we
explore more fully the
world we live in.
We return to solidity when we need to touch the earth again,
to feel the sun and wind and rain, to breathe the air.

— *Journal of Malaik*

16

White skin, shadowed with bruises, stretched across an ethereal face, lips full pink and parted, black eyes framed with a feathering of eyelashes. Dark hair, cold and brittle moved in time to breaths she wasn't taking. A scream whirled around the face and gurgled to a keening moan. The pink lips turned dull, the black eyes grey and dead. Spidery lines of blue spread out from her eyes to ears, to mouth. She didn't say a word. The dead didn't speak. A tear formed in the corner of her eye, a silver ball of anguish and pain. It hurt him to watch it fall, to see the trail of black ash it left behind on the slowly rotting face. Skin and muscle pulled away revealing bone and teeth. The tear dipped near lips, caught for a moment, collecting in its corner before overflowing and marking the way to chin. It stopped there, a solid mass quivering on the edge of a void.

Unfathomable, he knew. Nothing existed beyond that face, beyond the soft yearning of the song that welled up from its depth, the heat that licked at his senses. The face melted into the heat, the song, strident and pleading. Flames stretched outward, upward. The void shrunk beneath the bite of the fire until it was nothing and the face was gone, and he too started to burn.

He held his hands up, blackening claws, flame consuming his skin and muscles, chewing their way along his arms.

A second face appeared. A mouth slid against his, whispering, kissing; sandpaper tongue licking his lips. The mouth widened, extending over his eyes, until he saw nothing, felt nothing but hot breath and then not even that. He couldn't breathe. His hands lay dead beside him. The mouth was sucking the life from his body, one foul breath at a time. His lungs strained to fill and failed. Vomit, rushing up in a burning, putrid wave of disgust and fear, exploded from his mouth.

Rick sat upright, staring straight ahead, breathing heavily, no idea for the minute where in hell he was, knowing only that he needed air, lots of it. He reached for the window controls and stopped, staring now at his hand. Incomprehension filled him and then drained away. His hand wasn't burned. All five fingers normal, functional appendages.

No dead face assaulted him, no funereal voice, no gaping, sucking mouth.

'You okay?'

Gabriela seemed to be asking him that a lot lately.

'Yeah, fine. I dozed off, I guess.' He still felt woolly with sleep. He wiggled his fingers, just to make sure, and opened the window. A warm breeze filled the car, cooling the sweat on his face and arms. His shirt, still clammy, stuck to his chest and armpits and he pulled it away, his hands trembling. Gabriela was talking and Rick realised he hadn't heard a word.

'… snoring so loud I couldn't hear the radio.'

'You should have turned it up.'

'Nah, didn't want to wake you. You look like you haven't slept for a year, figured you could do with it. Snoring wasn't so bad.'

Rick thought back to the dream, to the face and the fire, the suffocating panicky feeling hit him deep in the gut. He shuddered and flexed his fingers, stretched his arms. 'Next time, go ahead and wake me.'

Gabriela looked at him, concern etching her face, and shrugged her shoulders. The wind coming through the open window pulled at her bun, loosening the hair. Mirrored sunglasses hid intelligent eyes that could see an untruth as easily as a new possibility or an old hurt, eyes Rick couldn't hide from no matter how hard he tried. Trying to had taken up a better part of the last year or so.

'I've been sleeping plenty,' Rick admitted. 'Just been dreaming a lot. The kind of dreams where you're never really sure if you're awake or sleep, even after you've woken up.'

Gabriela spared a glance away from the road and Rick took it full on.

'What sort of dreams?'

Rick shrugged. He didn't know how to explain them. Most of the dreams were forgotten on waking, even the bad ones. Vague memories and bursts of déjà vu were all he had to go on. *Bad enough when each time I remember something I get the creeps worse than any kid.*

'Did you just have one then? I saw you jump and your face is still white as a sheet, must've been a bad one.' Gabriela didn't look across again and Rick was grateful for a moment of privacy. It'd been a bad one for sure, but not the first time he'd dreamed it. He didn't remember when, but the face was as familiar to him as his own, and he didn't have a clue who it was. *The photograph of the dead woman …* It reminded him of her though he didn't think they were the same.

Gabriela kept her eyes on the road now. They'd gone from suburbia to wide valleys and sporadic heathland to dense rainforest. The breeze dropped away and the temperature rose with thick humidity.

Rick didn't mention the dream and Gabriela didn't ask.

A barricade and detour sign blocked the turnoff into Bellbird.

'What do you think?' Gabriela slipped her sunglasses to the top of her head and looked at Rick. The trees were tall enough along this stretch to cast the road in permanent shade.

The sign appeared innocuous and the road rough enough that repair or possibly a tree fall might be assumed to have closed the road.

Rick stared out the window. Sunshine filtered through gaps in the rainforest, sending yellow bands of light through the deep green foliage. The road twisted out of sight a few metres in and a hint of something dark beckoned. Anthony hadn't elaborated on the situation in Bellbird, but Rick had the feeling that it was going to be bad. Real bad.

'I'll move the barricade.'

Bird calls, raw sounds in the treetops and scrub below, and rustling beneath the carpet of rainforest litter, put Rick's nerves instantly on edge. He whistled without realising, a breathy ghost of sound that made no difference to the wildlife. The barricade, two metal frames for legs and a slab of yellow and black striped wood, was easy to move. Rick swung one end, gate-like, to the edge of the road, waited for Gabriela to drive through and then swung it back. By the time he was back in the car, his mouth and lips were dry.

Gabriela watched him; eyebrows raised, and turned the radio up. For once, Rick was glad for the noise.

They reached the outskirts of Bellbird fifteen minutes later.

The first house stood with its front door wide open and screen door closed, a Jack Russell jumping and scratching and barking for all its worth to get out. A cat sat slumped on the letterbox, one leg straight up in the air, licking its backside. It didn't look up as they passed by, apparently unconcerned by the car or the mad dog inside the house.

Rainforest thinned out into small farms and yards; a bushfire brigade station, a semi-neglected town hall and an open square of land accommodating soccer, football and netball. Gabriela turned the radio down.

'You notice something odd, Rick?'

'Quiet town.'

'Dead as a doornail.'

The last bend into the township proper slipped by with a faded 'Welcome to Bellbird' sign and the road widened into a main street with a few shops and not much else. Several cars were parked on the side of street, though they looked more as if the drivers had decided to simply pull over and stop rather than pay attention to the parking signs. One of the cars was a blue and white patrol car. Another was a station wagon marked with an FSG logo.

'The forensic science guys are here.' Gabriela idled the car past the police units and pulled over.

'That's Baglio's car there. The other must be an unmarked. What do you think's happened?' Rick opened his door to get out. Gabriela was already out and rolling up her sleeves, sunglasses perched firmly on her nose.

'Damn, it's humid here.' Gabriela moved away from the car and into the shade of the covered footpath. 'Well, there's no people … except for police.' Gabriela pointed down the street.

A uniformed policewoman and a couple of science techs in blue overalls had just come out of a building. The woman saw the two new arrivals and started walking toward them while the others stood and watched. Her face was as brisk as her walk and Rick decided attack would be their best defence. She'd probably picked them as reporters as soon as she'd seen them.

'Morning, officer. Anthony Baglio around? He asked us to meet him here.' Rick held out his hand as the woman approached and she shook it.

'Could I have your names, please, sir?'

'I'm Rick Hendry and this is Gabriela Salek …'

'Mr Baglio told us to expect you. If you'll come with me, I'll take you to him.' She held her arm out and gestured to the street behind them. 'He's just around the corner.'

'Thanks.' Rick wasn't sure when a police officer had last been so polite to him. He glanced at Gabriela who seemed just as surprised.

'She obviously hasn't read any of your articles lately,' Gabriela whispered as she joined the policewoman.

'I just need to get my gear from the car,' Rick said, ignoring Gabriela, and was surprised again when the woman nodded and patiently waited. He'd become used to stolid silence and grim faces when it came to dealing with the police of late. *Maybe I should ask her name, might be a good contact later …* Rick opened the back door of the car and reached in for his camera bag. The bag was more like a schoolboy's satchel than a camera bag, but it held his notebooks, a digital recorder and assorted pens as well, and had the added feature of a comfortable strap.

'Let's go,' he said when he had everything, smiling at the woman who didn't smile back.

'So what's going on?' Gabriela asked as they walked. 'Bellbird looks like a ghost town.'

'Mr Baglio will fill you in on what he wants you to know. Just down here.'

They came to the corner of a laneway that made the road into town look like a freshly paved highway. Cobbles had, at one time, been tarred over, but only the one time. Jagged potholes scored the bitumen exposing the older cobbled road. In other places, patches of the grey surface had thinned to a point that it only existed in between the cobbled bricks; a testament perhaps for the durability of older construction compared to modern.

'Watch your step,' the policewoman said, as Gabriela's shoe caught the edge of one pothole and she stumbled.

Anthony sat on the front step of the fifth house along.

'You made good time.' He stood and nodded to the policewoman. 'I'll take it from here.'

'We have a car at the southern end of town and another will be arriving soon to block the northern end. Officer Parry has set up tea and coffee, cold water if you want it, in the café. We'll have some food arriving soon too if you get hungry.'

'Some water would be good. Could you bring some bottles back here later?'

The policewoman nodded and walked off, leaving them to the house.

'Thanks for coming,' Anthony said, as if he thought they might not have.

'What's happened, Anthony? There's no people around. Has the area been evacuated?'

Rick was happy for Gabriela to ask the questions. He'd recognised the house as soon as they'd reached the front gate. The one with the body and the woman with fire in her hands and stars in her eyes, the house from his dreams. Anthony was talking and again, Rick wasn't listening. The words were there, buzzing around his head, but they couldn't reach through the awful feeling that he knew what was inside the front door. *But she removed that body …* Rick stopped as that part of the dream came back in full force. A body wrapped in wire and hooked on the wall. A dead face with a silvery sheen. Like the nightmare he'd had in Gabriela's car and the photographs from the morgue. All the same and all different. Rick held his breath. *Oh, God!*

Anthony led them into the front room, a living room–study lined with a massive bookcase along one wall and a collection of prints, paintings and photographs of trees and flowers. A desk was positioned in the corner of the room between windows and wall, and beneath a covering of loose-leaf notebooks, magazines and newspapers. The floor was covered by one huge Persian-style rug.

'Crime Scene haven't been through yet so don't touch anything,' Anthony warned.

Touching anything at all was the furthest thought from Rick's mind. He didn't want to breathe in this room, let alone touch. He shoved his hands in his pockets to be safe.

Gabriela didn't feel so inhibited. Her hands had been reaching out to the one bare wall even as Anthony spoke. A square of white showed where a large picture had once hung, the picture, ornately framed, now leaning against the bookshelf, face in.

'This looks familiar.' She turned to Rick and pointed about a foot higher up the wall than his head. A nail, strong enough to take a good deal of dead weight, protruded from the plasterboard. Smudges of blood near the nail and a trail of dirty brown further down the wall were enough to indicate what had been hanging there. A body, somewhat larger than the Sutherland woman, had been crucified on that wall.

'It's the same as the Sutherland crime scene, I'm told,' Anthony confirmed. 'Or near enough. The nail, blood traces, white powdery substance and ...' Anthony crouched down, with one gloved finger, lifted a piece of barbed-wire from the floor. He looked back up at Rick and Gabriela. No need to say more. They'd all seen the photographs. 'I've contacted Ulladulla police. It appears they have a few recent missing persons on their books. They're going to check into them and ring back. I told them we were interested in anyone living on their own. Someone that may have gone unnoticed for a while by the neighbours.'

'Did you tell them to look for barbed-wire and nails?'

'I did.'

'What about smell?' Gabriela was watching Rick now, reading God knew what on his face and Rick knew Gabriela was asking him, not Anthony, about smells.

'That too,' Anthony answered anyway. 'It's almost gone from this room, but the smell is certainly reminiscent of Elizabeth Barton's house. Hard to tell.'

'Rick?'

Rick shook his head. His throat didn't want to work. Anthony was right about the smell. Similar to Miss Barton's. More like Sutherland. Less though, he thought, like there's a rotting body tucked away behind the furniture. He glanced around anyway, just in case, then let his gaze go to Gabriela, still watching him and waiting for an answer.

'It's the same as Sutherland,' Rick said. 'More … kind of rotting flowers than Elizabeth Barton's house. Not as strong.' *Like it's been cleaned …*

Gabriela nodded and turned to Anthony. 'So the town was evacuated for a serial killer?'

Anthony straightened, face pained as if standing straight again was the hardest thing to do in the world. Judging by the creak of knees, Rick figured that right then, it probably was.

'The town wasn't evacuated.'

Rick didn't want to hear any more. Black scuffmarks stained the base of the wall above a scattering of crushed dead leaves. More leaves, some dirt and the edge of the rug bunched where someone, or something, had caught it, and suddenly Rick was seeing a trail leading out of the room and further into the house.

'Well, where is everyone then?'

Figure it out, Gabriela. They're all gone. Just like Lizzie and the couple on their honeymoon, and all the others on Anthony's growing list. All gone and never coming back.

'We don't know.' Rick didn't have to see Anthony's face to know that the detective was thinking about his list of the Missing. He wondered how long that list would be now, wondered if it had grown into a life of its own in Anthony's mind, as it had in his. *The Missing … The Damned!* Rick gave himself a mental shake, barely avoiding a physical shudder. They would find a similar crime scene down south, he knew it, and more people that had vanished. Ulladulla was a thriving tourist town with a transient summer population in its thousands. How could they not?

He left Gabriela and Anthony to discuss the ins and outs of a whole town gone and followed the trail of leaves and dirt out of the living room and to the back door. The yard looked a little different in the daylight with the moving shadows of the treetops swaying a lonely dance across the patchy lawn. The bush behind the yard only slightly less dark than his dream. The path through the trees clearly visible now as a natural cut in the ground caused by erosion and widened by use.

'You're not whistling.'

Rick jumped. He stood at the start of the dirt path with no memory of having walked the distance between house and bush. Gabriela waited beside him, Anthony behind her.

'There's something you're not telling me, isn't there?' Gabriela put her hand on Rick's shoulder and applied enough pressure to make him turn away from the path. 'You were sure about the connection between the killing and the disappearances from the start, weren't you? What is it about the blood? Do you know who these people are?'

'No.' Rick thought his voice sounded small, plaintive. He didn't know, not really. Could a dream be called knowledge?

'Rick.' Anthony stood the other side of him now. He felt surrounded, trapped. 'This case isn't exactly your run-of-the-mill homicide and kidnapping. If you know anything, tell us.'

I can't … I don't know … Rick took off, following the path at a run, pushing past bushes as if they weren't there. Branches whipped his face, stabbed his arms and legs. Sharp fronds and grasses cut his hands. He stumbled on loose ground, fell to his knees, tore his pants on a jagged rock, and regained his feet without any loss of momentum. The bushes closed in on the path until he had to force his way through them, breathing heavily in the humid atmosphere, chest heaving, and mouth gaping for air.

When the clearing came, Rick nearly fell simply from the lack of bushes to fight his way through. He stopped and, with a stab of nervous expectation, took in the area in one encompassing stare. He could see it all as if looking into a crystal ball. The circular flattening of grass and absence of bush, the scorch marks in the centre and the way the bordering trees seemed to lean in, guarding the clearing from all sides and leaving a single clear view to the sky directly above where the body had lain.

Where the body had lain …

This was the place of his dream. Where he had witnessed bizarre funeral rites, experienced magic, had flown with the stars … He sat down in a boneless lump. *Shit, it was real.* And the smell was here too, though faded and hiding beneath layers of cold cinders and the heady aroma of the bush around him. The smell of death and fire and … he thought again of the woman in his dream.

He hadn't been sure before, but now he knew, the hands had been female, the long denimed legs, the voice full of grief and horror. He wondered who she was and the face from the photographs flashed before him. No. Similar, but not her. He was sure of it. The face from the recent nightmare? Possibly, but, God, he hoped not. That face had been dead and rotting.

Thudding footsteps, swearing and the swish of branches being swept out of the way heralded the arrival of Gabriela and Anthony. Both swore some more when they nearly tripped over Rick's inert body.

'Damn, Rick! What the hell's the matter with you? Didn't know you could run so fast.' Gabriela dropped down beside Rick, peering intently into his face. Rick closed his eyes to avoid the questions.

He could hear Anthony gasping for breath. The run uphill and through such densely packed bush had been hard for him too, yet he felt as if he'd surpassed the need for breathing. He listened to Anthony control his lungs, heard when his need for air was taken over by his curiosity, and he started walking around the clearing. Forest litter crunched under his feet. Rick listened to him circle, walk to the centre, stop and kneel down.

A touch on his knee and Rick opened his eyes to Gabriela. 'His name was Malaik.'

Gabriela glanced at Anthony and Rick's statement was confirmed with a brief nod. 'Who was he?' she asked.

Rick shrugged. He didn't know, only that the woman had loved the man.

'She brought him here. Laid him down there.' Rick pointed to the blackened rocks in front of Anthony. 'She sang in a language I couldn't understand. Fire …' How could he say the fire had come from within her, had been drawn from the air and trees and bushes around them. How could he tell them how hotly it had burned, how high the flames, when not a single plant was singed and even the burn marks on the ground were not deep or wide enough to show that a body had been cremated here?

'What woman?' Gabriela had an arm around his shoulders and with a start, Rick realised he was crying.

'I don't know.' Rick wiped at his eyes with the back of his hands. They stung. His cheeks burned with hot tears.

Anthony dug his hand into the burned leaves and sand, and lifted it, letting the sand sift through his open fingers. He frowned, chewed his bottom lip and met Rick's blurry gaze. 'How do you know this?'

Rick could see suspicion in that frown. He faced Gabriela, could see a trace of it in her face as well. He didn't blame them. He'd be suspicious too if Gabriela started acting as strangely then blurted out a bunch of stuff about bodies that she really shouldn't know. He swallowed, that heavy gulp of air, spit and fear that preceded admissions a person would really prefer not to admit.

'Thursday night,' he said. 'I was here …'

Gabriela pulled away from Rick, sitting back and staring at him as if he'd either gone mad or just said the stupidest thing ever spoken. 'No way.' She held her hand up to Anthony who had jumped to his feet and started walking over. 'You couldn't have been.' She looked at Anthony then shook her head. 'There's just no way. Thursday night we had dinner together. He had a stomach full of beer and food; all but unconscious when I left. ' She stopped then and had the grace to look guilty. You were practically dead on your feet then …'

Gabriela didn't say how Rick must be now. He knew. Thursday

night was only two nights ago. It felt like a month.

'Well, how could he be at home asleep and here at the same time?' Anthony had his hands on his hips, confused.

Hell, join the club!

'Both. I was both. At home sleeping. Here in my dream.'

Gabriela turned her frowning face from Anthony to Rick in a wrench that Rick was sure must have hurt her neck. He could see the 'don't be ridiculous' comment lurking on her lips. To Gabriela's credit, she held the words back and Rick was glad for it. He knew how ridiculous it sounded without being told.

Anthony was back to chewing on his bottom lip, his gaze directed at the ground, or Rick's feet, he couldn't tell which. He turned away from Rick and walked the perimeter of the clearing.

'What else did you see? From the beginning.' Anthony's measured paces spiralled in until he reached the centre rocks and he looked down on them as if answers could be found in their crumbling remains.

'From the beginning? She found him in that room. I don't know who she is, but I've dreamed about her a few times, maybe more than I remember … He was already dead.' Rick nodded before Gabriela could ask. 'Yes, the same as the woman. With wire wrapped around him and that white stuff on his face. She called his name, that's how I know it. She dragged his body here because this is his circle. I don't know what that means.' He stood up and joined Anthony in the centre. Gabriela followed. All three now stood around the rocks, staring down.

'She placed a rock on his chest, cleared all around the body, then collected some leaves and started a fire with a match. There were more rocks, more fire and the singing.' And he was back to figuring out how to explain the internal fire.

'Go on,' Anthony said. 'What next?'

Without looking up, Rick continued. 'She sat down.' He closed his eyes and tried to remember how it had felt when she called on the power within her. 'It was hot from the inside out. Felt like, I don't know, lightning maybe. Like I'd been struck and was on fire. It came out of her like white light, from her fingers, her eyes, her mouth. Controlled at first, directed at him and then bubbling over until he was consumed. After that …' How could he go on? He had no words to describe what happened next. 'After that, I don't know. It was like we were flying and I could see her looking at me and could see my reflection in her face.'

'Was it real?'

Rick opened his eyes to see Gabriela with a doubtful expression on her face, doubt tinged with scepticism and belief. Anthony's face told him nothing. His lips stayed still, eyes unblinking, and Rick thought that maybe this was too much even for him.

'I didn't think so, but then … the girl at the morgue, the crime scene …' He nodded his head toward the path. 'The house and now this. I didn't think so, but how could it not be?'

'It's real,' Anthony said and Rick could hear the conviction in his voice. 'Like you said, how could it not? Your dream is the thread that ties everything together.'

Gabriela snorted. 'That, or it's a response to everything that's happened. Your subconscious putting two and two together and coming up with five.'

'Before it happened?' Rick took some gratitude in her sceptical statement. Gabriela being Gabriela kept things on a more even keel.

'Maybe it wasn't before at all, did you think of that?' Gabriela kicked at a rock. 'That woman's murder was in all the papers. You knew about it just like the rest of us did—even the wire was reported. You'd already been talking to Baglio here about people mysteriously disappearing.' She wiggled her fingers in the air.

'Then what about this house? What about the circle?' Anthony took Gabriela's opposition personally, and for a moment Rick wondered just what it was that had hooked the detective so fully on this case. Most cops he knew were down-to-earth, practical types who believed in good guys and bad guys, not supernatural spirits that could vanish people without a trace and communicate through dreams.

'Easy. Rick was pretty spooked up at Sutherland earlier. He just brought the creeps with him, even had a nightmare dozing off on the drive down. And as for this circle, Rick took the only path available and it led here. How could he not find it?'

Rick's shoulders slumped. Every one of Gabriela's points had merit. Everything that he felt and knew, or thought he knew, could be explained away by lack of sleep and an overactive imagination. He was surprised at how dejected that made him feel. How lonely. *The woman's not real at all.*

'I disagree,' Anthony said. 'I don't know how, but I think it's as real as anything else in this case. The murders, the missing people, everything. I also think that somewhere in Ulladulla or nearby there's a house with a body in it hanging on the wall. Unless, of course, this woman has already disposed of it. That another one will turn up sometime soon, and that whatever is taking these people is escalating. There are nearly fifty-five empty homes just down that hill. They did not suddenly pack up and leave en masse like a bunch of lemmings. They're gone! Forever!'

Rick felt stunned. Gabriela stood still, apparently unaffected by Anthony's outburst.

'Well, I have to agree with you there.' Gabriela's grin was slight, but there.

'But you just said …'

'I know what I said. What I didn't say was that if it was anyone else but Rick, I'd think the whole lot a bunch of bullshit someone dreamed up to boost magazine sales. If it was anyone else but him, Rick would think the same thing. He doesn't make that kind of shit up. I've known him long enough to know that for sure. Therefore, as unbelievable as it might all sound, coming from Rick, ah, and with you and all your facts, I've got to believe. I'm many things, but I'm no fool.'

'We have to find out who she is.' Relief raced through Rick faster than the burn of cheap Scotch.

'We have to get back to Sutherland.' Gabriela turned away from the circle and started back for the path.

'Right then,' Anthony said, sounding a little confused. 'I'll call ahead and see if anything else has been happening in the shire or anywhere else. Let's look up some local news on the way. They'll pick up stories of missing people quicker than the bigger papers.'

'What about the body at the morgue? We should probably still try to view it …' Rick didn't really want to, but as the only physical evidence, it surely wouldn't hurt.

'I've got a phone number. I'll ring ahead.'

They walked down the path, steeper than Rick remembered from his upward passage, more overgrown. The FSG crew was inside the house, checking for fingerprints, taking samples. The wire had been bagged. So had the thin trail of leaves and dirt and most of the contents of the desk.

The policewoman hovered near the front door, relieved, judging by her welcoming smile and friendlier manner, to see the three return. She had bottles of water in her arms

'Lunch is here. You must be starving.'

Anthony wandered over to the men in blue overalls, peeking over their shoulders and asking a few muffled questions.

'Yeah, I could eat,' Gabriela agreed. 'Stomach feels like it's been cast off and set adrift. Rick?'

'Yeah,' Rick said. His stomach felt more like a block of lead than anything, but food was probably a good idea. 'I could eat.'

———◦∞◦———

Bledray take sustenance from the body and souls of the Rydri.
Consuming everything;
they do not discriminate between young or old,
female or male.
All are equal in the face of eternal hunger.

— Journal of Malaik

———◦∞◦———

17

'Look at that.'

'Look at what?' Jedidiah raised his head from the sand and squinted into the sun.

'Those children on the water's edge.'

Jedidiah forced himself to sit. He saw the children with a predator's quick eye, had been listening to them while he lay on the hot sand, feigning sleep and enjoying the quickening of hunger their laughter brought to him.

'They're not being watched. We could take one so easily.'

Moriah, apparently, had been entertaining herself with planning an attack in the middle of the day on a crowded beach. *Always did like a challenge.* Her voice was edgy, and as Jedidiah turned his gaze from the children to Moriah, he saw that more than her voice was sharpened by hunger. Her body, beneath its covering of filmy material, quivered with need, shimmered with anticipated fulfilment. He felt the quickening rush through him in response and contemplated taking one of the children, in the water or among the rocks nearby. He drowned the thoughts with a wave of willpower and looked further along the beach.

'Hunger is making you foolish if you think they're not being watched.'

Moriah turned to him, frowning, lips turned down at the corners. Jedidiah grinned at her, his grin widening as her frown deepened, and nodded toward the small group of adults lying around on towels and in beach chairs, chatting, drinking and occasionally venturing down to the water.

'At least one of them is watching all the time. No sooner does one turn away than another takes up the guard.'

Moriah hissed her impatience and flopped down on her towel. Eyes squeezed closed against the sun, lips forming a straight line across her face. She pulled her top down around her to cover the flash of white stomach exposed from unguarded movement and reached for her hat. Jedidiah leaned over and cupped her cheek with his hand before she could find it. Rarely did Moriah need comfort and sweet words. The chance to offer them could not be missed.

'The waiting will only make it better, my love. I promise you, as soon as the sun dips a little, I'll help you catch as many wayward children as you can.'

Moriah opened her eyes, less annoyed now, but dark with hunger. 'You always know the right words to say.'

'That's because I love you.'

'You do?' Moriah's lips were plump and red.

'Burn for you.' Jedidiah tightened his hold on her head, lifted it until their lips met.

'Feed me.'

Jedidiah crushed his lips against hers. He could afford a Sharing. They would feed tonight and he'd regain anything he lost here on the beach.

The beach stretched either side of them, lined by the bay waters on one side and houses on the other. The murmur of voices mixed with waves hitting the sand, a lawnmower, a radio up too loud, the ever-present boats … Jedidiah liked the background noise, the life that came with it, washing over him with a sense of place and belonging. Even if the belonging had more to do with taking. He wanted the children now too, wanted their laughter bubbling inside him, the innocence and naivety to soothe his raging desires, their youth. So sweet.

Moriah stopped him before he could lose himself in the Sharing, pushed him away with his strength in her hands. He stayed where she left him, loose-limbed and boneless on the sand.

'Can you smell that?'

Jedidiah could barely see let alone smell. 'Smell what?' His teeth ground heavily in his mouth, tongue felt like an engorged slug. *Bring on the night.*

'We've got company.' Moriah slid down in the sand beside

Jedidiah and kissed him gently on the cheek. 'You shouldn't have let me take so much.'

'Who?' Jedidiah breathed in deep and caught a taste of something in the air.

'More of us,' she said. 'More of us. There's going to be a Gathering.'

Jedidiah stopped breathing for a minute, let himself relax in the sand, a smile drawing across his shivery lips. *A Gathering…* Ages had passed since the last Gathering. He didn't think enough of their kind were left for such a thing, had long since given up hope for another.

'We'll rest here a little longer then go and meet them, perhaps take a walk through town. The sun will be setting by then. You'll be stronger.' Moriah ran her fingers around his face, brushed back sandy hair, smoothed out eyebrows, kissed his lips, nibbled on his chin. Strength returned with every touch. 'We could do a little feed, like the Guardians do.'

Jedidiah shook his head, clawed his fingers into her arms.

'All or nothing, Moriah. I can outwait the sun.'

Cooler air and ravenous hunger woke Jedidiah hours later. Moriah was swimming—or as close to swimming as she'd ever get. The children were gone. He scanned the beach. So were the adults that came with the children and most everyone else as well. The sun hadn't quite set, but the way the shadows from the houses stretched across the beach to mingle with sand and fade into the oncoming tide indicated it certainly wasn't far from it. And he was hungry. So hungry.

He sat with aching muscles and stretched. Moriah waved to him and he stood to join her at the water's edge. Sand, glued to his skin with sweat, made him feel rigid and unbending, and cascaded from the folds of his shorts. The bottom of his feet cramped, making his toes curl as he walked hunched over with stiffness and dehydration. He needed to feed.

Water swished the sand from his feet and ankles, and he stepped in deeper to rid himself of the rest. He didn't like to swim, but he liked the feel of the caked sand even less, and dived in with clumsy movements, his eyes and mouth closed tight against the salty sting of the sea.

He felt tight as a drum, hollow, skin stretched across wasted muscles and brittle bones. Sand clumped in his swimming costume, trapped by cloth and body, and he wiped roughly at it, pulling at the clothing to free the offending particles. He broached the water, hair flat on his head and in his eyes, and his eyes stung anyway so he had to wipe at them too. He hated the sea.

Moriah slithered beside him in the water, pushed the hair away and wiped his face for him.

'Walk time,' she said. 'If you don't eat soon you'll shrivel away to nothing.'

Not quite nothing, Jedidiah knew and feared. More like a husk too weak to shift and form another body, too weak to feed at all. Death wouldn't come easy or quick, tacked on to the end of untold suffering. He shivered. He'd rather face instant death at the hands of a Guardian than that. He looked at Moriah, coaxing him now from the water he hated. No, he'd rather live. Leaving Moriah would be more unbearable than any fate.

'A group of people just got off that boat.' Moriah pointed to a green and gold ferry chugging across the bay, back to wherever it had come from. 'They had packs and tents.'

Jedidiah felt his lips tighten in a smile. An easy catch at night, campers, if he could last the distance. He wasn't sure he could.

'Let's make one little stop on the way,' he said.

'Ooh, take out?' Jedidiah goddess she really was. He nodded and took her hand as they walked to their towels.

'Let's see what's open.'

*Oh that we could be as quickly adaptable as the Rydri.
We barely survived the holocaust yet we could see that our future lay
with the Rydri more than ever, and we could see what we would have
to do to ensure even that against the Bledray.*

— *Journal of Malaik*

18

'We've been invited out for dinner.' Ben walked into Jamie's flat, hands in pocket, face serious.

Jamie was about to remind him they weren't meant to be seeing each other at the moment and then thought better of it. She needed to talk to him, to have him close.

'Who with?'

'Gabriela Salek.'

'You're kidding me? The reporter? It's bad enough my being with you, let alone some reporter. They asked about you today, you know. Knew you weren't that woman's uncle, know your background, and your reputation.'

'Have they checked the security tapes yet?' Ben didn't seem concerned in the slightest.

'Yes and they found nothing. Nothing they shared with me anyway. One of the techies said the tape had a glitch in it, some sort of shadowy thing that disrupted recording. Highly suspicious, but doesn't prove anything. The time lapse was really too short for someone to sneak in, steal a body and sneak back out.'

'Though that's exactly what's happened.'

'Well, yes …'

'It wasn't me so even if they do find me they can't make any links …'

'Yes, they can. They'll make any bloody links they like. There's already talk that you're actually the killer come back to gloat.'

'That's not true either.' Ben frowned and rubbed his hand through his hair.

'I know that. It's just rumours because they've got nothing better to go on.' Jamie folded her arms and then let them drop. She fervently wished she'd never called Ben in the first place, that she hadn't found the blood irregularity. 'But if they suspect you they'll dig deeper and as soon as they discover I called you, that I have a relationship with you, they'll start looking closer at me and you know how the higher-ups are about proper procedure. I'll be under investigation quicker than you can say … let's have dinner with a reporter and splash everything across the news!'

'Stop. Jamie, just stop.' Ben took her useless hands and held them together, his touch warm and gentle as if she were some skittish colt. 'I'm afraid this is bigger than you and your job, bigger than any rumours or procedures or any of that shit! I want you to get all your notes together on this woman, everything you've got on her blood and the dust. All the test results, everything. We're meeting Gabriela Salek in 40 minutes along with Rick Hendry and a Detective Baglio. They're working on this case from a different angle and they need us, or rather you and your findings …'

'No.' Jamie pulled her hands free to fold her arms, wrap them so tight around her they ached with the force of her grip. 'No. I don't want to be involved.' She walked away from Ben, put the lounge between them.

Ben didn't try to close the distance, but Jamie could sense his disappointment. She turned away from it and wished she could turn just as easily from the fear that twisted her inside. *Coward!* Did Ben think her a coward too? She glanced back at him, but he was looking at the floor, not her, and scratching his head. He was thinking what to say, she decided. Thinking of the right words to change her mind, to give her courage. She turned away again. *Fuck that!*

'It's too late to say that, Jamie. Whether you help them or not, you're in it up to your neck. This, at least, is a legal investigation now. You'll be working with the police …'

'But with no authority!'

Ben gripped the back of the lounge and Jamie could see he was getting frustrated. *Too bloody bad!*

'Jamie. There's been another murder. The same MO. They suspect now that there may have been others. And that's not all, people are going missing …'

'I don't know anything about that.'

'They believe it's all connected but they need proof. Physical and scientific proof. They have more blood samples. They need you to test them. You know what to look for, you already have the background. Think about it, Dr Morell. You're on the verge of making a scientific breakthrough. Are you going to let bureaucratic procedure keep you from this?' He skirted the lounge in quick steps, held her shoulders and forced her to face him, and then waited for her to look up, into his eyes. His voice dropped to a harsh whisper. 'We're talking non-humans here. Proof of another race, Jamie. An answer to that clichéd question, "Are we alone?" What if we've been looking in the wrong places? What if other life is not out among the stars somewhere, but right here with us? What if we're not the top of the food chain at all?'

'You think too much, Ben, and you ask too many what ifs. That woman's body, you know the one we don't have any more, is not proof of aliens or other humanoid races or hidden civilisations on Mars.'

'Either way you win. You'll be in on solving a murder that's got the police stumped, you'll have physical evidence either way of aliens and you can publish a paper on rare blood types. That job is not the be all and end all of your existence. Take a risk with me, Jamie.'

She had to admit all of Ben's what ifs were tantalising, his enthusiasm catching, but what if … She shrugged out of his embrace, she needed to think and she needed space to do it in. The papers were in her desk drawer. Her gaze wandered to the desk in the corner with its laptop and printer neatly stowed, the pens in their jar, dictionaries and a thesaurus, and a shelf full of medical texts on the wall above it. She thought about those papers and the résumé, and file full of job applications underneath them. Who the hell was she kidding? Looking for a new job had been high on her priorities right up until she found the blood anomaly.

She looked at her watch. If they were going to make that dinner, they'd need to leave pretty soon.

Anthony sat back in his chair and looked at the people circled around the table. They'd eaten and talked most of the evening tucked in a corner of this out-of-the-way restaurant, comparing notes, sharing stories, gaining a broader understanding of what had been occurring. An understanding, he noted, that helped them not one bit in knowing what they were facing. In reality, they were really not that much further along in the investigation than they were three days ago. They had more, true, but still the case was held together with conjecture and supposition, and tied up with a supernatural thread that would see them laughed out of any court.

He outlined the case in his head. One, the count of missing people had risen dramatically. Two, no bodies. Three, number of people being murdered and wrapped in barbed-wire also rising. Four, no bodies. Five, Rick, respected investigative reporter and man not prone to histrionics or wild ghost stories, had a vision about one of the bodiless murders. Six, Rick's 'murder' had taken place in a town with a missing population. And seven, five people were missing, or last seen, in Sutherland Shire since the death of the woman. A folded copy of the local newspaper sat on top of his briefcase, the lead story about a young man missing from Cronulla.

Police resources were concentrated on containing the Bellbird situation at the present moment, not the dwindling population of Cronulla and neighbouring suburbs.

The connection between the murders and the missing rested on location only. *Not nearly enough!*

Dr Morell's friend, Ben Sokoloff, appeared to be leaning toward aliens. What could Anthony say to that? The thought had more than crossed his mind several times, but he'd put that down to growing up on a television-fed diet of science fiction. Dr Morell, more contained in her beliefs than her associate, had honestly stated she didn't know what to believe. However, the blood raised questions with extremely cloudy answers. She had researched all other known instances of the irregularity and come up against brick walls. Scientists no longer working at universities, patients whose records were confidential, out-of-date or just plain missing.

Something else waited to be found.

He'd spent the afternoon checking out of his city motel and shifting base down to Cronulla, obtaining a room at one of the larger motels near the beach, not too far from the scene of the latest missing person. Well, the latest missing person so far recorded. He and Rick had walked the Esplanade, north of the motel and up to Wanda Beach, a busy area. So easy for one person to vanish in the crowds. They'd explored the sand hills behind the beach and found exactly what they expected to find. Absolutely nothing, not even a smell with the constant sea breezes to clean the air.

Meeting the doctors hadn't been a waste of time. They now all knew that the white silky powder found at both scenes and on the dead woman's face was a mix of the powdered herbs belladonna, morning glory and some other that remained unidentified. The two known ingredients—highly poisonous all on their own, Dr Morell had informed them—when mixed together and powdered resembled a toxic bomb similar in strength to the individual as the atom bomb was to Hiroshima.

Gabriela's tanned face had gone pasty at that pronouncement. Rick looked ill as well. Anthony had been wearing latex gloves whenever he touched the substance. But the doctor had assured them all they had to inhale a large quantity to have any effect and had then looked at them all closely.

Anthony stopped thinking about the case at that point and noticed that a woman stood outside the restaurant watching them. She looked familiar, though he couldn't place her and was about to point her out when Dr Morell happened to turn and see her as well.

'Oh, my God! That's the woman from the café this morning.' She pushed back her chair and started for the door.

Rick saw the woman too and froze, hand halfway to bringing a glass to his mouth. 'That's her,' he said, as if the others should know who 'her' was.

Dr Morell was almost at the door.

'Who?' Gabriela asked, straining to see past Rick.

Dr Sokoloff turned and now all four were staring out the window.

Dr Morell opened the door.

She was nice-looking, Anthony thought. A bit on the thin side, about 5'8" in height, dark hair, strong face, and … gone. Dr Morell stepped out onto the footpath and the woman vanished.

'How the hell did she do that?' Dr Sokoloff dropped the fork in his hand.

Rick finished the rest of his drink in one gulp. Anthony followed Gabriela out to the footpath.

'Did you see where she went?' he asked Dr Morell, peering into parked cars, striding to the next restaurant along and looking in there.

'She was gone by the time I got out here.'

'No,' Anthony said. 'She was here right until you stepped out and then she vanished. Did you see anything?'

'What? Like puffs of smoke and magic wands?'

'Yes, anything like that. Anything not like that.'

'Don't be silly, she just walked away, maybe got into a car, that's all. People don't just vanish into thin air.'

'She did.' Gabriela told her, but the doctor shook her head in disbelief and walked back into the restaurant. 'How could that happen? You saw it, didn't you?'

Anthony replied that he had and then he looked through the window, at Rick, Ben Sokoloff and Dr Morell, and the two empty chairs belonging to him and Gabriela. 'We all saw it. We all saw her. But I think your questions would be better suited put to Rick, don't you? He recognised her …'

'Do you think it's the one he's been dreaming about?'

'Perhaps. Let's ask him.'

He watched as Rick placed his empty glass on the table and ordered another drink from the waiter. The man looked like he'd seen a ghost, and in all probability, he had. They all had.

⎯⎯⎧⎤⎧⎯⎯

Cold. That's how he felt. Bone aching, teeth chattering cold. He needed another drink, more alcohol to warm his blood. Hold the ice, he told the waiter. Straight up whisky and be generous with the serve. His hand shook as he passed the empty glass up. His whole body was fucking shaking. Damn! But it was her, she was real, he knew it just as well as he knew that one glass of whisky was not going to be enough.

He listened to Dr Morell tell Ben that she'd seen the woman in the café near the morgue, not that long after the body had been taken.

'She looks familiar, but I don't know why.'

Ben nodded. She was familiar to him as well.

And Rick knew the whys about that too. She was the one who had taken the body. Somewhere, sometime on this hot Saturday, she had fashioned a fire with unexplained power that had sent the woman off to … Rick didn't know. Off to whatever these people thought of as heaven, he supposed.

Anthony and Gabriela came back to the table, both staring at him as if they'd just realised he had two heads when all they'd ever been able to see was one. *They know* … He looked up into their faces, both frowning, both a little scared. *No, they suspect.* He nodded at them. They hadn't shared that part of the story with the doctors yet. Sokoloff might understand, but Morell seemed more focused on reality, very much interested in hard facts.

Relief chased the cold away. Everyone had seen her. That meant he wasn't nuts. That meant she was someone real who had contacted him telepathically in his dreams. *Oh, my God! I am nuts!* But the proof was there. The woman was real. It was the woman from his dream. Now she was here, or had been here. What did that mean for him?

'You and Jamie have seen this woman before?' Ben watched him with a thoughtful expression. 'In different places I assume.'

'Explain how you know her, Dr Morell.' Anthony ignored Rick for the moment, opening his briefcase instead and questioning the doctor.

'She was at the café at the same time as me. Not long after the body did its vanishing act. I was talking to Ben on the phone and saw her walk in. She ordered coffee or whatever, went to the back of the café and started reading a newspaper. I bumped into a chair right then and nearly spilled my tea. I looked away for a minute and when I looked back she was gone.'

'So she vanished then too?' Gabriela asked the doctor, but kept her eyes on Rick.

'I presumed she'd walked out. There was probably a back door. Why? Who is she?'

'Rick?' Ben's thoughtful look shifted to penetrating.

The waiter arrived with his drink and Rick gratefully accepted the glass—and the time he needed to formulate an answer. He'd tell them everything, of course. Sokoloff was obviously as involved as the rest of them. Jamie Morell was less of a sure thing. He'd have to risk it. He thanked the waiter. Emptied the glass. And with liquor seeping into his bloodstream and giving him something firmer, if a little fuzzy, to hold onto, he said, 'Let's pay up and get out of here. This isn't the place to tell you the rest of the story. It only gets weirder from here.'

He watched their reactions. Ben nodded and leaned forward to retrieve his wallet from his back pocket. Anthony did the same and Gabriela picked up her purse. Dr Morell's face showed astonishment followed by consternation chased off by resignation and the start of curiosity. *She's in too. Hooked just like the rest of us.*

Rick glanced at the other tables. Everyone else was busy eating or talking. No one but them had seen the woman evaporate before their eyes, no one but them. *What does it mean?*

He didn't know, but he had the feeling that the knowing would be his all too soon. The thought made him want to order another drink.

———◦•◦———

Change will be slow;
following the path of the Hunters and their Companions.
It will be reflected in the
stories and songs
of those Rydri who remember Miaheyyu in whichever form
their culture permits.

— Journal of Malaik

———◦•◦———

19

The woman lived in a little house on a big block of land that backed onto the Royal National Park. It had been her father's house once, back when getting to Bundeena necessitated detailed planning and an itinerary. A car or wagon ride along a muddy track rutted through with the tracks of other cars or wagons all eager to get to 'paradise'. That was before she was born, before her parents had met and married.

Bill Ward had seen an opportunity in procuring property on land that, at that time, was in the middle of the wilderness and, therefore, not worth much. Many of his neighbours had been encouraged to move to the tiny village when the Depression had put renting a decent home out of the reach of most people. Bill sniffed a bargain and followed them in, and he'd been right. Dorothy Parden's land was worth at least a million in cool, hard cash, and she wouldn't trade it for anything.

She sat on her white plastic 'outdoors' chair on her front porch when the southerlies were blowing and watched bushwalkers and beachgoers walk along the road below. When it was too hot out front, she'd retreat to the back porch to watch ships and fishing boats sail past, or feed the birds who escaped the bush to feed on the sweet offerings of her garden.

Dorothy bustled around her house, tidying and moving things; chatting to her husband, firmly ensconced in his workroom turning rocks; or talking on the phone to her grandchildren and daughters, discussing Christmas—just around the corner, you know—and who would be doing what where and with whom. Dorothy was happy with her life. She had a husband still, being of an age when most of her friends no longer did, who she got along with quite well, and a family that visited regularly and were all reasonably happy with their own lives, as far as she could tell or wanted to know.

Answering the knock on the door and providing help to lost strangers was nothing at all. Yes, they could use her phone. Yes, she loved living this close to the bush and the ocean. No, the isolation was hardly noticeable, though the walk down to the road was getting longer every year. 'Would you like a cup of tea, loves? The kettle's already on the stove, just about to boil. I'll just call Roger in …'

———

Jedidiah and Moriah sat on the back porch of the Parden residence watching the path of the walkers Moriah had seen alight from the ferry.

'They've left it late to start a trip,' Jedidiah commented. He felt refreshed, rejuvenated.

'They won't get far before they have to start pitching tents. Make it easier for us.' Moriah turned to him with a greedy smile.

There'd been a time, not all that long ago, when they could get by with feeding only a few times in a year. A time when hunger was a constant companion and they'd survived as washed out apparitions of their true selves, lurking around the edges of towns, eating tasteless human food to keep from fading away altogether.

Something had changed in them, linked with the discovery of how to defeat the Guardians. Hunger grew; the occasional feeding no longer enough. They were driven by the need to take human life, to consume it, own it and become it. The need drowned every other. *Nearly every other* … Jedidiah reached for Moriah's hand.

They were like starving children, Jedidiah decided. Swallowing everything they could, taking more than they needed because it was there and the taking was so easy, so fine. He loved the power and strength that coursed through every vein, pumped vitality through every cell, felt drunk on it and longed for more. Before the morning came again, the campers would be theirs. Not because they were hungry, but because they wanted them, and they could.

Moriah stood up and Jedidiah's hand dropped against the armrest of the plastic chair. 'Let's go down to the beach.' She stared down the white strip of sand between the dark blanket of the sea and the barrier of bushland that separated township from ocean.

'Time to meet the others?'

Moriah didn't answer. She jumped the short distance from porch down to grass, jogged to the fence line and, with one hand holding a decrepit looking fencepost steady, lightly jumped over. A wide path followed the line of houses down in the direction of the beach. Moriah didn't wait.

'Time to meet the others then.' Jedidiah shimmered, changed form and in an instant caught up with Moriah, caressing her shoulders with his cool, airy touch before reforming and matching her determined stride. *Others, others, others* …It had been so long since they'd met others.

*Guardians and Hunters must beware the temptation
of Hunger.
To fall so will be as to live in damnation and torment;
neither Alffür nor Bledray,
neither living nor dead.*

20

Tonight. She would meet him tonight. But they'd all seen her, and Lael was confused. A whole group of humans to learn the Way of the Hunter? How bad was this going to get? One was all she was used to dealing with. One Hunter, one human, and as far as she knew that was how it had always been. The strength engendered by the coupling had always been insurmountable in the past. *Shit! Am I meant to couple with all of them?* Lael paced the shadows of the shop entryway across the road from the restaurant. *No, no, that can't be right. I didn't know about the others. I would have known if that'd been the case.* Lael stilled and watched the group exit the restaurant, looking around, though they tried to hide it, and walking up the street, away from her. Shoulder to shoulder and protective, as if already on the defence. She could see their strength even now, rippling around them in a blaze of colour and wondered if they'd any inkling yet of the challenge ahead.

Probably not. Humans rarely did. Their concept of reality was, on a general level, narrow and rigid. Even those few enlightened ones saw the dimensions of life as a construct of ideas and thought rather than a world teeming with possibilities. Modern education turned alternative dimension into fantasy.

Lael followed them, tempted to sneak closer to hear their words and arguments. They were an articulate lot if the body language and throwing of hands was anything to go by. *Five. Five people to communicate with.* The reason behind the number escaped her for a moment; left her baffled with the technicalities of first convincing and then fighting with such a large number of humans.

An old memory, passed down to her from Malaik, her mentor and partner, came to her. He'd taught her the Ways of the Hunter before taking up Guardianship. Too old, he'd said, for wandering the world. Too hurt from the last Gathering to ever want to do it again.

She could, he'd said. She had strength that would remain untapped until she needed it. Until the next Gathering. For there would be one, he told her. The Ghouls had not been wholly defeated, only controlled, weakened for a time though, no one knew how long that time would be.

Lael had the definite feeling that time was up. The Ghouls were gathering.

Midnight. The cusp of days, bridge between night and morning, old and new, dream and truth. *And they're all still awake, dammit!* Lael waited with draining impatience for the five humans to shut up, stop thinking, and get to sleep.

She had a lot to find out, a lot to share with them, had to figure out what to do and where to do it. The stench the Ghouls gave off grew stronger with every lost hour. They were coming to this area like ants to the honeypot. Somewhere to the south, she thought, though distinguishing their location from smell alone, when she was trapped in her motel room waiting for gabby humans, was difficult.

The atmosphere in her room was close and hot with the window and door locked. Candles, flames fluttering as she paced past them, smoke eddying in mini-tornadoes of air, filled the spaces in the room with a lingering fragrance. Lael had enjoyed their smell when she first lit them, appreciated the mask they threw over the tainted air of the Ghouls. Now, she found the aroma sickeningly sweet, corrupted by the Ghouls and the lack of ventilation. She needed air, needed action … needed those humans to sleep so she could get on with things.

'Bugger it!' She had to find out where the Ghouls were.

Lael unlocked and wrenched open the door and nearly swooned at the acidity of the night air. She ran then, urgency gripping her as the screams of dying souls mixed with the stars and faded into obscurity—even the heavens closed to them, the flames of hell a passing fancy when existence and being has been snuffed out of the universe.

Her footsteps clattered on the stairs, thudded along the drive and then vanished from hearing as she hit the shadows, changed form and flew into the night, an invisible hawk hunting for its prey.

The scent sharpened as she drew away from the buildings and trappings of humanity, crystallised into an aromatic arrow pointing out the path she should take. Glittering trails in a broad expanse of blackness acted like a giant X, marking the spot. The black area was the Royal National Park, a long tract of natural bushland that divided the cities of Sydney and Wollongong. Not the usual feeding grounds of the Ghouls, but skirted by enough blinking lights indicating townships to turn the area into a killing field.

The trails led out from those townships like a spider's web, if the spider was tripping on cocaine; straggly lines showing no discernible pattern, following no pre-planned strategy. Like the Ghoul at Cronulla, indiscriminate and careless.

Lael had feared that the Gathering had started, that she was defeated before the battle had begun. In truth, knowing that the telltale sign of the Ghouls hunting and feeding meant that people were dying, she knew that even now the battle was still to come. It could not be joined too soon, could not be faced unprepared or all indeed would be lost; and all was the much larger worry.

She swooped down, disregarding discretion for speed and surprise, and attacked a pair of Ghouls too involved in a Sharing to realise their danger. She surrounded them with an almighty roar and rush of power, clenched their struggling forms to her, crushing, strangling, draining the stolen essence of their beings until their vaporous forms were little more than atrophied fragments of airborne molecules. Then she released them to dissolve in the breeze. Not enough left to do anything else.

Vibrating with the intensity of her attack, enlivened by fierceness and the true nature of her calling, Lael searched for more Ghouls. Staying low, swerving through branches and long grass, she reached out with her senses. Passing over alarmed animals, feeding deer that startled, ears swivelling and noses sniffing for danger, foxes scurrying to dens leaving behind kills, she found a lone Ghoul engrossed in feeding on a cliff top that sheered away to the ocean below.

Another loner? Lael flashed on Carena's red dress. Unusual enough for there to be one lone Ghoul when they paired for life and rarely survived separation, but two? She paused at the edge of the low scrub. A fishing rod leaned against a sun-whitened rock of calcified sand. Its hook and line hung carelessly free. Lael was too late to save the fisherman. She looked out to the verge of the cliff. More fishermen cast their baited lines out to the ocean. Torches and lamps sent circles of light around their gear, colourful glow sticks marked the lip of the cliff. This fisherman was lost, the others wouldn't be.

Lael knew she should take the Ghoul straightaway, before it sensed her presence and fled, but she wanted to know what its separation meant. She waited a few seconds longer, until the Ghoul had almost completed the feed, but had not taken the last, vital quintessence of the human. When that moment came, she circled the Ghoul and its victim, and ensnared it in a tightening noose of power.

'What are you?' she whispered. 'Tell me your name.'

The Ghoul whimpered and Lael was surprised at the waves of despair that pummelled her embrace.

'I am David . Take me now.'

That was even more surprising, but she could feel the sincerity of the desolation this Ghoul felt, and something else, flashes of red, a woman's name … Carena.

'Why are you alone?'

The Ghoul flinched and moaned his grief. 'She cast me aside. Changed she is, changed in a way I would not follow. They all are.'

Lael flexed her power, drawing another low moan of desolation. She suspected a trick, as with Carena, and would not be fooled again. Yet no trick came.

'Destroy me. I cannot fight the need any longer. I don't want to be drawn into the Gathering …'

'What are you?' A Bledray Ghoul with morals?

'I took little feeds. I touched life without taking and it was enough, but now the fire of Taking controls me. Carena was repulsed. She left. The fire burned hotly within her.' His voice dropped to the softest of whispers. 'She found out how to defeat the Guardians. The knowledge spreads through us, feeds the flames … Kill me now before I am truly destroyed.'

The Ghoul held back its instinctual drive to defend itself, laid itself bare to the Hunter's deadly touch.

'Why are you not a Guardian?' Was this how Guardians were made? Emerging from the ashes of a defeated Ghoul like a phoenix.

'I cannot live without Carena, and now she is …' He looked into Lael's indistinct face. 'She is gone. I don't want to be anything without her.'

It had always confused her really, that the Alffür Guardians and Hunters could live alone for millennia if they so chose, while Ghouls partnered with a love that knew no boundaries. She'd never heard of one casting aside another. Ghoul partners attuned to each through unfettered Sharing.

'But she left you. She took life and kept the Sharing to herself. Even for a Ghoul she was a monster.'

David said nothing. Slowly, achingly so, he transformed into the fleshless being they all were really—Ghouls, Guardians and Hunters alike, ghosts that had haunted humanity through the ages.

She could taste his disgust in himself, his despair over the loss of Carena. Lael took him with an aversion she had never felt before. Choice was not given; roles could not be changed. He was a Ghoul and she the Hunter; no fuzzy lines could be drawn between the two. Power trickled through her as she encapsulated the Ghoul and forced him into nothingness. She flew high into the sky, over the heads of the surviving fishermen and out to sea where she dove, hit the water and kept going, howling anguish and pain and sorrow at the inevitability of life and death.

The remains of the fisherman lay where David had dropped him. An ugly dried out husk of a man whose last recognisable thought would have been of pleasure. The man's pants, ragged tracksuit pants stained with years of fish guts, seawater and whatever else he'd come into contact with, tented over his groin in a grotesque comedy of sexual arousal.

Lael sat on the white rock above it, a pool of water collecting beneath her and forming rivulets that ran down the rock face to the body. No amount of water would rehydrate the barren carcass of this human, and no trace of him could be left behind. Lael slipped down the side of the rock, graceful and intent. She would have to finish what the Ghoul started.

She kneeled beside his bony hand; his fingers had clawed deep gouges into the eroded surface of the sandstone. She ran a hand over his long, wind-scruffed hair, and shed a tear when it broke like dried grass with her touch. The others were calling out, missing their friend gone too long for rebaiting and taking a leak. Their voices grumbled and scoffed at what else their friend might be up to.

'If they only knew,' she whispered to him. 'If they only knew.'

She opened her mouth, almost kissing him now, not daring to touch just yet and then stretched it wider to encompass his gaping mouth, his nose. She couldn't look into his eyes, glazed and milky as they were, wouldn't touch him anywhere else. Stilled breath, waiting, waiting until the need to breathe overcame her disgust at what she was doing and then a long, indrawn gasp for air that robbed the body of any remaining soul and sent it through the dusty realm of void and into the complete emptiness of the non-being. Never to be reborn. Never to know the eternal spirit.

Lael wanted to sink into the rock and stay there forever, huddled beneath its hard protective walls. She'd tasted human soul complete, the whole cake instead of the pieces she took only when necessary, and she liked it, wanted more. Wanted to gorge and drink and kill and destroy. The other humans were not far away, coming closer, concern rippling through their base jokes and taunts. *Take them all. Feed and be strong. Feed and come to us …* Lael was aflame with raw, agonising hunger.

The fishermen came closer, within her reach. They hadn't seen her yet, though she was still in flesh form. Moon-striped shadows hid her crouching at the base of the rock. A foot came close, the leg … she stretched out her hand. Oh, the frisson of that touch, so delightful, so desirous. *More* … Her hand ran up the leg, curled around it as she changed form and swirled around his body.

The man became aware then, aware of the hunger she couldn't hide, the danger he was in. *Be mine, be mine, be mine* … she sang to him, but her need was too strong. Fear emanated from him like a splash of icy cold water, doused her senses and brought her back from the brink of unspeakable horror. She pushed away from him even as he stumbled, back stepping across the rough ground, a gargled scream caught in his throat.

Lael left the scream and the men behind on the lonely cliff, flying aimlessly, ensnared still in the horror that she'd been about to commit and finally, dropped to earth, gracelessly, uncaring, great sobs of abhorrence renting her apart cell by cell. She landed at the end of a beach covered in broken shells and shattered coral, waves thundering as they crashed against rock and shore. White foam washed over her feet, the pull of the water sucking her into reach of the waves. They broke around her, the waves, cold and full with torn seaweed, sand and pulsing, living water. She cried as they pounded her, not for the beating her body was taking, but because it was not enough. Not enough punishment for what she had nearly done, for what she still felt—the lingering traces of a hunger that yawned inside her, a cavernous hole that would never, ever be filled.

The waves carried her out to sea, unable to kill her, though she'd hoped they would. Moonlight silvered the surface of the water around her. Somewhere further out, she heard the sound of ships passing, of whales broaching. Her eyes were open, staring at the stars and the moon, and she was more tired than she'd ever been before. The horror started fading, removed from her now as the cold of the sea penetrated the shock, and she closed her eyes. Realising as she did so, that the humans she'd been waiting for had finally gone to sleep.

The means of the Hunt
are the steps of every journey
past and future,
and must be weighed and balanced
within the heart of the Hunter.

— Journal of Malaik

21

Rick sat around a campfire. Ordinary fire, he realised, with crackling flames and burning sticks, circled with rocks and set into a hollow in the sand. He looked down. He was wearing the clothes he'd had on all day, faded jeans, pale yellow polo shirt, and his hiking boots. He must have left the jacket he'd worn to the restaurant in his car. What the hell was he doing at the beach? The last thing he remembered was dumping his clothes on the floor and crashing into bed, feeling like a zombie to the grave. He most definitely did not remember getting up, dressing and venturing out to the beach in the middle of the night. He looked around him and realised he didn't recognise the beach he was on.

'Hey, the fire!'

Rick turned and peered into the blackness behind him, orange licks of flame still flitting across his vision.

'Rick? What're you doing here?'

Gabriela appeared out of the flickering darkness, hair messed up, and for all the world looking like she'd just woken up. She sat down beside Rick, head cocked to one side either listening for something or waiting for Rick to answer.

'Where's here?' she asked instead and felt dumb for not knowing.

'You know, I think we're dreaming ...' Ben said from the other side of the fire, though no one had been there a second before. Jamie Morell was curled up beneath his protective arm, half-asleep and flushed, lips pouting.

'Don't be silly,' she said, her voice roughened with sleep and sex.

Rick felt a little embarrassed, as if he'd walked into the room and caught them in the act.

'Group dreaming?' Anthony stood beside Gabriela, hands in pockets, tie loose, shirt untucked. 'That's unlikely, isn't it?'

'Maybe it's like group learning or group memory or something.

You know where the same or similar ideas pop up all over the world.' Gabriela rubbed her eyes then stared blearily into the fire. 'I could do with a cigarette right about now. And a drink, or at least eight hours straight of sleep.'

'You don't smoke.' Rick felt stupid again. He looked at everyone's face in turn. Other than each of them appearing to have just woken up, they looked pretty much how they had when he'd left them sometime around midnight. Except Gabriela, who, temporarily single, had decided to crash on his spare bed rather than drive home, and had stripped down to underwear and a tank top. She'd been snoring before Rick had even made it to his own room. Midnight. *What time is it now?* Rick glanced at his watch, but the face was blurry, the hands swam like tadpoles caught in a net. 'Does anyone know what time it is?'

'I'd rather know where we are and why?' Anthony walked around the fire, pausing behind Ben and Dr Morell to frown before shaking his head a little and continuing on. He stopped again beside Rick and sat down with crossed legs, letting his hands hang limply over his knees. 'Well?'

'Well what?' They all stared at Rick now, waiting for answers he didn't have. *A couple of weird dreams doesn't make me an expert.*

'No,' Gabriela said. 'But they make you more experienced at this stuff than us.'

Rick screwed up his face. He could feel the creases, the drag of his eyelids over his eyes. *I didn't think I said that out loud?*

'You didn't.' Dr Morell this time, sitting up now, alert. 'But I heard it as if you did.'

'Me too,' Ben said. 'Do you think that's normal for a group dream?'

'How the hell should I know? Last time I had a dream this weird the only other person in it was that woman and we were kind of one and the same.' Rick looked down at himself again.

'Don't worry, Rick. You still look as manly as ever.' Gabriela smirked, and if Rick didn't feel so surreally out of place, he'd have liked to wipe that smirk off her face.

Gabriela frowned and Rick added, *Just kidding …* to his thoughts.

'Is this in any way similar to your dream of the woman?' Anthony tried hard to remain professionally distant about it all, but Rick could hear the whisperings of doubt and fear in his thoughts.

'There was a fire before, that's all. Not the same kind of fire though and look …' He pointed to the flames. 'No dead body either.'

'So no murder then …' Gabriela twisted until she was on her knees and reached out to the flames. 'Do you think if it's a dream that means it won't burn? If I put my hand in the flames and then wake up in the morning with blistered fingers, we'll know whether or not this is real.'

'That's about the dumbest thing I ever heard.' All five faces turned to the new voice. Gabriela froze mid-reach.

The woman had joined them. Hair curled damply around her neck, hung in her eyes, some stuck to her hollowed cheeks. She took Gabriela's arm and pulled it away from the fire, kneeling beside her as if she'd been there the whole time. *Maybe she has …*

'Whether or not you burn your hand and whether or not it's real, you'll still be in a lot of pain and I'd rather you were whole and thinking clearly at this point.'

'Who are you?' Four of them asked at once.

The woman looked at Rick, kept his gaze and answered in a voice that sent shivers down his spine. 'You can call me Lael.'

'Are we dreaming?' Ben asked, he and Dr Morell inching closer to the woman.

Gabriela seemed frozen, transfixed by the hand on her arm. Rick could hear Anthony stand up and step closer. *Sit down.* Anthony did.

'You are and aren't. The only one actually sitting at the fire is me,' Lael answered, releasing Gabriela and turning her gaze on the others. Rick felt lost without its steady anchor.

'So, it's a real fire?' Ben put his hands out to feel the heat.

'Yes, it's real. Keeps the Ghouls away.'

'And this is a real beach?' The woman, Lael, Rick reminded himself, flashed a slightly annoyed look at Dr Morell.

'Yes,' she answered levelly. Rick could feel her aggravation though.

Aggravation and something else he couldn't quite work out. 'This beach is just south of where Anthony is laying in his suite with a view and the doors locked tight.'

Anthony stifled a gasp. 'Closer than Bellbird?'

'Much closer.'

'Tell us what's happening?' he blurted out. 'Tell us about the missing and the dead.'

'Did you take the woman from the morgue?' Dr Morell, awake now, wanted to get some answers.

Lael had drawn in on herself with Anthony's questions. Rick could see it, sense it, as if it were a physical shrinking rather than a gathering of wild thoughts. He could sense those too, tangled strings of memory teetering between terror and insanity. He wondered what had happened to her between the last dream and this. What had caused the breakdown in her surety?

You don't want to know.

Rick flinched. She stared straight at him, resolute, strong despite the grasping mind, and stronger perhaps because of it. *No … I don't want to know.*

She told them then, a campfire story about monsters and ghouls … the Bledray … their natural killing grounds the civilised areas of the human race, and their prey: humans, known as the Ryrdri. Tales of the Alffür, those that guarded against the monsters, fought when they rose up, died to protect a race that could not even imagine their danger. Guardians ever vigilant and Hunters, the itinerant travellers who moved from one area to another, watching, waiting, taking action as needed.

They'd started out the same, treating humans like humans did cows and pigs, until humans learned to communicate and those who would become Guardians learned to listen. The split between the people became violent and permanent, yet it was centuries until Hunters emerged from the Guardians. Born to roam and protect, passionate and cold in their outlook, they were a paradox created to allow Guardians to draw back from the frontline and concentrate on protection and nurturing.

Humans thought they were pretty close to the top of the food chain; no natural predator that actively hunted them and enough smarts to keep those that would at bay. Humans were wrong.

The end of the world as they knew it wouldn't come in some distant future with a bang or the spread of toxins, or as the result of some unknown war. It would, Lael said, come in the next twenty-four hours, forty-eight if they were lucky, with the lusty kisses of a billion Bledray Ghouls. The human race would be wiped out before they knew they were in trouble.

'Are they vampires?' Ben leaned forward, intent on the story. 'What other monsters exist that we don't know about?'

'No, and many, some of them are even human ...' Lael answered with bowed head, hair falling across her face in a protective curtain.

'What would happen after?' Gabriela asked. 'When everyone's gone and they've got no more souls to raid. What happens when there are only them left?'

Lael shrugged. 'They'll move on to the next feeding ground. There won't be only them left.'

'Has this happened before?' Ben asked, apparently thinking worlds ahead and behind any of them.

'Once that I know of. Malaik told me ...' Lael's voice broke and Rick recognised the grief the woman had shared in their previous meeting. 'It's said they slept after, hibernated I suppose, waiting for a new spring and new growth.'

'Us?' Rick didn't know Ben well enough to gauge quite where he was going with his thoughts. He sensed though, in this dream-awareness they all shared, that he was thinking of evolution; apes to human, brutish animal to thinking brain-developed being. But if he was thinking that, then who was it that the Ghouls had fed off before ... us?

Rick stole a glance at the others. Their faces were rapt, intent on the woman, the stories and her answers. The woman was intent on him, and now he wondered ... why him?

'Why us?' Dr Morell asked, the sleepy, just been screwed expression completely gone. 'Why us five? Why Rick?' She obviously hadn't forgotten that the connection had been made first with Rick on a bushy hill behind a ghost town.

'When they stir, as they have been, the Hunter finds a human and together they fight them. The close connection between them keeps the Hunter sane; prevents them from becoming the enemy.' She tore her gaze from Rick and turned it to the fire. 'Both Hunter and Human are made stronger by the contact. Perhaps someone somewhere deemed it necessary that a human help in defence of their kind.'

'You're the Hunter? One of these Alffür?' Gabriela laid a hand on her knee.

Lael nodded.

'And Rick is your chosen human?'

She locked dark eyes with Rick, not able it seemed to look away for long. There was no need to answer.

'Then where does that leave us?' Gabriela touched them both now, a human bridge between the real and unreal.

'That'd bring us to the deadline of twenty-four hours, wouldn't you think, Gabriela? The little uprising that will kill us all and wipe even the memory of us from the earth. The battle to end all battles that so obviously can't be fought by only two.' Anthony sounded panicked and Rick didn't blame him.

How wrong it felt to go from reporter, or cop or doctor to warrior against the undead hordes, last defenders of an entire race. *Oh, shit. Oh, fuck! And what did Gabriela just call him? The chosen one! Oh, God, that was going too far. Too damn far!* Chosen Ones nearly always died at the end of the story. That's why they were the fucking Chosen Ones: sacrifices for the surviving grateful ones. Hell, he'd read every Stephen King book, watched every horror movie and had absorbed plenty of science fiction when he was a kid. The odds for the Chosen Ones were never good. *No way in hell …* He started to stand, his legs clearly telling him to run.

Before he could go into full-blown panic, Rick heard a low hum in his ears, a soothing noise that sounded almost like words being sung, or the wind blowing through a valley. A memory of another time came to him. He and this woman standing on the crest of a hill, a lake as still and clear as freshly blown glass below them. Birds in the trees, children off playing somewhere in the woods, people laughing, living … and he knew it wasn't him that stood there holding Lael's hand, but one that had come before. Come before and survived, better than survived, had lived a long life.

The panic reared back, on the edge of bolting, but held in abeyance for now, pushed away to a corner of his mind where Rick hoped it would stay.

'What do we do?' He spoke at last and the others sat back, visibly relieved that he'd taken control. He was relieved himself, amazed really, at the strength that flowed into him with those words.

Lael smiled, and then leaned close to Gabriela. She kissed her, a light touch of breath and promise and strength.

'Rest,' she said. 'Go back to your dreams and sleep.' She released Gabriela, who started to waver and fade. She stood, traced her fingers down Lael's face, turned and had gone within two steps.

Lael, without need to stand or crawl, moved closer to Dr Morell and Ben. She kissed them both. 'Jamie, hold him tight and love him well. Therein lies your strength.' When the doctor had faded from view, from the dream, she leaned forward to Ben. 'She needs you.' And when Ben too had gone, she sat in front of Anthony, holding his hands, rubbing her thumb across his knuckles. 'You are so strong, so strong. In another time, you would have been the one chosen. Perhaps, in time to come, you will be.' She kissed him then, parting his lips with her tongue and delving between his teeth with more passion than she had shown the others. Rick felt jealous and scared, and relieved all in one, sure then that he would need Anthony's strength.

And then he was gone as well, walking along the beach into the moonlight and back to his bed.

'And you,' Lael said, facing him squarely and alone, the fire still crackling, burning wood still popping with heat. She pressed the palm of her hand to his forehead, her touch cool, the scent of her skin so inviting, alluring. 'You can wake up now.'

Rick opened his eyes and sat up. A tangled sheet slipped down his naked chest. *Yes, I'm naked and in bed, right where I left me.*

The light from the bathroom down the hallway dimly lit the room.

'I'm home.' *And I'm safe and …*

Lael stood at the end of his bed, waiting for him.

Memory of life before is sketchy.
We who once could
remember everything
have found that
survival and grief
combine to scrape away
the un-needed and the painful.
Too many of us were killed
and so our story too is
destined to pass
from this world.

— Journal of Malaik

22

Gabriela woke with a grunt and a groan; groggy in the way of a hangover, and automatically pushing hair from her face. She itched and felt grubby all over and contemplated the merits of a hot shower versus more sleep. The room had the washed-out look of early morning and a glance at her watch proved the light levels correct. Early morning, indeed. 5.30am. She groaned again, stretched, and opted for a shower.

The shower was pelting down on the back of her neck, as hot as she could stand it, before she remembered the dream. She turned the water off with a harsh yank of the tap, slammed open the shower door and grabbed a towel, flinging it around herself as she left the bathroom.

'Rick?' She paused before bashing on the door and tapped instead. 'Rick, you awake?'

When she received no answer, she pushed the door open and peeked in. Rick lay, sprawled across the bed, sheets tangled around his legs, one pillow on the floor and the other held tightly to his chest, covering his face. Soft snores came from beneath the pillow. Gabriela didn't have the heart to wake him. What could another hour hurt? For chrissakes, it was—she looked at her watch again—5.45 on a Sunday morning. *'Course, when the fate of the world rests in your hands, time and catching up on sleep probably doesn't mean much.*

She returned to the bathroom to finish drying off and to dress, and by the time she made it out to the kitchen had nearly convinced herself that the dream had been only that, and there were no such things as soul-sucking Ghouls.

Seeing Lael, doubled over on the back lawn and apparently spewing forth every bit of food she'd ever eaten, changed everything.

'Oh, fuck …' Gabriela watched her, hand stalled over the tap, and marvelled at the absolute wreck of a picture she made. She turned the tap on, filled the kettle, and went out to help her.

Couplings usually went a little longer, usually occurred before both parties were so immersed in events they felt like shit and preferred a cuddle and sleep to sex. Yet they'd completed the first step, brief as it had been, and sometimes quality could not be measured by quantity.

Rick's touch had been electric, his adoration addictive. He'd buried himself in her in not so much a physical way but in an act of absolution that seared their souls together. Hot, raw and urgent, they had come together with little foreplay and plenty of denied passion, and had blown their world apart.

Later, as Rick dozed toward sleep, and Lael lay entwined in his arms, she felt the pungent disgust of what she'd done on the clifftop come back in waves of putrid memory. She'd had no choice, she knew that, and after she'd been caught up in the blood-lust the act had caused within her. Her stomach rolled at the fleeting images that crossed her vision; her hand reaching for the second fisherman, her body wanting every fibre of his being. The horror of what she'd been capable of, still was capable of, erupted in a gush of scalding liquid. She shifted, vanished and reappeared in Rick's backyard, unable to control either her gut-wrenching reaction or the tears that flowed down her cheeks.

She didn't notice Gabriela's approach until a hand lighted on her shoulder and pulled her hair back and out of the way. A glass of water appeared beside her and she took it as if she were dying of thirst. Perhaps she was; she'd certainly vomited up much more than she'd drunk in the last few days.

'Rinse and spit,' Gabriela said, before she could gulp the entire contents.

So she did, so easy to do as one's told without thought, to not have to think for oneself. Gabriela clasped both her shoulders and knelt down behind her, holding her against her chest and offering her strength to get through the violent bout of illness. Lael hadn't realised the chill in the air until she felt her warmth, or the loneliness that she carried wrapped around her like a blanket until she smelled the freshness of her scent, soap and shampoo and another less-identifiable quality that was hers alone. She produced a warm, damp handtowel and wiped her hands clean, finger by finger, and then her arms and face. She closed her eyes and breathed deep of the fresh air. How she missed such simple acts of caring.

'I'm done,' she said. *For now …* A tingle in her skin told her that something was not quite right, something else remained, but she felt too rent apart, too sorrowed to search it out. She stood when Gabriela stood, she walked when Gabriela walked, and she sat right where Gabriela put her.

'I'll have some tea ready in a minute and I'll make you some toast.' She twisted back, mid-step. 'You do drink tea and eat toast, don't you?'

'Yes. I'm no Ghoul.' *Yet.* 'But I'm not hungry.'

Gabriela continued her passage into the kitchen, listening to the rattle of cups, short burst of whistle from the electric kettle, and the swoosh and gurgle of water being poured. Lael didn't move from her seat, didn't turn her gaze from the open kitchen doorway and the sight of Gabriela making her a breakfast she truly didn't want.

The toaster popped with a satisfied grunt from Gabriela and less than a minute later, she was back at the table and placing down a tray filled to the edges with teapot, cups, toasted bread, butter, plates and knives.

'Hang on, forgot the jam,' she said and sailed back the way she'd come. 'Hope you like blackberry, that's all Rick has.' She plopped it down on the table beside the toast and began to serve. 'I know you probably don't feel like eating, but a bit of toast, dry might be better, and some tea will help settle your stomach. I know. Made it through plenty of day-afters on not much more.' She looked at her, frowned and asked, 'Sugar?' Then went ahead and put a teaspoonful in any-way. 'Strong and sweet is better.'

Lael thought the smell of the tea rather bitter, but it didn't turn her stomach so she sipped it when Gabriela handed her the cup and was pleasantly surprised by the release of tension that simple act caused. She sighed, returned Gabriela's tentative smile and reached for the toast; dry in her mouth, but when washed down with the tea, the exact food that she needed.

'So that whole group dream thing was real?'

'Of course.' Lael nodded, bit, sipped, swallowed. 'And you didn't have to burn the skin from your hand to prove it.'

Gabriela laughed and flushed, embarrassed.

'Yeah, well, I can be a bit …' She looked away a moment. 'Rambunctious at times.'

'I would never have guessed.' Lael finished the toast and took another, starving now that her stomach had settled, relaxed with her wild thoughts tempered by the casual routine of eating breakfast and chatting with Gabriela. 'You're allowed to ask questions.'

Gabriela picked up the mug of black tea she'd poured for herself and blew into it, a cloud of steam billowed out, masking the intensity of her eyes for just a moment. She sipped, carefully, testing the heat of the tea. 'Is this happening anywhere else?'

'Not yet, but it will spread quickly. You're worried about your partner?'

'I need to warn her, but what do I say? Annie, scary as shit monsters are about to suck everyone into an eternal vacuum … She'll come racing back to Sydney thinking I've had a nervous breakdown.'

'Anywhere but here is the safest place for her to be. Ring her if you need to, but don't tell her anything … yet.'

Gabriela ran her hands over her face. *Fuck* … Annie was going to be pissed off. She should have gone to Canberra with her. She'd much prefer to face the end of days completely oblivious.

'What are the chances of any of us not making it through the next forty-eight hours?'

'High, for us all.'

'When do we start?'

'We already have.'

'Well then, when do we move on to the next phase of the mission?'

'Why don't you let her finish her breakfast first, Captain Salek? What's an interrogation without crumpets and coffee?' Rick leaned against the doorframe of the kitchen. He hadn't showered, Lael could smell the sex on him still, and his hair spiked out from where he had tried to tame it with his hands.

'My, my,' Gabriela rejoined. 'Aren't you the picture of "Most Eligible Bachelor" first thing in the morning? Sit down and I'll get you a mug. Did I hear you say you had crumpets? And honey?'

Rick leaned forward and let gravity pull him away from his leaning post and toward the closest chair. 'Yes, you did and yes, I do. On both counts. Crumpets in the freezer, honey in the fridge and be quick about that mug. A man could die of thirst out here.'

'Aye, aye, Commander Hendry,' Gabriela muttered, head already in the freezer looking for crumpets.

Lael laughed and felt her spirit lighten when Rick met her gaze and leaned forward to kiss her lips.

'Mmmm, tea and toast … who needs crumpets and honey?'

Lael brushed crumbs from his lips.

'I thought I was dreaming,' Rick said, catching her hand and leaning in close to whisper. 'Not the beach with the others. I knew that was real, but after, in my bedroom.'

'No dream.' Rick kissed her fingers, nibbled on her wrist. *I could take him again, right now …*

'I'm glad. I haven't felt like that … like this … ever. So buoyant, strong … so alive. I'm so fucking horny right now, I feel like knocking everything off the table and making love to you right here.' He eyed the table, patted it with his free hand as if to test the strength of both the table and his desire.

Lael averted her eyes from Rick to Gabriela, toasting crumpets now in the kitchen, putting the kettle back on, fixing coffee. Oh, what a fucked up world! Right here, right now, things would never be this perfect again.

The telephone rang and the bubble burst with an almost audible pop. Rick grumbled curse words under his breath and let go of Lael's hand to answer it. Lael drank her cooling tea and listened to his half of the conversation.

'Yes … Yes … Right here … Her too … I don't know when, hang on, Ben, and I'll ask …' Rick lowered the phone from his mouth, but didn't bother to cover it. 'Do you want everyone to meet? When and where?' His expression was a fine mix of disappointment, realisation and growing apprehension.

'Anthony's hotel room.' She stood and moved to the open sliding door that led out to the backyard and the scene of her loss of control, and breathed in. She ached too much to exert herself any more than that. The air that filled her remained untainted, clean in the dawn when the Ghouls slept. Already the light had cleared to the brightness that came before another hot day. They had some time, but not much. Lael turned to Rick, waiting patiently. 'One hour.'

Rick nodded, passed that information along and hung up the phone. 'I have to eat and shower. Is there anything else I need to do? Anything I need to bring?'

'We may need to make fire. Bring matches. Water to drink, food … wear comfortable clothes and shoes …'

Gabriela placed a plate piled high with golden honeyed crumpets and a jug of coffee on the table. 'Can't you just, you know …' She waved her hands in front of her face. 'Wiggle your fingers and make fire?'

'Well, yes I can, Gabriela. As a matter of fact, I can wiggle my fingers and do a great many things … But you can't.' Lael walked to the table and took a crumpet. Honey dripped down her fingers. She licked it with a sudden greedy need for sweetness. 'Thanks for your help this morning, Gabriela, and thanks for breakfast.' She turned to Rick, walked close enough by him that their hips brushed, and said, 'I'll meet you in the shower. Hurry up and eat.'

She left Rick to Gabriela's spluttering questions and to breakfast. The brief time of normalcy, or near normalcy anyway, was over. In less than an hour, she'd be on the road again. In just over an hour, she'd be back on the hunt; a pack now to support her and the prey firmly set in her sights.

*The Hunter knows the
worth of the journey;
each step leading to the fulfilment of the end task.
Each step must be considered before life can be taken.
Even the life of the enemy has value and cannot
be extinguished lightly*

— *Journal of Malaik*

23

'Why exactly are we on this boat instead of driving in air-conditioned comfort?' Anthony stood, as casual as Rick had seen him so far—except for the state of sleepy scruffiness in their dream—dressed in cargo pants, long-sleeved t-shirt and hiking boots, a cap pulled down low to shade his eyes. He didn't look too good, with dark circles under his eyes and terse lines around his mouth even though he appeared relaxed, propped in the corner of the wooden bench seat, the side railing and the wall behind him.

The ferry rose and dipped with the heavy swell of the bay, listing precariously at times to the side only to right itself on the crest of a wave and then list again in the other direction. In the main cabin of the ferry, the bobbing effect had clearly delineated daytrippers from locals. The tourists crowded windows with a combination of excitement and anxiety in their faces. The locals didn't spare the nervous visitors or the waves a look, unless it was to vaguely sneer and shake their heads before returning to their newspapers or books or snotty-nosed toddlers. The crew balanced themselves with wide-set feet and long years of practice in such conditions, collecting fares and smiles and questions, returning change, patient weathered expressions and calm assurances.

'No, mate. The ferry's never sunk, not even close, mate …'

'That's twelve bucks eighty for the two of you and three-twenty each for the bikes …'

'Yes, ma'am. The ferry's keepin' perfect time. Twenty minute trip each way. We'll be back at Bundeena an hour after we leave. No, ma'am, this swell isn't anything to worry about. Just a bit messy out here in the middle. No problems tyin' up at the wharf at all …'

'Seen your dad yesterday, Bob. Dressed to the nines, mate! He have a hot date or what?'

The fare collector's voice was a soothing litany in the rabble.

'Hear that, Anthony? We'll be off this boat in a minute or two, feet on solid ground again.' Jamie, Rick decided, just looked plain queasy. She huddled beside Ben and crossed her hands in her lap.

Practically joined at the hip ... It bothered him, but only a little. Ben didn't seem to mind having the good doctor so close all the time. Why should he? His ex-wife had been like that, needy, clingy, acting scared to cover up her basic bitchy manipulative self. Rick shuddered, as he nearly always did when he thought about her and turned to Lael instead.

Lael, leaning over the prow of the boat as it cut through wind and waves. Lael with her hair blowing back as free as the rest of her. He envied her yet at the same time recognised that freedom for Lael was a misnomer. Her days and nights were spent hunting and protecting, guarding the human race from extinction with no thanks, no acknowledgement or payment of any kind. Invisible and separated, even, he suspected, from her own kind. What that kind was, he didn't really understand either. She'd told them about the Bledray monsters and the Alffür Guardians, but not much about Hunters, or nothing he could clearly remember. Hints that the Guardians were not human and, therefore, neither was she, which would, of course, explain her talent for astral travel.

Yet, she looked human. Ate and drank and laughed, when her worries were momentarily forgotten, like a human; cried and felt pain just like a human. Gabriela had told him what had happened that morning, as Rick too had eventually shared the secrets of the night, and they'd speculated on what had transpired within their knowledge and without.

Rick stumbled and steadied himself with one arm on the railing, shifting just enough to observe Lael's face, eyes closed, expression beatific with the brush of the wind. He felt a lurch within him, not caused by boat; a swell completely apart from the heaving waters they travelled, and turned to find Gabriela, sitting a few feet away, watching him. He shrugged and ducked his head. *What can I do?*

Gabriela shook her head and slid her sunglasses down onto her face. She didn't know either.

A hand on his arm brought him from his reverie. Lael's voice reminded him that they were not on this boat to enjoy sunshine and sand. She pointed to the row of beaches that the ferry now faced.

'The third beach along, without the houses as back-up. That's where we need to go.'

Rick nodded. It looked familiar. 'Is that where we were last night?'

'Yes. Near the headland. We'll go back to that spot and work out a battle plan.' She stopped long enough to look full into his face, reading what from his expression he couldn't guess. 'The ferry's crowded. I need to get off first. You get off last. I'll wait for you on the top level of the wharf.'

'Okay. Why?'

She didn't shrug or look shamed or however Rick thought one should look when telling you about non-human appetites.

'I need more than tea, toast and crumpet to power my day.'

Rick didn't want to know exactly what that meant.

***

'Really, deep down and compared to us, she's a Ghoul too, isn't she?' Anthony hefted his pack onto his shoulder and looped his arm through the free strap.

He'd thought about it. Written copious notes, some rambling, some pointed lists of facts and near-facts, and recorded as many details from the dream as he could remember—including a near word-for-word rendition of everything that was said. He'd concluded, somewhere around 4am, that the only thing differentiating Guardians and Hunters from Ghouls was preferred diet and a few scraps of philosophy.

As Anthony watched Lael now, touching in some way every passenger off the ferry and growing visibly stronger from the contact, he understood that she was feeding. That she too needed human essence to survive.

'I suppose she is.' Rick was watching her too.

'She said last night that you and she would couple. Does that mean what I think it means?'

'Probably.'

'She told me, right before I left the beach, that if it wasn't for you, I would have been the Chosen One.'

Rick looked at him then, face expressionless, eyes searching. Anthony met the look, unblinking.

'You jealous?'

Anthony turned back to the wharf and Lael. 'Probably … Yes, a little.'

———⬥◦◦⬥———

The Bledray set traps
like a spider spinning its web.
Each strand is gossamer thin and so light to the senses
to be barely noticeable.
Each touch draws the prey to the centre;
where power pulses and
cannot be withstood.

— *Journal of Malaik*

———⬥◦◦⬥———

24

The white-blonde woman standing at the corner of Bundeena's two main streets tapped her foot impatiently, puffing in exasperation and nervousness at a stray lock of hair across her face. Her cargo pants, low and baggy, hid all but the pink-polished nails of her toes as they beat a frantic pattern on the tarred path.

'I'm sure this is the right corner.' She glared at her watch for the tenth time in as many seconds. 'Definitely the right time. Where. Are. They?' Each word hissed from between pearly white grinding teeth.

Bridget had just come off the ferry, happy and excited that Sunday had arrived at last and promised to be a beautiful, sunshiney day. She loved coming to Bundeena, the pace of life here suited her right down to the ground. She even thought she could handle the ferry ride across the bay to and from work each day, or at least, the twenty-minute drive through the park to Sutherland.

'Now, if only the others would show up and we can get this show on the road.'

She wanted to pace, but that would look just too weird, some mad blonde woman pacing and muttering to herself on the corner undaunted by the thronging crowds … Undaunted. Yes, she could definitely do undaunted.

A small group of visitors broke from the back of the crowd that had been on the ferry with her.

'That had been one crowd, let me tell you.'

Bridget recognised the group. She'd stood near them at the Cronulla wharf, all waiting for the ferry, and then sat near them at the front of the boat. They were a bit of a strange lot as far as she was concerned. *Not that talking to oneself while stomping around the street was at all strange, nosiree!* Alternatively, excited and serious, pale-faced then blushed, full of courage and possibility and then plain old scared.

It looked like they were going in the same direction she and her friends, whenever they arrived, were going, up the hill, past the RSL club, maybe to Jibbon, or the ocean track, she supposed, if they turned off.

'Hurry up!' Bridget had the urge to follow the group, see what they were up to. A couple of those guys were pretty good looking, kinda spunky even. She grinned and then jumped a foot in the air as her shoulders were grabbed from behind and she was spun around to face the laughing faces of her two friends.

'Bridget! You've got thongs on!' Mei looked aghast at Bridget's feet. 'We're going bushwalking. You can't wear thongs in the bush. It's not safe.'

'Yeah, girlie,' Wendy chimed in. 'Bull ants, snakes, spiders.'

'Not to mention sticks, stones, tree roots … syringes.' The smile dropped from Mei's face to be replaced by worry. She chewed on her bottom lip and looked back, with a trace of desperation on her face, to her car parked on the other side of the road. 'Maybe we should just go down to that beach there.'

'Yes, mums,' Bridget answered. 'There's way too many houses along that beach, Mei. We want bush, nature, you know, the real deal.' She picked up her backpack, a pair of hiking boots swung by the laces from the shoulder strap. 'The thongs are just for now and the beach, so I can kick about in the water. I'm a good girl, I brought appropriate footwear.'

Wendy and Mei looked down at their tightly-laced, booted feet in a perfectly synchronised move.

'Oh,' Mei said. 'Thongs are a good idea …'

'Don't worry, we'll figure it out. Let's go. A bunch of hotties just went up the street. If we're lucky we can follow them all the way to the beach.'

'Oh, Bridget.'

'Where?'

'C'mon, Ashley. I want to get to the beach before it gets too crowded at Devil's Hole.' Marty, a slender, bordering on skinny, youth, shuffled from one foot to the other, switched his boogie board from one arm to the other. Ashley was always so slow. Didn't girls understand the importance of riding waves solo? He knew he should have gone ahead with his mates an hour ago instead of dropping by Ashley's on the way.

'I'm ready … Sorry.' Ashley burst out the front door in a flurry of beach towel, hat and shiny sarong. Her long hair was tied back in a thick plait. 'I brought some food …' She patted the bulging bag hooked over her shoulder and Marty had to smile.

Ashley might be always late, but she always came prepared, and her mum made great sandwiches.

'Seeya, Mrs Wilson,' he called out as he grabbed Ashley's hand and started dragging her down the drive.

A car full of women drove past and Marty sighed. The beach was gonna be packed.

<hr>

'What a beautiful beach.'

'Drew! Abbie! Don't run off without your hats!'

'Don't worry, Cam. We'll catch up to them in a bit. They can put their hats on then. Let's just relax and take in all this sun and sand.'

Cam, still frowning after her twins, rested the heavy cooler bag she was carrying on the ground and inspected Samantha's 'beautiful beach'. Divided into two, there was a small section, already crowded with teenagers and boogie-boards, and a long section dotted with groups of picnickers and swimmers, all of whom looked to be settled in for the day. Just offshore a mini-flotilla of boats anchored in orderly lines; people lazing around on them, drinking, eating, talking, kids dive-bombing into the water. It did look good, she supposed. Everyone so relaxed. The water relatively clean.

'Okay, where do we want to sit?'

Samantha pointed off in the distance and Cam groaned. The

cooler bag weighed a tonne and Sam too had her arms full of towels, an umbrella, a bag stuffed with kids' stuff: bucket and spade, Frisbee, tennis ball, blow-up balls, and grown-up stuff: newspapers and a paperback.

'There's a nice gap between groups about a quarter the way up and some shade from the trees. Why don't we dump our gear there, then go for a walk and check out the rest of the beach?'

Cam nodded and picked up her load. 'Sounds good to me. Here we go. Sam and Cam doing the beach thing. Drew! Abbie! This way!'

The twins swerved away from the water and started running along the sand without a pause in motion or any indication that they'd seen where their mother pointed. They skipped around a bunch of wave-jumping, chatting backpackers and shot off to the exact spot Samantha had pointed out. Cam shook her head and followed after, Sam beside her.

Sam and Cam walking along the beach. Sam and Cam, Sam and Cam.

Time is relative to all actions.
The strength of the Hunter and Hunted is measured by the
rise and fall of night and day

— *Journal of Malaik*

25

Ben and Jamie fell back a little from the rest of the group.

'You don't think it'll happen today, do you? In broad daylight?'

Ben glanced behind them. 'I'm not sure how important light or the lack of it is in these cases, Jamie.' He looked ahead and then eyed the people they passed by. 'I suppose night time's better for not getting caught, but if the Gathering is a big enough force, I suppose "getting caught" is immaterial.' Small craft, rowboats and canoes, journeyed between shore and the much larger boats. 'Course, there's always habit.'

'What do you mean?'

Ben shrugged. 'If the Ghouls are used to being circumspect, feeding in the dark and being sneaky, then old habits can be hard to break.'

'What are you doing?'

'What do you mean?' Ben glanced at Jamie, the wide-brimmed hat, the shirt that covered arms, shoulders, waistline, breasts and the cotton drawstring pants that flowed out of it.

'You've looked behind us and in front, checked out the people sitting on the beach, the ones in the water and the ones on their boats. Are you looking for monsters?'

'No, I'm not … well, maybe a little, but … do you think there's a lot of people here? It is an out of the way kind of beach and a lot of them seem to be slowly gravitating toward the east end.'

'It's already hot and it's Sunday. Probably like this every weekend.'

Jamie was right, he supposed. It was hot; sweat trickled down his back and stained his shirt. And maybe it was only a Sunday crowd, but Ben didn't think so.

They draw the humans to them … That's what Lael had said when they'd met in Anthony's motel room and gone over the essentials of the dream. Like a Venus flytrap releasing irresistible pheromones into the air, tempting its prey with lush promises and then closing the trap around them. Alone, their special brand of 'attractiveness' only worked *in situ*. The Ghouls had to be close up. They would come across as friendly, trustworthy.

Their kiss is heaven in your grasp, but the soul-dead do not even make it to hell …

Ben still wasn't sure what was expected of him. The only surety he did have was that a few days ago he'd been excited beyond measure of the path Jamie's phone call had opened up, the mythic trail of knowledge it hinted at. Now, with realms of understanding before him, links to other worlds, truth to ancient legends all but in his hands, he was scared to death.

Jamie was suspicious. Copying his tracking behaviour, looking for signs.

'You know though, that a few of these people, the ones walking mostly, were on the ferry with us. That blonde woman up ahead of us definitely was. Maybe it's not Ghouls, but Lael who's attracting them.'

Ben stopped. What if she was? Hadn't they all fallen in with her and her story with barely a word of dissent? Yesterday, Jamie didn't want to be involved in any of it; today she was as hooked as any of them. What sort of control did Lael have over them? Were they warriors or fodder?

Jamie tugged at his arm and he moved on, staring now at his feet and the sand. Lael had come through to them in their dreams for a reason. The human mind was more susceptible while asleep, more accepting of strangeness, otherworldness. Pliable to manipulation too, hence the success of hypnosis as therapy, and its entertainment value.

A smell wafted past. Like something dying in the bush or the rotten remains of fish on the shore. Ben tried not to breathe too deeply. Jamie too had smelled it, he guessed. Her pace quickened, strides more determined. No doubt hoping to put distance between her nose and the smell as fast as she could. Ben looked around him at the people. *Strange how no one else seems to smell it …*

Glare from sunlight hitting the water cut across Anthony's vision and penetrated his eyes, hit the back of his eyeballs and shattered into a shards of pain that lanced his brain and cut it to shreds. At least, that's what it felt like anyway. Even with sunglasses, hat pulled low and head down, eyes cast away, the glare got him. He tried walking with his eyes closed and stumbled into Gabriela, feet clumsy in the soft sand.

'Watch it,' Gabriela warned, and Anthony mumbled an apology.

He cracked his eyes open and allowed the barest sliver of light through, just enough to not fall flat on his face. Rick and Lael were shapeless blobs in front of him, distorted by the packs they carried and the fragmentation peering at them through his eyelashes caused.

Too much reading, he decided. Too much scanning of websites and documents, statements and photographs. Too much nervous tension and not enough sleep. *No sleep, actually.* The dream had started as soon as he'd closed his eyes and felt the pull of the sandman. He didn't think what he'd experienced after counted as sleep in any way, shape or form. Especially, when he'd walked away from the fire, straight into his room and seen his body lying on the bed, pale and still as if close to death. A glow of light had seemed to emanate from the body, pulsing with every rise and fall of the chest. The body didn't seem real somehow, didn't look like him without him inside to make it come alive. He'd looked in the mirror behind the door wondering what he looked like without his body and saw a rainbow of sparkling colour that moved and swayed in the vaguest form of a man.

Looking back at his body on the bed, the light, almost blinding in its startling brilliance stretched from the bed to him. There'd been sharp stabbing pain, a roar of sound like a jet engine starting up right outside the window, and then a hard tug that precipitated being sucked back into his body. A loud clang in his head—the dungeon door being slammed shut and dead-bolted—and he was back, lying on the bed and staring up at the ceiling. No pretty lights. No magical threads of being. Just him and the headache from hell.

Which he still had, thanks to his inability to stop thinking and get some rest.

Still, the experience had been wonderful, delicious in a way he couldn't describe even to himself, except that it was better than the most tender steak, the finest wine, the sweetest, stickiest dessert. Better even than making love on a warm night with satin sheets and the most desirous partner one could hope to lure into bed. Anthony laughed and winced with the pain it caused his head. Better than sex!

He wanted to do it again. Wanted to fly and soar with the birds. He had the indistinct memory of doing exactly that to and from the fire, but couldn't now distinguish that experience from past more innocent dreams. He only knew he wanted it. He closed his eyes for two steps before guardedly opening them wider.

Gabriela matched him step for step along the beach; their arms brushing every now and then, the touch supportive every now and then. Anthony looked down at his arm. More than supportive, he realised. Gabriela's hand held his arm in a strong grip, guided him to walk around clumps of dried seaweed, sand-covered children and their instinctual need to dig bloody great holes, anchor ropes, lapping water and any other bit of debris that littered their path. Gabriela was literally holding him up and keeping him moving.

'Ummm, you can probably let go now, Gabriela. I think I've got it from here.'

Gabriela's answering look was disbelieving. 'Anthony, you've crashed into me three times, tripped over air and seaweed in equal amounts and you've been talking to yourself since we hit the beach. I don't think you've got anything. And I'm sure Lael would be happy if you made it to the end of the beach at least without falling into the water and drowning while you recited poetry or whatever it is you've been gabbing about.'

Anthony would have stopped walking and protested if Gabriela hadn't been hanging on so tight and forcing him into forward motion.

'I don't know what you're talking about,' he spluttered and then blushed as it occurred to him that was exactly how it had come out. *Spluttering? What next? Drooling and dancing naked?*

'I don't know what you've been talking about either. That's the point,' Gabriela said. 'Up this way.' Her grip became a gentle push and Anthony changed direction to follow Lael into the shade of some trees. 'Sit here.' Gabriela guided him down, taking his pack off his shoulders, pushing him over. 'Close your eyes.'

Anthony tried to sit, feeling wild-eyed and frantic. The others were also dropping their packs, sitting or pacing the expanse of the shelter the tree provided. Dr Morell leaned over him, touched the palm of her hand to his forehead then let her hand slip to his neck and carefully pushed him back down.

A few feet away, clear of the trees, a circle of rocks surrounded the grey black ashes of a dead fire. Anthony stared at it until his eyelids dropped, too heavy to open and then saw it anyway, in the dark, now with dancing flames and a solemn figure seated beside it.

I want to fly, he told the figure.

The figure turned to him, leaned closer, and parted her lips in the semblance of a smile. *You'll fly higher than any human has before,* she said.

He dissolved into her kiss … and flew.

*To mingle with all life is the fulfilment of the
Hunter's commitment.*

'Does anyone want coffee? I brought a thermos.'

Dr Morell—Rick hadn't quite got the hang of thinking about her without the appellation—pulled a silver flask and a couple of plastic cups from her pack. *How practical.*

'Oh, baby,' Gabriela answered. 'How did you know? I haven't got nearly enough caffeine in my system and the withdrawals are killing me!'

Rick didn't think he could handle anything right now. The smell had smacked him full in the face as soon as they'd walked off the narrow path from street to beach. It was the same putrid odour that had permeated the house in Sutherland, stolen through the houses and streets of Bellbird, and waited for him with lingering malevolence in the little clearing behind Malaik's house.

'Drink.' Lael pushed a bottle of water into his hands.

It tasted metallic, tainted. A bit like that first sip after a visit to the dentist, when you'd sat for an hour, reclined in an uncomfortable chair with an armoury of instruments protruding from your mouth. He drank it anyway, because Lael squatted in front him, watching him closely, as if nothing he could say or do would convince her that he wasn't thirsty.

Anthony looked like shit. Red-faced and sweaty, almost gasping for air and eyes darkened to coal pits in his head. They hadn't walked that far and he knew the man was fit. He'd been a bundle of nervous energy since they'd met, always on the move, never still. *Well, he's still now* …The detective wasn't moving from where Gabriela had dropped him and the doctor had encouraged him to sleep.

'It's not the walk.' Lael left the bottle in Rick's hands and started sorting through her duffel bag. The rest had packs and Lael had a scrappy old duffel that separated at the seams in more than one spot and was quite possibly older than Rick was.

'What is it then?' Rick took the packages Lael handed him, collecting them in his lap.

Gabriela, on guard at the edge of the shade turned her face toward them. 'I had to practically carry him here. He's been muttering and stumbling around. He was okay on the ferry ride over.'

Lael continued with the search through her pack. Dr Morell passed Gabriela a mug, poured more for Ben, looked at Rick—and when he shook his head—poured some for herself. 'Did you want some coffee, Lael?'

'Thank you, no.' She handed a final packet to Rick and then pushed the duffel bag aside. 'He feels the presence of the Ghouls. He feels my presence. He's quite sensitive really.'

'It doesn't look like that's a good thing.' Ben took his coffee closer to the trunk of the tree. The bush started in clumps of sharp-leaved grasses behind it.

'He needs to assimilate. It's harder for some than others. Circle around, come closer.' Lael waved to Gabriela and Ben, motioned to the semicircle Dr Morell, Rick and the sleeping Anthony already formed.

With the forming of the circle, Rick noticed that the tang of death in the air faded. Anthony groaned and flung his arm out so that his hand lay in the centre, fingers half-curled in an unconscious pointing gesture toward Lael.

'The battle will not be enjoined until dusk,' Lael said. 'It is necessary for us to be in place early, while they're not paying much attention.'

'You mean they're here already?' Dr Morell looked at Ben with something akin to astonishment on her face. Rick didn't understand the look at first, not until Ben, nodding sagely, met her look and explained.

'I could feel something as we walked. I thought it might be the people, attracted to the Ghouls … or you …' Rick saw mistrust cross Ben's face as he fixed his eyes on Lael. 'They seem to me to be following … yearning … What makes us follow you so willingly?' The last blurted out in a bubble of doubt and suspicion.

'Ben …' Gabriela sounded angry and when Rick turned his head, she looked it as well. Her hair had escaped its noose and stuck to her face and neck like a tattoo, sticky from the salt in the sea wind and the sheen of sweat that covered her skin.

Rick cocked his head. Gabriela seemed different to him, less laconic and laid back, more … *passionate.* Certainly ready to defend Lael at a moment's notice.

Lael held her hand up.

'You follow because you know you must. You're all sensitive in varying degrees to the presence of the Ghouls and to me, but you are not following blindly. You have free will to leave whenever you like. Go ahead, Ben. Why don't you? Take Jamie with you. I won't mind. I won't try and stop you.'

Ben didn't move.

Jamie looked affronted. 'Well, I have free will too and I bloody well want to stay!'

Ben touched Jamie's shoulder. 'But why, Jamie? Yesterday you didn't want to know and today you won't be left behind. What's changed in you?'

'Yesterday, Ben, you talked me into seeing this through and today you're the one having second thoughts. What's changed in you?' When Ben didn't answer, the doctor went on, jerking a thumb in Lael's direction and then facing each of the group in turn. 'She's not human, yet she looks and acts it … for the most part … how many more of them are out there? That blood anomaly has shown up all over the world, not much of it, but enough to indicate that her kind have obviously infiltrated our kind. I want to know more. I want more evidence. I want to write the book that's going to document what we're all doing here and why. What led us to this point? Not just us either …' She lifted her hands to include each of the group. 'But all of humanity. Are we on this earth to be food for these Bledray Ghouls? Cows to their McBurgers? I thought, Ben, that's kind of what you wanted too. Isn't this what you've been searching for all this time, chasing your musty old legends and fragments of myth? Isn't this exactly what you wanted to know?'

Ben sat looking as stunned as Rick felt. Dr Morell had shown none of this passionate quest for knowledge over the last day. If asked, Rick would have said that she didn't believe a word of it and was tagging along to keep Ben company.

Lael smiled. Rick thought it creepy, as if she'd known what the doctor's response would be all along.

'Jamie wants to know. Ben, you want to understand. Both of you are searching for the ultimate truth. That searching will arm you against the call of the Ghouls. And you others … Anthony is fine-tuning himself to their presence. He will be able to track them without need of light or even sight.'

'And Gabriela?' Rick had to ask. Of them all, Gabriela had seemed the most unlikely to jump right into something as out there as this little quest was.

'Gabriela is here because she stands in the sure knowledge that she can't be defeated. Her loyalty, to you, Rick, and to Anthony …' She pointed at the prone man and to Gabriela's guarding hand on his shoulder. '… and to all of us is the strength that will keep us fighting.'

'Typical,' Gabriela huffed, only a little nervousness evident in her sarcastic grin. 'I'm the bloody sidekick!' Her hand, Rick noticed, didn't move away from Anthony.

'And you, Rick, are equal amounts doubtful, brave, scared, determined and horrified, angry and full of great love. Not knowing what you'll face, you'll face it anyway. You are the only one without free will because it is not in you to back down. It is not in you to deny either your destiny or me …'

'Because they are one and the same.'

Everyone looked at Anthony, awake and moving into a more upright position.

'And now, I think we have more of a grasp of why us. Perhaps you'd care to explain just how we're going to defeat this monstrous horde. You've managed to sidestep that little problem till now.'

Rick, with Anthony's declaration of his destiny echoing in his ears, remembered the packets Lael had given him. Five packets, wrapped in leather by the look and tied off with string. He picked one of them up and pulled the string. It fell away easily and Rick saw that the leather wrap was a drawstring bag, and the bag was full of … white powder.

'Don't touch it,' Lael warned. She took the rest of the bags from Rick and handed them out. 'You can't fight the Ghouls one-on-one. You will not defeat even one of them that way. Instead, we will attempt to set a trap.

'Deeper in the park behind us is a lagoon …'

*The Hunter keeps with the wind and the trees and the sky,
and knows when a quarry must fall or be rescued*

— *Journal of Malaik*

<h1 style="text-align:center">27</h1>

The humidity rose exponentially the further they travelled into the bush. Gabriela's skin itched—with sweat, with the sand that had found its way into her clothes, with the prick of every leaf off every branch off every damn bush she'd had to push her way through on the animal track they'd followed in from the beach.

True, the lagoon wasn't that far from the beach; if you were a bird. They'd finally cut through to the sandy fire trail and it was wider so they could walk fast, but still the track was windy, hilly, and soft sand all the way. She could barely hear the waves crashing and people shouting on the beach. To reach the lagoon they'd needed to leave the trail and find their way through the thick bush again. The walk had been long and with each step, the heat had risen.

Lael had gathered them in again to feed them yet another snippet of information of what they could expect. She'd stood, facing the way they'd come and told them the town was uphill to her left. To the right were rocky beaches and the ocean, behind her, kilometres of bush, twice as dense as this little patch.

'Where are the Ghouls?' Dr Morell whispered.

'In the town,' Lael answered and then she'd closed her eyes and kind of swayed, and Gabriela felt all shivery like someone had walked across her grave. 'They're resting,' Lael had continued on after she opened her eyes again. 'Too hot for them perhaps; turgidity does that.'

'You mean, they fed last night, here?' The doctor's whisper was starting to sound a little strangled.

'Here, in the town … out on the cliffs.' The colour in Lael's face washed out, leaving the even tan a jaundiced grey and Gabriela remembered her illness from the morning.

She looked out to where she thought the cliffs would be, further down the coast if memory served her right, but still within walking distance. It'd been a few years since Gabriela had come down this way, not long after she and Annie had become a couple, before work had become all-consuming, and they had more time for leisure than the date nights they now scheduled into their diaries.

'How many people have to die for a Ghoul to be turgid?'

Gabriela didn't think Ben was helping the matter. 'How about we just get on with the job at hand and worry about what's coming instead of what's already been?'

'Sprinkle the dust around the edges of the lagoon.'

'Isn't it poisonous?' The doctor wasn't much far behind Ben with the annoying questions.

'It won't harm you, but it is flammable, so no smoking.'

Yeah, right … We're in the middle of the bush in the middle of a drought in the middle of summer and she's worried about the powder being flammable. The whole damn park will go up like a tinder-box if just one spark gets into it …

Gabriela recalled the matches in her pocket and started getting a very bad feeling. *Surely, she wouldn't …*

'Don't use all the powder. In the event that you get attacked, some of that thrown in their faces will ward them off. They don't like it any better than we do, and they especially won't like this recipe.'

'I'm almost afraid to ask what it is,' Ben said, opening his bag and shaking the contents around.

'Then don't.'

Rick and Anthony had already started the job of sprinkling the powder, not interested apparently in the ensuing conversation.

'Do you think she means to set this all alight?' Gabriela asked Rick.

Both he and Anthony straightened up and sent grim looks at the dry grasses and scrub of the lagoon.

'I'm sure she has good reason for everything she does,' Anthony said.

'I think this is a trap meant to lure them in.' Rick shrugged. 'Hell, maybe it's her version of crushed eggshells and snails. The snails can't pass the eggshells and the Ghoulies can't pass this powder.'

'You think?'

Gabriela could see the shrug in Rick's shoulders without him having to move a muscle.

'Makes sense.'

'If only it could be that easy.' Anthony returned to his sprinkling.

'We aren't here for the easy.'

Gabriela was forced to admit, even if only to herself, when Rick was right, he sure was right. They weren't there for easy.

———◆———

It took the rest of the sticky afternoon to finish setting the trap. The dark of night still a few hours off when Lael called a halt with a brisk, 'That'll do.'

Thank, God. Jamie slipped the bag and its remaining contents into her pants pocket and wiped her forehead with the back of her arm. Her hands glistened white where the powder stuck to them and, though Lael had said it wouldn't harm them, she wasn't taking any chances.

A wave of something went past in the air, and she stopped breathing until it faded, eyes watering at the acidity of the stench. Ben covered his face with his arm, his dark hands appeared to have been sunk in baker's flour they were so white with the powder. *He smells it too …* She looked around at the others. Gabriela made sounds of disgust; Rick was bent over double and retching; Anthony stood stock still, sniffing like a hound on the hunt. *How can he stand it?*

'Get inside the circle,' Lael ordered and they all acted on her command.

Jamie sought out Ben's hand and held it tight. Lael searched the sky for danger, her penetrating gaze surely enough to burn out stars if she wanted to.

'Stay low.'

They all crouched down even though lagoon water, thick with weed and slimy mud, crawled up their legs to their knees. Jamie tried not to think about what else might be in the stagnant water. Knowing it was a class 'A' breeding ground for mosquitoes was bad enough. She shifted position, felt and heard the squelch of the mud, and shuddered.

Lael, also hunched down low but outside the circle, had started singing. Her voice, soft and soothing, reminded Jamie of the wind in the trees, of the ripple of water and the gentle lapping sounds it made. She felt warm and comfortable, and sleepy. Ben's arm came around her shoulders and she rested her head against him, thinking of the morning and how fine it was to wake up in his arms.

She heard a whispered, 'Stay here,' and lazily watched as Lael seemed to shift and fragment into a million spots of light. *How odd …* The tiny lights spread out like wisps of clouds over their heads and faded until they were invisible. Or almost. Jamie thought she could still see one or two flicker and change colour.

And then all the lights were gone and the sky was clear again. Jamie heard Anthony whispering.

'Did you hear that?'

Rick answered. 'Voices not far away.'

'Do Ghouls chat and giggle when they feed?' Gabriela now, her voice betraying the tenseness behind her light-hearted words.

Rick must have made some move because Gabriela dropped all attempts at cheerfulness as she spoke again. 'Don't be stupid, Rick. She said stay here. Anthony, no!'

Jamie twisted around to see. The hazy feeling of only moments ago was fading fast without Lael's song in her ears. She sensed danger and the oily scent of something wrong. Rick and Anthony were going, no matter what Lael had ordered, or Gabriela could say. Well, her mother had certainly not raised a stupid daughter.

'You go and watch their backs, Gabriela,' she found herself saying. 'That's what she said, they'll need you. We'll stay here.' She grabbed Ben's arm and squeezed. 'We'll stay right here and watch and wait.'

Ben had been on the verge of following as well, but relaxed in her grip. 'Be careful …'

Gabriela moved through the bushes like a wraith after the others. *A vengeful wraith …* Jamie lost sight of her quickly, stared after her for a handful of long seconds and turned around in Ben's arms.

'I hate waiting,' she said.

'Me too.'

They held each other tight and watched the sky and surrounding bushes. Night hadn't quite arrived, but the Ghouls were on the prowl.

'Can you see them?'

'I can.' Anthony slit his eyes to filter out the dulling sunshine. The trail of the Ghouls as they skimmed the tops of the trees gleamed with unnatural brilliance, the bloody exhaust of killing machines. 'Can you smell them?'

Rick's face, even in the patchy shadows of the bush, was white as a ghost's, pinched around his eyes and flaring nostrils. A rustle in the branches behind them and Gabriela appeared, angry and ready to do battle judging by the fiery light in her eyes. With her hair sticking out and littered with broken twigs and leaves, she looked to Anthony like a pissed-off archangel in search of butts to kick. He saw a fraction of what Lael must have seen, the pool of strength that ran through Gabriela Salek like liquid steel.

'Are you guys idiots or just plain deaf? She said stay at the lagoon. I definitely heard her say to stay!'

'She needs help with this,' Rick said, and looked so confident in that knowledge that Gabriela nodded and gave in without another word of protest.

'This way,' Anthony told them.

He crept through the trees, making as little noise as he could. He needn't have worried, around them the low hum of cicadas was turning into a cacophony of sound. Rick was so close behind him that he could feel his hot breath on his back. No doubt, Gabriela was just as close behind Rick. He broke through the bush and onto the wide sandy track as suddenly as falling down an unseen staircase and winced as he felt his knee pull in ways knees weren't meant to. Rick must have great reactions, he figured, to avoid tumbling down the eroded bank on top of him.

'You okay? One minute we're struggling through jungle and the next we're practically on a highway.' Gabriela put one hand under his arm and helped him to a standing position without losing a breath. Anthony was beginning to feel like the veritable damsel in distress; Gabriela his knight in shining armour. Fuck, his knee hurt.

'You're not okay, are you?' With the look Rick was giving his leg, Anthony half-expected to see bones poking through, blood gushing. He rolled up his pants leg to check—no bones, no blood, but it was swelling by the second. *Fuck!*

Anthony saw a flash of colour out of the corner of his eyes and jumped back, nearly knocking Gabriela over. 'What the hell was that?' Another flash and a riot of giggles, and Anthony realised it had been kids, the fastest in the world apparently.

'Drew! Abbie!' The voice that called after them sounded impatient and extremely cross. The woman jogging around the bend appeared every bit as cranky as she sounded. She spared them a pained smile and kept jogging. 'You kids get back here!'

Anthony could hear her calling, hear the anger turn to worry edged with panic. 'Kids, where are you? This isn't funny. Please come back.'

Anthony registered the lull in the cicada chorus as a sudden burst of light coalesced into a beam of rippling, shifting form.

'No!' Rick yelled and ran off after the woman.

'Go, go!' Anthony pushed Gabriela to follow. 'They're attacking that family! Go!'

He hobbled after them, watching the play of light; staggering under a wave of hungry pleasure and finally halting, almost crying with the pain of his knee. Ahead of him, kneeling in the sand, vomiting and retching and sobbing and cursing, was Rick. In the middle of the track was a lone tennis ball, too new-looking to have been sitting there long. The sand was scuffed and gouged, drag marks crossed harder patches. A doll hung as a dismal epitaph in the branches that bordered the track.

They were too late. It had happened in an instant and they were too late.

Gabriela came running back down the track.

'No sign of the mother or the kids. Completely …' She saw the doll and the ball, and Rick chucking his lunch in the sand. '… Gone.'

Rick's head came up, red and wild, even as Anthony saw the tell-tale sparkle of Ghoul. 'Back to the lagoon,' he yelled. 'Back, back!'

Gabriela grabbed Rick first, yanked him upright, and then Anthony, spinning him around and making no allowances for sore knees or upset stomachs. The Ghouls were hot behind them, she could smell them now too. She risked a look behind and saw not the glinting lights she expected, but two men, smiling lustily, greedily at their retreating backs. And no matter how fast Gabriela ran, the men kept pace, toying with them, running them down, she suspected, until they dropped with exhaustion.

Then she remembered the leather pouch in her pocket. She pulled her arm free and cried out, 'The powder. The powder!' Found the bag, opened it with a dexterity born from sheer terror, and grabbed a handful of the powder, flinging it in the faces of the leering couple and cursing them with words she'd never before heard.

The Ghouls reared back, screeching, changing from solid to vapour and back again and then vanished in a cloud of phosphorous-laden dust.

Anthony could barely hear over the thud of his heart in his ears. *Oh, my God!*

'What did you say?' He couldn't tell who asked, but it was Gabriela, again, who helped him stand. Gabriela, again, who guided him along the track to the spot where they'd left the bushes.

Rick's T-shirt hung damply from his arms and chest. His jeans, stained with dirt and vomit, hung low on his hips. He was thinner; skin, stretched tight across his arms, showed scratching, bruising and bony wrists grown fragile in the space of a few hours. Anthony spread his own hands out in front of him, wondering what havoc all this was taking on him, wondering what Rick might see when he looked at him, and hoped it was more than a reflection of his own hurting self.

They reached the lagoon within seconds, stepped over the circle of powder and dropped to their knees in the marshy safety of the centre. It took only seconds more to realise that Ben and Jamie were not where they'd left them.

*Awareness of surroundings is innate. The Hunter senses the
quarry through sight, sound, smell, and taste.
Even the smallest trace of emotion and need can be detected*

— *Journal of Malaik*

28

Ghouls could hide all they wanted from humans and rarely ever be found, but there was no hiding from a Hunter. Lael didn't bother with formalities or questions. She had all the information she needed and no time for anything more than quick and permanent results. Even as she drifted beneath the pink flowers of a honeysuckle bush on the precipice of a kill, other Ghouls were hunting and feeding. Lael put them from her mind, swirled around the feet of the Ghouls and rose up in a living shawl of power. The pair were covered, smothered and despatched within seconds. Just in time.

Two teenagers wandered, hand in hand, along the track, eyes only for each other, talking, kissing, and not paying any attention to where they were going. Lael doubted they really knew where they were, or how they got there. The scent trail of the Ghouls was strong along the track, drawing the couple onward through the bush and eventually back up to town.

She waited for them around one of the many bends, a harmless woman, a little flustered, a lot lost and smiled brightly in relief when they approached and noticed her presence.

'I thought I heard voices,' she said, arms outstretched in welcome. 'I'm so glad to see you. Can you tell me which is the right way out of here?'

The teenagers walked right up to her and she clasped them both on the shoulder, smiling and exuding trusting confidence.

'Sure,' said the boy. 'You got a map? Where're you tryin' to get to in particular?'

'Sorry, no map and the beach would be best. Is it far?'

'Not at all.' The girl turned and pointed down the track. 'It's down that way. Just keep to this trail and it'll take you right there …'

'Or close enough you'll be able to see it anyway.'

'That's right. You really can't miss it.' The girl had a dazed cast to her face. She would probably never know how close she'd come to death.

'We were just going to head back ourselves …'

'We could show you, if you like.'

'I would like it very much. Do you live around here?' Lael herded them back in the direction of the beach, ran her hands lightly over the back of their heads, down their backs, let the conversation carry on without her and slowly faded out of their world.

Carrying her mark, no Ghoul would attack … she hoped. She whispered a few words into the air, both a prayer and a benediction for safety, and lifted into the air. Any peace she felt at having saved the teenagers evaporated with the realisation that while she protected the young couple, someone else had died. Even now, Rick and the others fought for their lives. Failure filled her even as only moments ago success had rallied her convictions. Not even into the fight proper yet, and the fine line of defence she had developed was wavering close to destruction.

She consolidated into a seething ball of invisible matter and propelled herself through the air toward Rick, reaching them as they defeated the Ghouls attacking, and turning to the area of the lagoon when she realised Ben and Jamie were not with the others.

The lagoon was empty.

'Hi. You all right out there?'

Jamie and Ben waved at three women that appeared from nowhere at the edge of the lagoon, looking hot and raggedy, and pretty close to collapse.

'We're fine,' Ben called out. *If you don't count mosquitoes and snakes and Ghouls waiting to suck every drop of life from your body.*

'Are you lost?' one of the women asked. 'Or is there a path through this …' she looked at the sodden ground with distaste, '… bog?'

'No path,' Jamie called out. 'We were just looking at a bird.'

'Oh … birdwatchers.' The women discussed this among themselves for a short moment. The first speaker, the shortest of the trio, shrugged her shoulders and whispered, 'Ask them then,' to the others.

'You wouldn't be from Bundeena, would you? We've been going round in circles trying to get back up to the town, or the beach, or a better marked trail …' The woman, white-haired and slim, looked worried, and Ben didn't blame her. A night lost in the bush would be anything but fun … especially this night.

A man's cry came from the east—the direction Rick, Anthony and Gabriela had taken.

'The beach is that way.' Jamie pointed it out with a flourish. 'Not far.' Her smile was broad and entirely forced, and then to Ben she said, 'Maybe we should go with them.'

She produced the bag Lael had given her and bounced it in her hand, and, as much as Ben wanted to stay and wait for the others, he knew the women would have no chance against a Ghoul.

'We haven't seen how this stuff works yet.'

'Now's a good a time as any, and if we're quick, and lucky, we can slip past anyone's notice.'

'I don't know, Jamie. Even on the beach they won't be safe …'

Jamie took pause then. He could see it plainly in her face. She had presumed the beach to represent safety when safety couldn't be guaranteed anywhere. She came to some kind of resolution, frowning and grim at first, clutching the bag tightly, and then a lightening of face and sincere smile this time.

'This is still the most dangerous place. We'll be drawing the Ghouls to the circle, maybe during all that they'll fail to notice any people left on the beach.'

She had a point.

The women meantime had walked around the edge of the lagoon, bickering and laughing, and were about to disappear in the bushes.

'Come on, then,' Ben said and grabbed Jamie's hand. 'Let's do this before it's too late.'

They splashed through the shallow lagoon, their noisy approach halting the woman as they turned back in curiosity.

'Do you mind if we take the rear? We were just going to leave ourselves.'

Ben couldn't shake the feeling that something was wrong. The light was fading fast, casting the crooked branches of the trees in gloom and the women's bodies in awkward shadow. Their chatter silenced. Birds, brain-achingly noisy only moments ago, were absent, the crack of sticks underfoot sounded hollow.

'Stop,' Ben said. 'Stop.'

The women stopped, craning their necks to see back along the trail to where Ben stood in a flushed-face sweat.

'Ben, what is it?' Jamie whispered. She looked all around and then back at Ben. 'For Christ's sake, what is it?' Fear and the odd light in the sky made her face hawkish and strained, her cheeks so angular they appeared cut from marble.

He saw them first in Jamie's eyes, pinpoints of light in eyes so velvety brown any reflection caught in their depths was absorbed and thrown back out tenfold. He loved those eyes, was a slave to every flutter and nuance of emotion they expressed. Right now, they were telling him that Ghouls lurked behind them. Jamie's gaze passed from Ben to over his shoulder, her eyebrows dropped in a concerted effort to see into the shadows and then widened when she did. Ben turned to see what she'd seen.

What had Lael told them? Fright threatened to chase every sensible thought out of his head.

They can appear as humans, beautiful and alluring, and as tiny stars almost imperceptible to the eye.

That was it. Tiny stars in Jamie's eyes, a diaphanous cloud in the air behind them.

'Run,' he said, too softly. The women were confused, eyeing him strangely. First stop and then run. He was obviously off his nutter.

'Are you all right back there?'

'What's going on?'

'This is bloody ridiculous.'

He knew how crazy he sounded, even to Jamie, petrified beside him, digging into his arms so hard he felt every imprint of her fingers as a puncture wound.

A smell might come to you, something dead.

A chill might shiver its way down your back.
Don't turn around, don't let them close.

'Can you smell that?' Ben sensed the odour even as Jamie spoke.

The women had started walking again, but not fast enough. They needed to run. Didn't they understand that they need to fucking run?

'Snake!' Ben cried. 'Snake!'

The order to run became instinct; the word 'snake' an alarm unto itself. One of the women screamed. One swore and all three ran, disregarding of sharp branches and nuts. When one slowed, more curious than scared, Ben shoved both her and Jamie forward.

'Big snake,' he warned, and forced them on. 'Bad time of day for snakes … and spiders.' The woman looked convinced then, a shifting glance into the bushes for webs, and she ran—as Ben wanted her to, as Ben himself ran, hard and fast, and with head down.

They broke through the bushes and onto the beach, almost reaching the water before they could stop. Wild-eyed, all of them, hats askew, shirts torn.

'Oh, my God, oh, my God,' they each whispered. 'I've never been so scared.' 'I've never run so fast.' 'Did anyone see the snake?' 'Was it big?' 'Must've been huge.'

The beach, almost deserted, was a haven after the thick, hot atmosphere of the bush. Cool breezes caressed their sweat-slicked skin. The light evened out here, without the reach of the trees to splinter it into prisms of off-key perception.

The smell was stronger.

A few boats remained anchored offshore, their lights off, no sign of life. A couple of dogs chased each other further up. The headland loomed beside them in rocky sanction over the waters that lapped its feet.

The peacefulness of the scene razored Ben's already edgy nerves.

A Ghoul materialised at the top of the beach, another one in the centre of the path the group had just taken. Shadowed heads bobbed around the cabins of the boats.

'Did that person just appear out of thin air?' The woman who hadn't been scared of the snake pointed up the beach. Her hair glowed ghostly white in the eeriness of dusk.

'Where, Bridg?'

Ben gathered them into a tighter group. 'You should go now. It's not safe here after dark.'

'You're scaring me,' the short woman said. 'I think we should do exactly as he says, girls, now.'

Ben stole a look back into the bush. The Ghoul hadn't moved. A flickering around him became a plague of firefly light. More Ghouls. *Cutting off our path back to the lagoon.*

'We're going,' the woman said again as if talking to a bunch of parent-deaf pre-pubescents.

'Ben?' Jamie's voice hissed out. 'We can't get back and we can't leave them.'

'I know that. Don't you think I know that?' Ben moved after the women. They would have to trust that the others would be okay, hope that Lael would come to their rescue. A phantasm appeared between the departing women and themselves. Jamie opened her bag and dug out a handful of the powder. Ben did the same. 'If we're not careful the women will think we're attacking them. They have to see the Ghouls themselves.'

'They already have.' Jamie started running.

The women had stopped and were talking to an unpretentious looking young man. He reached out and touched the white-blonde woman, put a friendly arm around her shoulders, drew her close to him. Ben could see her smile of pleasure, hear the voices of the others.

'Bridg, what the hell are you doing?'

One put out an arm to her friend in a bid to pull her back. Another started to push him away. Both let their arms drop to their sides as all three fell under the spell of Ghoul and waited their turn for his kiss.

Jamie yelled a war cry and a string of obscene words that shocked the women out of their daze. Ben was running, running so hard his feet pounded into the sand with the thudding danger of an enraged bull-elephant. Blood rushed through his veins in a red-hot blinding torrent. Jamie pushed the blonde woman away from the Ghoul, broke their kiss and flung powder into its face. Ben surged after her, scooped up the woman coughing and choking for breath, threw her over his shoulder, took the wrists of another and screamed, the bull-elephant's trumpet of dire warning and action. 'Run, dammit. Move!'

He felt Jamie beside him, dragging the last woman after her, sprinting so fast in the soft sand her feet barely touched ground. He wouldn't have been surprised to see the woman flying in the air behind her.

'Run, run, run, run …' Jamie used the litany of the word to fuel her escape.

Two more Ghouls emerged from the sand, blocking any hope of escape along the beach.

If you can, find water, dive under and stay under as long as you can.

They could take to the water and hope they didn't drown before the Ghouls gave up or they could head back to the lagoon and the safety of the circle. It wouldn't take so long to reach it now they all knew where it was. Ben veered into the bushes.

The women struggled to free their hands.

'You've got to keep running,' he urged them without slowing. 'Head back to the lagoon, keep the houses on your right if we get separated. Don't stop for anything or anybody, even each other.'

They nodded and didn't slacken their pace, keeping at his heels even as he ducked and wove a path through nearly impenetrable scrub. The blonde woman struggled to put her feet on the ground, almost swinging Ben off balance. He let her down, but kept hold of her arm.

A cloud of rancidity on his left made him swerve automatically to his right, another directly after and he realised they were being herded away from the lagoon. They came to a small clearing and he stopped, causing Jamie and the last woman to crash into them and fall in a tangled heap.

'What is it?' Jamie said, pushing the woman off her and helping her to stand at the same time. 'Why did we stop?'

Ben pulled his bag from his shirt pocket. He hadn't realised he'd stowed it there. 'Sprinkle the powder on our heads and shoulders. Do it!'

Jamie obeyed, reassuring the women that the powder was safe, it would protect them, would ward off the Ghouls. Ben hoped she was right. The women were too exhausted and gasping for breath to argue. One came to him to check on her still unsteady friend.

'She'll be okay,' he told her. He could hear and feel the woman's shuddering breaths.

Decay swept through the clearing in a fierce gush of depraved longing. They couldn't afford to wait any longer.

'Time to run again. Same instructions as before. Keep as close to me as you can. Jamie …' Jamie's face was scratched, her hair in a snarl around her head, but he could see her strength shining through. 'You'll have to take the rear. I want you to call Lael. As loud as you can, call her, scream for her, demand she get her butt down here to help us. We can't hide from these monsters and we can't fight them all off alone.'

Ben turned and ran. The women once again followed right behind him. Jamie shouted until her voice grew hoarse. He didn't know if they could outrun them, didn't know whether or not they were being played with, didn't dare hope they could escape unhurt. He just ran … and ran.

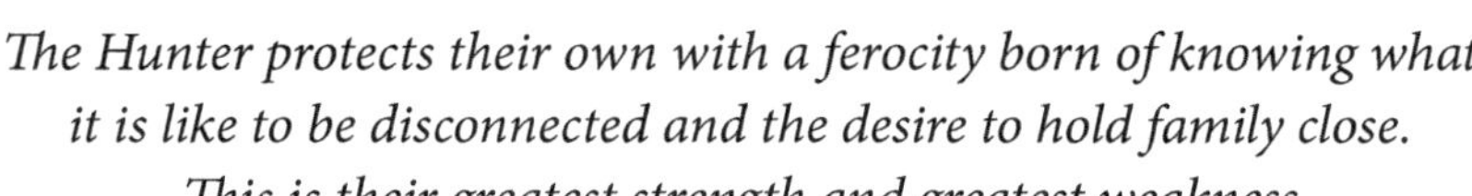

The Hunter protects their own with a ferocity born of knowing what it is like to be disconnected and the desire to hold family close. This is their greatest strength and greatest weakness

— Journal of Malaik

29

Lael stormed toward the three men as they lay panting in the lagoon, heedless now of the water and mud.

'I told you to stay!'

'There were people, kids … we had to help,' Rick protested. His ribs ached and his stomach still twisted itself in knots. He'd never been so sick in his life. If the mere scent of Ghouls wracked him so completely, surely he could only be a hindrance. The thought chilled him to the bone.

'They were already gone … Others were at risk. Others still are!'

'They were children! A mother … vanished …' Rick couldn't believe that this was the same woman he had shared his bed and shower with just that morning. So soft then, so hard now.

'That is nothing compared to what will happen if we fail here tonight.'

'Are you so heartless that the death of innocent children means nothing? How long have you been at this game if the lives of two kids and their mum is a mere by-product of the hunt?'

Lael's eyes flared red and Rick saw, finally, the Hunter that she was.

'How many children do you think there were in Bellbird? How many do you think are left in this town? The neighbouring town, across the bay, the rest of the city, the country? How many do you think I have seen fall already because I am only one person, one Hunter, woefully little and ineffectual in the face of a full-scale Gathering. Hundreds of Ghouls could descend here tonight—thousands—and the next closest Hunter is just as many miles away.'

Anthony pushed between them, but Lael gripped Rick's arm, some of the fire leaving her eyes. 'They died, yes, but others were saved. You must do what I tell you, when I tell you …' She paused and turned her face, her concentration averted to something else. Sound on the rising wind.

Rick heard it too. Someone calling for Lael, pleading for help. Ben and Dr Morell. Shit, how could he be so stupid? They weren't here and he'd allowed his weakness to affect his thinking. They'd said they'd wait. Had they too gone to someone's rescue?

'Go,' he urged. Lael dissipated into the gloom of dusk in an instant. The only sign of her presence was the lingering pressure of her hand on his arm.

'Well, then …' Anthony looked all around him and gave up with a shrug.

Gabriela stood, attempted to smooth out her dripping jeans. 'This time, we're staying put.'

Ben seemed to find trails where there were none. Jamie hoped he knew where he was going. Her legs were starting to feel like lead weights, lungs like they'd burst apart any minute. She kept yelling though, calling Lael's name, using it like a safety rope and an incantation all in one. The woman in front of her stumbled and Jamie steadied her before she could fall, kept her moving before she could even think of stopping.

Faces popped out of the bushes, hands reached out, tugged at her clothes, clawed her hair. Jamie punched out, ducked, hit aside everything that came at her until even branches snapped under her defensive blitz. She could hear the women crying, near hysterical and scared out of their wits.

'Lael! Lael!' she called. Where the hell was Lael?

And then Lael was right behind her, a ball of white fire in one hand, the other, reassuringly on Jamie's back.

'Keep running,' she said. 'You're nearly there. Call for Rick now. He's at the lagoon waiting for you. Let them know you're coming.'

Lael must have jumped on a fallen tree then, or a rock, because she rose above Jamie and threw her fire over their heads. It left a comet-trail of sizzling embers that spread out to cover them and marked the way to the lagoon.

'Rick! We're coming in!' Jamie shouted. 'Rick!'

She sensed Lael had gone again, heard frustrated cries come from the bushes, saw a dazzling clash of light and thought it the after-burn of the heat on her eyeballs. A surge of hatred filled her, a danger-survived thrill of bloodthirsty rage. *Kill them,* an unbidden voice in her mind swelled. *Kill them all!*

Rick heard his name, saw the sky light up, and stood in time to be nearly bowled over by a hurtling Ben, a trail of women and Dr Morell. He caught Ben by the shoulders and pulled him around, halting his forward motion and helping him to the ground slower than the undignified heap he was heading for. Gabriela and Anthony caught a woman each, as another sank to her hands and knees. Dr Morell came in half-turned to see whatever chased them, fell over the woman and landed on her backside on the safe side of the powdered circle.

'Lael, Lael's in there,' she gasped. 'Killing them. Oh, my God. So many … Did you see the fire?'

'Calm down, calm down. You made it.' Rick held her clutching hands still, enfolded her in his arms and drew her upward to stand on unsteady feet. 'You did it.'

'Yes, yes …' Rick could feel her violently shivering, felt her bring it under control with a final shuddering lurch, and let her go when she reeled to the women collapsed on the ground around them. 'Ben? Is she okay?'

Rick saw too then that one of the women was near unconscious. Dr Morell dropped beside Ben. Anthony had already peeled the woman away from him, laid her in his own lap, and tapped his fingertips on her cheeks.

'She's shook all to hell,' Ben said. 'There wasn't time to be gentle.'

Rick helped Gabriela see to the other women. They removed their packs, retrieved water bottles, had them drink—though the act of breathing seemed hard enough. Dr Morell's voice was soft, reassuring, even made Rick feel better, but the woman was too dazed.

Lael stepped out of the bushes, haggard and weighed down with exhaustion. He wondered how she could possibly last the night. He was at her side without thinking, taking her hand.

'I'm sorry, I didn't mean to infer …'

'Yes, you did,' she said, her voice ragged but her face understanding. Then she looked at the women and the understanding turned to worry and enough fear to make Rick nervous. 'What are we going to do with them?' She pulled away from Rick and circled around the crowd with her hands on her hips and her face down.

He hoped she had a plan, some sort of backup to use. A curl of dread expanded low in his back at the thought that maybe she didn't. She stopped opposite him, face now to the sky, eyes closed as if hoping to divine a clue from the heavens. She transferred her divination to him and Rick saw she'd found her answer.

'We won't be safe here for long. There's too many of them and now too many of us.'

'Where can we go?'

'We need an enclosed space, somewhere big enough to fit these women, but small enough to guard.'

'One of the houses?' Anthony faced the houses now. Lights had come on along the ridge. Many houses stayed in darkness.

'Getting there from here isn't that easy,' Gabriela said. 'There's a pretty steep hill and some deep gullies. We won't be able to see more than a foot in front of our faces soon.'

'And they're not easy to defend. Too many windows and doors. South of here, on the cliff face is a cave …'

'I know where that is.' Gabriela joined Rick and Lael. 'Fair walk from here though and these women are about played out.'

'We can go as far as we need to go to get away from those monsters,' said one.

'If that's what they are,' said another. 'I've never seen such a thing …'

'That's what they are,' said Lael, as final as God on matters of heaven and hell. 'We can cut from here to the coast. The trail's good. Won't take long.'

'It's rougher along the coastline and dangerous in the dark.' Gabriela didn't look happy. 'The town would be easier.'

'But not safer.' Anthony still stared, squinting up at the houses. 'If we're going to attempt this cave, we should do it now.' He turned his stare to Lael. 'Right now.'

The pain in Rick's back tightened. The women started getting ready to move; picking up their bags, closing off water bottles, helping each other. One came across to Anthony and her injured friend.

'And Bridget?'

'You will have to take turns helping her. She's coming too now. Keep her moving as fast as you can. Let's go before the Ghouls regroup.' Lael brooked no further argument or comment, turning on her heel, retrieving her duffel and stalking out of the lagoon.

Rick and the others were left to catch up. Bridget was helped into a standing position cradled between her friends. They followed Lael out, in single file behind Ben, Dr Morell and Gabriela in single file behind them. In the rear and with a hand on Rick's elbow, to urge him onward, was Anthony. Rick shook his head.

'This isn't a democracy, Rick. Lael knows what she's doing.'

'Action, not talk?'

'Exactly. You might not be able to see it, and with the easterly breeze, maybe you can't smell it yet, but up on the hill, where families are sitting down to dinner, there's a rainbow of light hovering over the rooftops. We have to get to safety before that rainbow finds its pot of gold.'

'Us,' Rick muttered, thinking of every vampiric movie he'd ever seen and suspecting they all came distressingly short of tonight's reality.

'Us,' Anthony answered.

They stepped out onto the path, wary of the drop in the ground. Rick lifted Anthony's arm to his shoulders, wrapped his own arm around the detective's waist, and helped him, as fast as he could, limp along the trail.

*The sun and moon are connected as is Alffür to Rydri;
as is Bledray to Bledray. Each needs the other in order to
tread the true path*

— *Journal of Malaik*

30

Grey fingers of cloud extended across the sky hiding the rise of the moon and distorting the last of the sun's rays. Night would come early because of them. The heat of the day, trapped between earth and cloud, oppressed most of those living without benefit of air-conditioner—and the dead didn't care.

Neither did Moriah. She liked the heat, lying on her back in Dorothy Parden's garden, arms and legs flung out, soaking it in. Dorothy's window-unit cooler clanked a steady beat of tepid air into the house and dripped a staccato of water onto a rock slab below. Moriah liked Dorothy's garden too. Bushrock shelves fitted with succulents and groundcover runners, loamy beds of vegetables, a whole corner taken over by broad pumpkin leaves and sun-yellow flowers, the whole surrounded by house, fence and a nasturtiumed wall that led to a front porch and the long drive Dorothy so detested.

Jedidiah stayed inside with his air and Roger Parden's rocks, playing at human with protective goggles over his eyes and a white mask over his mouth and nose, tumbling a pile of rock, grit and water, and making a mess. Lucky Roger wasn't around to see it.

Moriah squirmed in the grass, sang out loud for the pure pleasure of making sound, and filled her lungs with humid air and the scents of the garden. She stopped singing as soon as it registered that some of the scents did not come from the lawn or plants, or the bush on the other side of the house, or the sea the other side of that. More tantalising than any of those came the smell of her own kind. Jedidiah inside all covered in white dust, someone out on the street, and a great wafting cloud rising up from the beach.

Moriah didn't know the name of her kind. The Guardians and Hunters called them Bledray Ghouls. They knew themselves only as Us. Us who love and share. Us who are hunted without mercy, destroyed without leniency. Us who had found a way to come back. Outside of Us, there were Them and Ryrdri.

She lay awhile longer, drifting in thought with the smells, not noticing the subtle change from pleasant to dark until the sun had fully sunk and the moon, peeking through the cloud fingers, had risen.

Moriah opened her eyes with a snap … Hunter … and with fluid motion, rose and entered the house where no smells other than smoking oil and barren air polluted the closed-in rooms. She slid open the glass doors with a crash and recoiled at the pervasive fetor that had replaced the comforting perfume of Us.

<hr>

Lael had always worked on instinct, relying on her skills and senses to judge her next movement. Being a Hunter demanded it. No school taught what a Hunter needed to survive. Yet this lull confused her. Her body hurt, head ached and the tingle in her skin had changed to hot and cold flushes of electrical energy. Fire had come to her fingertips before the thought of it entered her head. Instinct, she told herself. Natural, yet the conflagration she had sent above the heads of the humans had been white hot and crackling.

She was no new Hunter exploring the limits of her power. Lael knew exactly what she was capable of, but energy of that strength had never figured in her abilities before. Neither had the vicious drive to kill that accompanied it. She had far exceeded her usual capability, slaughtering a dozen Ghouls with the speed and deadliness of a guided missile.

The bittersweet taste such slaughter left in her mouth scared her as little else did. It was corrupt, putrescent, and she wanted more.

Why weren't the Ghouls pressing the attack? Lael had seen the same lights as Anthony, had sensed the presence of the Ghouls even against the prevailing breezes. They grew in numbers with every second of the dying day, yet the majority of them were not feeding. Since when had Ghouls been able to resist an orgy? When did they start to hunt in packs and stalk their prey? What were they waiting for now?

Lael left the designated path at a patch of neatly nibbled lawn. A startled deer, caught in the open, thudded into the thick glades of the park. Several tents, the rooves sagging, poles leaning into the middle sat pegged in darkness. Whatever campers had been there were lost to Ghouls the previous night, back when Ghouls behaved as they'd always done, hunting in pairs and not playing with their prey.

Whispers along the line of humans carried their fear and growing horror forward, pushed her to walk faster. The grass thinned and tapered off into shell-grit and sand. Ocean waves pounded the rocks along the shore, foam from their spent force spraying into the air and rolling through cracks and crevices emerging as bleached-bones from the blackness of the water.

Weak moonlight filtered through the cloud cover above, lighting enough of their path to show them the danger of putting a foot wrong among the boulders and slabs of tide-pool pocked granite. Lael slowed her pace to allow Gabriela to fall in beside her.

'We'll follow the shore along then move up as the cliffs get higher. You know the way?'

'Yes. It's tricky.'

'Go slow where you need to, faster when you can.'

'Where're you going to be?'

'This lull in activity isn't natural. I'm going to have a look around, distract them if I need to. Get to the cave as quickly as possible. We need to choose our ground and not let the Ghouls do it for us.'

'I'll bring Rick up to the front to help you should you need it. Anthony will stay in the rear with Jamie.'

'Anthony hurt his knee fairly badly.'

'I'll take a look at it. I'll keep an eye on you so concentrate on not falling off the cliffs. Don't worry too much about the Ghouls. Rick can give you plenty of notice if they come, and between you, you can fend off any attack that might slip past me.'

'You're not filling me with confidence here.' Gabriela's teeth flashed white as she grinned.

'I'm very good at diversions.'

'Oh, well, that's just so much better.'

Lael laughed, soft and strained, but a laugh it was and she felt better for it.

'Stop before you get into the bush. Make the changeover then.'

'Whatever you say.'

Lael patted her on the back and stood aside, waving the women forward, and walking again when the others caught up to tell them the plan. She stopped Rick and Anthony, kneeling beside the detective to run her hand over the damaged knee.

'It's not too bad,' she told them, though the knee felt hot and the skin was stretched tighter than a drum. 'Nothing some ice and a few days rest wouldn't fix.' She looked into Anthony's agonised visage. Anthony tried to form a smile and failed dismally. 'Pity we haven't got that long.' She clasped his knee, let her hand feel the heat and draw it into herself, sucking out the pain and bruising, easing the stiffness.

Anthony choked back a cry and then let out a deep sigh, moving the leg, testing its ability to hold his weight and smiling as the vestiges of pain left his face.'

'Good as new,' he said, now hopping from one foot to the other.

'Probably better.'

'Thanks.'

Lael shrugged off his thanks. 'You have work to do that can't be done with only one leg.' Anthony moved on after the others and she turned to Rick. 'When Gabriela stops in a few minutes, walk with her. She knows the way to the cave, but needs you to watch her back. She can't be worrying about Ghouls and picking a way through the bushes at the same time. I'll be back as soon as I can.'

Rick held her when she would have turned away, bent his head to hers, encapsulated her lips to his. Urgency, fear and courage formed that kiss. Strength ploughed her teeth and tongue. He pulled away, left her lips throbbing, and cupped his hands around her face.

'Be careful,' he said and Lael thrilled at the husky timbre of the words.

He left, jogging to catch up with Anthony and the others, and not looking back.

Lael rubbed her lips together, ran her tongue over her teeth. The taste of doom had evaporated at his touch, replaced with a new flavour that was all Rick and nothing else. *I like that much better ...*

She turned back along the beach, shifted shape and went to learn what she could from the gathering Ghouls.

The moon gave out phantoms of light that alternately lit the path Gabriela followed, and plunged it into black slabs of space. Pounding waves on the left hand, trackless scrub on the right and twenty year old memories of walking this same path, kept her feet sure. *Yeah, but that was in broad daylight ...* Gabriela quashed the nervy voice in her head and used every scrap of moonlight to traverse the zig-zagging clifftop, cutting across the teeth of erosion when she could.

Time meant nothing with sweat running into her eyes and the surety that behind her, eight people relied on her capacity to find her way in the dark.

Fuck ... Her foot slipped at the edge of an incline and she went down on one knee, but the way was clear ahead for a few feet and speed meant everything. She sent back a warning and continued on.

They were nearly at the cave, she was sure of it. The cliffs rose steadily steeper from the sea, the scrub pulled back to expose the bare skeleton of white rock. They climbed a last steep incline as the moon illuminated the land in silver light.

'Tumbledowns,' she said and paused. Long ago, sea and wind had eaten away enough of the sandstone cliff to cause it to crumble into rock.

'Are we there?'

Gabriela heard Rick and pointed. 'There.' A black handprint marked the other side of the bouldered inlet. 'At the top.'

Moans of pain and exhaustion collected around hers, bags and bodies dropped, rocks scraped and jumbled under booted feet.

'Oh, God! We're not there yet?'

'Can we stop for just a minute?'

'Move downhill a little, so we can't be seen. Stay together. Keep quiet. One minute is all we can spare.' Anthony urged the group down from the high ground, into the edge of shadows. A sickness rose in Gabriela as she saw him constantly look back to the township.

'What do you see?' she whispered, and when Rick froze, face upturned to sniff the air, she quailed and added, 'What do you smell?'

The eruption of flame that spurted a kilometre into the sky, halfway between the cliffs and the town pre-empted any need for answers. An aurora of cascading light rippled down. Apparitions flew, screaming, tearing, livid gargoyles and chimera converged on a single point and were consumed in a ring of fire. A living white fire that reached out and seized as many of the enraged Ghouls as possible.

'That's the lagoon,' someone said in a halting breath.

'That's Lael.'

The women screamed.

'Rest time's over,' announced Rick, clutching at his belly and holding back retching sobs. He doubled over, hands on knees, choking, and then lifted his head, shocking Gabriela with the mask of illness and fear his face had become. 'They're on their way.'

The group found their feet as one and began running, tripping, falling and clambering up again, following the boundary of the rocky cliff, low to almost sea level and then up, up, up to the high cliff looming over it and the narrow trail that led into the cave.

Full Gatherings are rare.
Bledray do their utmost
to hide in the voids.
A lone Bledray
is just as rare as a pack.
To find either signifies the start of a Gathering.

— Journal of Malaik

31

By the time she reached the ridge, the lull had come to its end.

People stood in back yards and on verandahs, looking down into the morass of the Park. Some had started along the trails. None of them were human.

Lael let enough of herself be seen to attract their attention and retreated to the lagoon.

The circle had, in places, blown away or dissolved into the marsh, but enough remained to suit Lael's needs. She stopped in its centre, shifted to solid matter and waited.

A curtain of light washed over the treetops; beautiful, glimmering sheets that vibrated with the force of life. Life that came from the unrelenting pursuit of human spirit flesh. Shades of colour brightened, flared and faded to assume new colours. The leaves on the trees burnished with golden hues and brilliant greens.

Lael watched them come, refused entry to the beauty that would mesmerise her with a determined stance, feet apart, arms straight and hands by her sides. She narrowed her eyes. Ghouls stepped through the gaps in the circle, grins so wide they might have been sharks circling in for the kill. *They are circling in for the kill …*

More streamed down from the town, up from the beach, yet she sensed the gathering was not yet at hand. Many of these Ghouls had not fed. They starved yet they held their hunger at bay … *for the gathering!* Lael mentally reeled at the image of countless Ghouls circling in their light fantastic, sharing their passion and hunger, and joining as one before spreading out in a tidal wave of human destruction. She knew that this had happened and been stopped before. Success hinged on sacrifice and blood.

Heat started in her feet, the same tingling jolt of energy she'd been at odds with since her encounter with the fisherman not far from this very spot, not far from the cave the humans now sought sanctuary in. The name of the Ghoul she'd killed there came as an icicle of dread in her mind. *David* ... And the fire in her feet traversed the length of her body and burst the banks of muscle and skin, shooting skyward in a beacon of pure white. The circle erupted in matching white flames, trapping all the Ghouls within its perimeter and rendering them to ash in an instant.

Ghouls outside the circle shrank back in fear, but still too close, were sucked into the flames and consumed. Immense heat hit the trees in a blast that set them afire. Orange flame joined with white, licked down tree trunks and ignited grass and deadfall, sweeping out with unmatched ferocity, even by the Ghouls.

Embers curled high into the night sky, orange stars caught in the wind and sent further into the bush. Spot fires started. Trees exploded. All whipped by changing winds into a roaring bushfire.

The lagoon was eaten up within minutes, the shallow water not nearly enough to prevent its death under the torrent of fire. The circle of white flame extinguished, inhaled into the void of natural fire and snuffed out in a cloud of acrid, Ghoulish air.

———◦◦◦◦———

Bledray mate for eternity.
They live, feed,
and travel in pairs.
They contemplate no other. They need no other.

— Journal of Malaik

———◦◦◦◦———

32

'Moriah, no!'

Jedidiah wrestled Moriah back inside the house. He'd heard the glass door smash over the noise of the tumbler he'd finally figured out how to use and come running out in time to see all hell break loose in the bush below them.

Moriah was wild with anger and grief, and would have joined the conflagration in the bush if he hadn't been there to stop her. Even now, she fought his locked embrace. The mewing sounds coming from her throat ripped him to shreds, but he wouldn't let go, not when doing so meant losing her.

'You'll die alongside them if you go. Moriah, listen to me.' He peppered her with calm and logic. 'We'll have another chance, a better chance.' She kicked, gnashed at him with her teeth. 'Please, Moriah. We can get revenge if we wait … just wait.' He recognised the frisson of change as she attempted to shift and urgency overtook his attempts at reassuring calm. 'Moriah. That much power expended will cripple the Hunter. More of us will come and the Hunter will be useless against us. We will leave her behind in our wake. Please, Moriah. Come to your senses. Going down there only plays into her hand.'

Finally, when Jedidiah thought that his pleas would be nothing more than an empty epitaph, Moriah came round. Gulping air, tears drying, Moriah ceased her fight and stood limp in his arms. He scattered appreciative kisses over her face, relaxed his arms into a gentle embrace and rocked a slow dance of joy that Moriah remained his awhile longer.

When she moved to the doorway, he went with her, and together they watched the brilliant killing flames become a garden of fire.

'I'll destroy her myself,' Moriah said. 'I'll wait a little longer like you said, when the Hunter is weakened and our number reinforced, and then her spirit will be mine.'

Jedidiah ignored the hot tears coursing down his face, the lead weight of his heart in his chest already more than he could bear.

*Harmony of Songs
is the connection,
the pathway they travel from
one singer to another.
Harmony passes through everything, from rock to tree
to beast and bird,
Rydri to Alffür and Bledray*

— *Journal of Malaik*

33

The cave, known as Fisherman's Hut, had been fashioned decades ago out of the rock. On the cliff, so worn with erosion, so beaten by wind and sun, it was hard now to tell if the tiny hut was man-made or natural. A window had been carved out in the seaward wall, the doorway, low and narrow was angled to protect the interior at least a little. Furthest from door and window, a ledge had been cut out, a makeshift bed, seat and table all in one. The black scarring of untold campfires marked the cliff-side wall.

Sanctuary had come in the form of this tiny hole in the wall, a hole too small to fit them all. The women huddled on the bench-seat, Bridget wide-awake now and shivering with shock and fright, surrounded by her friends. The low murmur of their voices drifted out to Rick standing guard outside the doorway.

'We need a fire,' Gabriela said, crouching over the makeshift fireplace and sifting through the remains of previous fires. 'There's enough wood left here to get one started.'

'So start one.' Rick understood the security of a fire and didn't question the fallibility of that security against the Ghouls. 'I'm going up top.' He didn't add that Lael should be back by now. They all knew it.

Anthony straightened from his position leaning against the wall near the window. Dr Morell talked with the women, questioned them on injuries, checked Bridget's temperature and pulse rate. Bridget stared blankly ahead, maybe watching Gabriela with the fire, maybe reliving her experience on the beach. Rick couldn't tell. The doc looked worried though, kneeling in front of her, tapping her knees, rubbing her hands. Nothing could be done until they could get the hell out of there and get her to a hospital.

Ben, engrossed in sprinkling their dwindling supply of powder around the window and walls, didn't look up or acknowledge Rick in any way.

Rick left them to it and, with Anthony following, went up to keep watch for Lael.

'I bet this is real nice during the day time,' Anthony said as they scrambled over the lip of the cliff and crept to the protective shelter of some bushes. 'Scary as hell at night though. What do you think happened to Lael?'

Rick thought it an odd time to be making conversation, but if Anthony felt nervous who was he to deny his relief of tension. 'I don't know,' he answered, unhelpful but honest. 'Let's look around. Keep close.'

Rick scrambled from bush clump to rock, Anthony on his heels.

'Maybe we should split up?' Anthony peeked over the top edge of some crumbling sandstone.

'No, we stay together.' Rick had no intention of facing a Ghoul alone if he could help it. Ben and Dr Morell had only just made it through their encounter and they'd had Lael's help.

They left the safety of the rock to sprint across a flat open section of hardened clay and gravel, skidding to a halt at the edge of the bushes on the far side.

'I can smell those damn Ghouls,' Rick said. 'But I can't tell if they're close or if it's the wind.' He lifted his face to the breeze and was about to ask Anthony what he could see when smoke filled his nostrils and sent him into a paroxysm of coughing.

'Ah, Rick?' Anthony stood, his hand trailing on Rick's shoulder in a forgotten attempt to pat him on the back. 'You know that white fire down by the lagoon? It's changed colour and is heading this way.'

Rick's chest heaved with the need for smoke-free oxygen, but he pushed himself to his feet regardless and then wished he'd stayed down. They must have been protected by the natural fall of the land and unevenness of the cliff top not to notice the line of orange-red fire that tracked a path through the bush, cutting them off from town and beach with only the ocean at their backs. Rolling clouds of smoke and embers lit the sky and cast it with the dull glow of an unstoppable force. And all that was heading their way.

Rick noticed then the scatter of fleeing animals, squawking birds, the rumble of waves, the clamour of the fire itself as if someone had just turned the sound up. Rick thought of Gabriela making fire from pre-burnt stumps in the cave. He'd have all the warming flames he could ask for soon, and some left over to barbecue a few sausages as well. He shook his head from the triviality of Sunday barbecues in the face of being burnt alive in a bushfire.

'We have to find Lael,' he said, determination fuelling strength.

They forgot about discretion and furtiveness and started calling out. In the end, finding Lael was much easier than they feared. Rick tripped over her unmoving foot and fell flat on his face in the bushes beside her.

Sticks scratched his face, more than one tore his clothes and punctured skin as easily as bursting bubbles. But she was there and not moving, and Rick didn't care about anything else.

'Lael? Lael?' He smoothed a tangle of hair from her too-pale face. Anthony slipped his arms under her shoulders to lift her into a sitting position. Her head rolled back on his chest exposing the gleam of her long neck flecked with dirt and soot, awkwardly edged in the fire-stained moonlight.

'Touch her,' Anthony said. 'Put your hands on her bare skin, kiss her, anything, just touch her.'

Rick did what Anthony ordered, too flustered to question such a strange demand. Then he remembered the ferry ride. Was that just this morning? It seemed like years ago that he'd watched as the people brushed by her, bolstering her with the strength of their spirit. She needed some of that strength now. He leaned over and pressed his lips to her lax mouth, smeared his touch across her cheeks, tasted dead ash and bitter smoke. Anthony rubbed her arms, pulled her shirt up and touched his hand to her concaved stomach. Rick could feel and see it all, sense the slow warming of her body as she fed off their willing vitality.

Pleasant warmth tingled across the soles of his feet, covered his scalp and travelled through his body in a yearning to join. A glance at Anthony, at his closed eyes and barely-there grin around parted lips, told him the detective was experiencing a similar phenomenon.

The tingling reached his groin and the pleasant feeling turned erotic. Time to stop before he lost control and Rick directed his feelings into Lael. He sensed that they'd brought her back from the brink of wherever she'd been and rocked back on his heels, forcing himself to break the contact. He stole another desperate look at the oncoming bushfire. The smell of Ghoul mingled with the smoke and charring of bush and animal created a cloying, almost greasy odour. It thickened the air and warned of imminent disaster

'We need to get out of this scrub and get Lael to the others.'

Anthony nodded, a little dazed, and hocked one of Lael's arms over his shoulders. Rick took the other and they carried her toward the cave, feet dragging across the ground.

They almost made it.

There are not enough Alffür left to Guard the vast numbers of Rydri.
There were never enough Hunters to protect us all.
Only combined is there hope.
At the end, we will all come together.
We will have no choice.

— Journal of Malaik

34

'Where are you taking her?'

The woman appeared out of the air in front of them with such suddenness Rick nearly fell to his knees in surprise. Anthony too struggled to keep his balance under Lael's dead weight. Her hair was long and dark, tied in a neat plait that hung over her shoulders, glossy and smooth where it divided into a straight part on top of her head. Her face could have covered magazines the world over, so perfect were her features; from the delicate, arched eyebrows to the pouting lips. She sat, half-reclined, across a sandstone shelf that jutted from the cliff top like a sacrificial altar, long legs crossed at the ankle, one shapely arm languishing along her body, the other supporting her gorgeous head.

Rick hated her on the spot. He tightened his hold on Lael's arm, shrugged her into better positioning on his shoulders and made to walk around the Ghoul.

'Isn't she well?'

Don't answer … don't answer … just keep walking …

A shift in the atmosphere and the sharp pungency that came with it pulled Rick up short. Anthony's intake of startled breath confirmed what Rick knew already. The beautiful woman on the rock had not come alone. A man formed, tall and solid. A shock of black hair fell across his face and he pushed it back with disarming innocence.

'You know, Moriah, I don't think she's well at all.'

'Back, back, go back,' Rick hissed. He started to turn only to find that any retreat had been blocked by the arrival of more Ghouls, some swirling clouds of vapour, others in the flesh. Behind them, the bushfire paled into insignificance.

Rick could hear Anthony whispering to Lael, 'Wake up, wake up!' and could feel Lael making the attempt, her relaxed muscles tensing with the effort. Her feet stopped dragging as she took her own weight. Sparkles of static electricity stung his hands where they gripped her.

When Lael seemed to have enough strength to support herself, even if only partially, Rick let go of her arm and reached for the sack of powder swinging from his belt loops. 'Get ready,' he told Anthony. 'Take her weight.'

Rick plunged his hand into the sack and pulled out a handful of its contents to raise before him like a protective shield.

The woman's laugh shook him to the core.

'What are you going to do with that? Make me sneeze?'

Lael put her hand on his arm. *Go ahead*, that touch told him. *Make the bitch sneeze!*

He opened his hand, the powder sifting down between his fingers, a tiny pile of it in the centre of his palm. 'Gesundheit,' he said and blew the powder from his hand. A river of energy ran from Lael to him and through him, arcing from his open hand and lighting the powder with the same white flame that had killed so many Ghouls at the lagoon.

The woman screamed and vanished behind the flare of light. Rick recoiled from its brightness.

'No, Rick. Run through it. Reach the others and bring them back.' Lael's words sounded in his head as clear as if she'd spoken them out loud and he reacted on their command without thinking. The light singed his clothing and sizzled against his skin but did no further harm. He reached the cliff edge in a few bounding strides, skidded to a stop before he could go right over and dived down the trail to the cave, to be caught by Gabriela on her way up. She shoved him through the doorway.

'They're here … Just above us …' Rick forced words out on blasting breaths torn from his throat. 'Lael and Anthony are trapped … bushfire …'

Gabriela gripped his shirt and spun him around, pushing him ahead and back up the trail, forcing him to his knees near the top and holding him down. 'Sit tight,' she said and crept close enough to the top to sneak a look at the danger that faced them.

Rick's vision was starred with the glitter of Lael's diversion. Outside the flashing lights that felt seared into his eyeballs, everything was black. Rick hoped it was lack of light over the ocean, but his hand in front of his face proved that hope false.

Gabriela ducked down beside him. 'What did Lael do? On second thought, don't tell me. The Ghouls are raging around her and Anthony. I think they're herding them to the opposite cliff. It's flatter ground over there, less bush. We could probably sneak right up to them, use a little of our magic fairy dust and wish them into oblivion.'

Rick shook his head. 'There's too many of them. It's the fire they're scared of more than the powder itself and Lael's power is what ignites the damn fire.'

'So we need fire and we don't have it. We need Lael and we don't have her either.'

Rick wished he could see Gabriela's face clearly, read there what the woman was thinking.

'Well, that's okay, because I just happen to have a packet of matches in my pocket and the Hunter's favourite boy by my side. How could I possibly go wrong?'

Rick felt his shirt bunch in Gabriela's hand, felt himself being pulled along the track. In his eyes, the flare of Lael's fire drowned out everything else. He knew when he was at the top because he tripped over the last step up, landing on his hands and scoring them deeply with sharp gravel. Gabriela snatched him from a fall and half-dragged, half-pushed him, Rick prayed, to the nearest cover and out of sight of the Ghouls.

'What's wrong?' she asked, still holding tight as if sensing Rick was helpless without her.

'I can't see properly. Did you see the fire? I was looking right into it when it erupted.'

'Shit.'

Yeah, no kidding …

'How do they feel? Hot, gritty?'

'What's the matter?' Ben had come up behind them.

Dr Morell pushed past him. 'What is it?'

'He has some flashburn from Lael's fireworks.' Gabriela continued to swear fluently under her breath.

'So how do they feel?' Dr Morell prompted. Rick felt the splash of water on his face.

'A little hot, not too bad. I just can't see anything much past the damn fire.' Water flowed from his face down his neck and soaked his clothes. His eyes filled with it and he blinked, trying to escape the flood. 'Shit.'

'It will fade, but there's no telling how soon. He can wait here and hope the Ghouls don't notice him or you can keep him with you, Gabriela. Which is it?'

Gabriela's answer was to take Rick's shirt again and start moving, telling Rick as she went what she could see.

Rick didn't like the sound of it one bit.

Each Hunter carries with them a relic.
A petrified sliver of the Forked Tree from which all life falls imbued
with a glimmer of that which first brought the Hunters to us.
Forged by lightning and scourged by the fury of the Bledray, the pebble is conduit between worlds and a direct connection between
the energies of Alffür and Rydri.

— Journal of Malaik

35

Shock rooted Anthony to the spot.

'Remember when I said that, but for Rick, you would have been the Chosen One?' Lael sounded much too weak to talk let alone defend against the ravening Ghouls that tore at their eyes and clothes, swirled into fantastic, lurid displays of colour.

'I remember,' he answered her. He also remembered a time when he'd never met her, never knew of evil beings that lurked in the corners of this world, never would have believed that his life would end on a cliff at night surrounded by weird flying things and …

'Concentrate, Anthony.'

'Okay, okay … I'm good, really.' So no, he wasn't really, but saying the words would bring about the action, wouldn't it?

'Don't look at them, take small breaths only. You're strong enough to fight them. You have reserves you've never tapped.'

If you say so …

Lael coughed and the strain of it racked her body. 'The others will come, but we won't have time to wait. Take this and get ready for my signal.' She pushed something small and hard into his hand. It vibrated with energy. 'Hold onto it and don't think about what you're doing. It will all come naturally if you don't think about it.'

'What's the signal?

Lael pushed away from his body, lurched a step before gaining balance and yelled, 'This!' And the night exploded into day.

He hadn't seen the fire in her hands before this, had no direct experience that could prepare him for the sight of her hurling balls of fire into the ranks of the Ghouls. *Stop thinking, you idiot!* He ran after her, ducking the spinning fireballs and shouting out commands and insults. The thing in his hand grew hot and heavy, and when one Ghoul came close with her drooling smile, it emitted a bolt of electricity that struck her head and blew it to pieces. Gore rained over him, sputtered and disintegrated. He held his fist out throwing punches at the Ghouls that rendered them as innocuous as shifting wind over a garbage dump.

Lael staggered under the sheer number of Ghouls, cutting a swathe through them to reach the one issuing orders and screaming abuse. A path was opening up before her though Lael didn't appear to notice, and then Anthony realised: the woman was sacrificing Ghouls to further weaken Lael and draw her to a ghostly altar of rock.

'Be careful,' he yelled out, but his words were drowned in the melee. He shoved aside Ghouls, sent spine-shattering bolts of power through their bodies and vaporised those that shifted forms. He took hits that should have killed him; his legs and arms smouldered and bled. 'Lael!'

She had almost reached the rock, the way now clear and Anthony thought he could at last see her understanding that she had been tricked. Shouts issued from all around, familiar voices, clouds of powder flaring into flame, Ben's voice yelling for Jamie, rising in a world full of pain that threatened to flatten them all.

Anthony could see Ben running, diving, tackling the Ghoul that held Jamie's prostrate form in her hands.

Lael dropped to one knee, so used up now that she could barely manage even that.

The Ghouls swelled, victory incensing them to new levels of depravity. Anthony's fist ached, knuckles and fingers numb and cold. He had no power, he never had done. Lael had been feeding him hers, syphoning off enough for him to defend himself when she needed every drop for herself.

Hands grabbed him. Someone threw a bag over his head, dark and dank, yet pleasantly comforting. He sank to the ground, so tired now he thought he could sleep for a week. Dreams started in his head. He was walking along the beach with Lael. The water was cool on his hot feet. They swam out, further and further until the sea bed sank away. They floated together at first, holding hands, making love. Then sinking into the deep, sinking into forever.

Ben and Jamie circled in the opposite direction to Gabriela and Rick, trying to find a way to Anthony and Lael. The noise was horrifying, the sight of the Ghouls up close in their madness even more so. And behind all that, the approaching bushfire, flames leaping into the air, immolating everything in its path. Ben estimated its arrival at ten minutes, if they were lucky, twenty if God was in a favourable mood. So far it didn't seem like it.

Jamie clutched at his hand like a lifeline, scooting up close to him whenever he paused, running behind him to avoid being left behind when he moved on. She needn't have worried; he had no intention of letting go.

When he saw Lael leap into the middle of the Ghouls and start firing off the same twisting fireballs she'd used to aid their escape earlier, he took that as the sign to attack. The fistful of powder felt like sand in his hand—soft satiny sand warmed under the midday sun. He scattered it as far as he could and, on Gabriela's advice a few minutes previously, lit it with the flick of his plastic cigarette lighter. The fire that sprung up was somewhere between Lael's white flames of pure energy and the spit of a rocket fuse.

Jamie stayed behind him, hissing warnings in his ear as Ghouls came too close, pulling or pushing on his hand to urge him on. She picked up rocks and threw them, hitting a few unwary Ghouls, going straight through others, and Ben wondered why she didn't just use the powder.

He never got the chance to ask as two Ghouls emerged directly in front of him. Jamie pushed him into some low-lying bushes that snapped and flattened under his weight and turned on the Ghouls with nothing to protect her but a handful of pebbles and the dissipating dust in the air. Ben threw up his lighter and she grabbed it, flicking it on and punching fist and flame into the face of the closest Ghoul. The monster screamed and went up brighter than fireworks on Australia Day.

Ben was in the middle of a victorious yell when he realised that the flame had also lit Jamie's hand. Fire danced up the sleeve of her cotton top and she cried out with the pain of it, but she didn't stop fighting. The second Ghoul dived in and she sideswiped it with her burning arm. Ben fought to stand, the bushes tangling his feet. More Ghouls came in, so many now that the bushfire was hidden behind their tumbling mass.

Jamie rolled on the ground, patting her arm and putting out the flame. She smiled at him then, as if to assure him of her safety, and reached forward to help him to his feet. Their fingertips almost touched.

The Ghoul that attacked came from above, soaring in from the direction of the fire, over Ben, and close enough for the stink of her to stay with him for the rest of his life. She crashed straight into Jamie, lifting her from the ground and smashing her into the base of the rocks in the centre of the battle.

Ben screamed and was on his feet, berserk with fear and rage. Jamie lay like a rag-doll in the Ghoul's arms, blood trickled from her mouth, her blackened arm pointed toward him, not moving. The Ghoul cast him a derisive smile and leaned over her, mouth opening wide to take her in. Ben couldn't reach her. Ghouls swarmed around him. He pushed them off. Threw powder in their faces until his pouch was empty and then threw that in despair at the head of the Ghoul taking his Jamie.

He stumbled and crawled, ignored the Ghouls now that petted his face and hair, plucked at his clothes, groped his body. He saw Lael fall, heard someone yell his name, but it was nothing to him. Jamie was alabaster, even the burnt arm had bleached white under the Ghoul's foul touch. He stretched out a hand to her foot, whimpered her name and screamed over and over again as the foot degenerated into dust. The rest of her body followed into dissolution until nothing but the yellow plastic of the cigarette lighter that had lain beneath her remained.

The same Ghoul reached for him, cupped his head in her hand and pulled him to her. He had no power to resist, no thought to run or take up the lighter. Jamie's face shimmered in front of him, Jamie's smile; her hands holding his face, her lips on his. He was happier than he'd ever been.

He died that way.

*The unsworn covenant
keeps the Hunter
to their purpose.
Hunt only in defence
of the innocent.
Kill only to prevent holocaust.*

— *Journal of Malaik*

36

Bubbles of noxious fumes exploded in front of his face. He sneezed into clouds of Lael's powder and slowly his sight returned. Gabriela had hold of his arm, he'd felt the grip like a vice cutting off his circulation, jerking him in one direction then another. Gabriela yelled to duck and he ducked. Gabriela ordered him to drop to the ground and the ground smashed into his body with the speed of a Mack truck. He realised he could see when flashing lights became swerving shadows, when he could duck before Gabriela commanded it and judge the distance to the ground before he dropped.

But it was too slow. Frustration ate at him, the screams of his friends tore him apart. Light now emerged from the shadows, stripes of orange, swirls of white and pink and green. The glittering of his bedazzlement faded to a dull ache that pressed against the back of his eyeballs.

'Oh, my God,' he heard Gabriela say and wondered how many times they could say that before God either smote them down where they stood or took pity and delivered them from the horrors they faced.

'Oh, my God,' he heard again. He stopped thinking of God and started on what it could be that reduced Gabriela to three such useless words.

The swirling, mutating lights settled into a pulsing single light that illuminated the altar of rock the beautiful Ghoul had lay claim to. She stood there now, shimmering through a waterfall of cleaning tears and the shutter/click of his eyelids. The hair had come free from its binding, frizzed around her head in a bloody halo. Her boyfriend, the black haired bastard, sat at her feet, arms folded and a doting expression on his face.

Good, I can see faces …

Rick shifted his gaze from the two Ghouls to the figure heaving with exhaustion below them. Only Gabriela's hold on his arm stopped him racing straight in.

'Lael can look after herself for a bit longer. We've got to help Anthony.' Gabriela dragged him around to face him and slapped him across the cheek when he didn't respond. 'Anthony needs us now, Rick!'

Rick staggered under the loss of support and dizziness caused by his returning sight. He watched Gabriela duck and weave a way through the Ghouls, her bag of powder bobbing against her hip. *Must be empty* … Rick still had his. He squeezed it between his fingers, thin and near empty, but enough of a volume to give him confidence. He would save it. He would help Anthony and then he would go after Lael.

Anthony lay motionless beneath the writhing body of a red-haired Ghoul, unaware of the hands that held him in close embrace, the legs that pinned him to the ground … the mouth on his face searching in grotesque likeness of sexual need and response.

Gabriela threw herself into a flying kick that would make any martial artist proud and knocked the Ghoul away from his feast. The Ghoul howled and made to attack, assert his right to the kill. Gabriela picked up a rock and smashed it into the side of the Ghoul's head, crumpling it like papier mache and, if not quite killing it, at least rendering it immobile for the time being.

Rick slid in beside her, calling Anthony's name, shaking his shoulders and patting his face.

'Where's the doc?' Rick asked, searching the cliff top for her. 'Where is she?'

'She's gone, Rick.'

Rick quaked at the finality in Gabriela's voice, denied what it told him.

'Gone where? We have to get her back here.' Rick would have gone to find her, would have run through the crowd of Ghouls to bring her back for Anthony.

Gabriela stopped him.

'She's dead,' she yelled, impatient, grieving and scared shitless.

'Ben?'

Gabriela shook her head. She didn't know.

Rick looked around for him and saw only Ghouls. Ghouls and Lael kneeling in their midst with head bowed and chest heaving. Moriah, the exquisite porcelain-faced Ghoul, stepped down from her altar, approached Lael with guarded movements, circled her, and ran a finger over her shoulder.

Shit! Rick took Anthony by the shoulders and started shaking. 'Wake up, dammit! We need you here with us.' Gabriela's arm was again holding him back, warning him to be careful. Rick stopped shaking, drew one hand back and slapped Anthony across the face.

'Rick!'

'He doesn't have time to wake up on his own.' Rick made to slap him again and this time Gabriela did stop him.

'Water,' she said and started wriggling his back.

'I don't have any!' Didn't Gabriela see how urgent the situation was? Jamie, and probably Ben, gone. Lael pushed beyond her limits of endurance and at the mercy of the Ghouls!

Gabriela dropped her backpack between her knees, ripped it open and pulled out a bottle of water. She opened it with a savage twist and poured its contents over Anthony's face. Rick started shaking him again, gently this time, and calling his name over and over. And even though it felt like hours were passing, in truth, Anthony woke spluttering and fighting within seconds. Eyes opened blank and Gabriela pushed wet hair away, patted his cheeks, smoothed over eyebrows … 'Come on, come on …' She held his hands, rubbing them, clapping them together. 'Come on.'

Life returned to Anthony's eyes in a flood of energy that started at his feet and rushed upward, muscles contracting and flexing, back arching, hands clenching into fists, head snapping back and up, Anthony sitting even as the flood reached his brain.

Rick and Gabriela hurled him to his feet, holding him upright and steady as he found his balance and strength.

'What's happening?' he asked, his eyes wide and blinking. 'Where are we?'

'We're on the cliffs in the national park, remember?' Gabriela told him.

'We've got to get him up to speed and moving,' Rick hissed to Gabriela. 'Walk while you talk. I want to be out of the direct vision of that main Ghoul.'

'Anthony, you and Lael were fighting the Ghouls. One jumped you. Do you remember that?'

'Think so.' Anthony's feet stumbled over each other as Rick guided them to the shadows to the side of the Ghouls.

The Ghouls had stopped paying attention to them. Each had eyes fixated on their apparent leader and Lael. They hummed with excitement. Rick could see it in their rapt faces. The smell threatened to cripple him, sweeter than a hundred different perfumes mixed in a wooden vat that something had died in.

Above them the aurora of light returned, a pathway to the heavens on rolling, rippling waves of hue. No rainbow could compete, no artist's rendition could hope to capture the beauty of the sky at that moment. The light fell to the ground, washing over the edge of the cliff, spotlighting the bushfire now only metres away.

The Gathering was happening right now.

Rick had forgotten all about the fire.

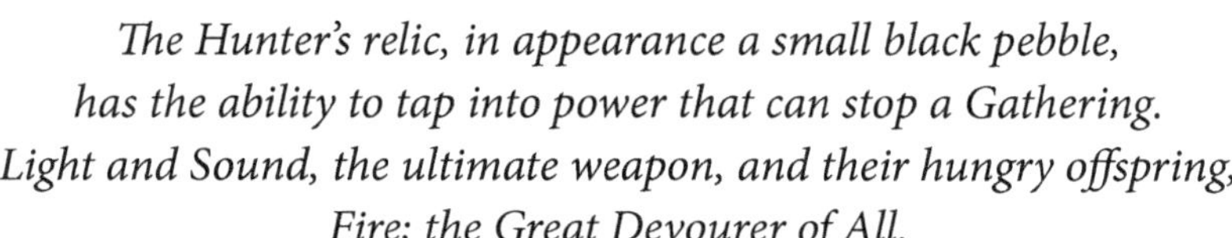

*The Hunter's relic, in appearance a small black pebble,
has the ability to tap into power that can stop a Gathering.
Light and Sound, the ultimate weapon, and their hungry offspring,
Fire; the Great Devourer of All.*

— Journal of Malaik

37

Anthony vomited; water and bile and not much else splashed over Rick and Gabriela's shoes, and stained the grey rocky ground black.

The three sank down. Gabriela filled Anthony in on what had happened, though Anthony looked more concerned with his protesting stomach.

'We can't wait any longer,' Rick said.

'What the hell are we going to do? Do you see how many of them there are now?' Gabriela turned to face the ritual happening at the foot of the altar.

Anthony stared at his open hands and started patting his pockets, searching the ground. 'Where is it? Where is it?'

The heat of the fire pushed the smell of the Ghouls around the cliff in a billowing fog of green-tinged smoke and vapour. Wind-warped trees and bushes joined the rest of the park in the burning. In the distance, sirens wailed, and Rick took comfort in the proof that they weren't the only humans left this side of Port Hacking. The shuttering chop of blades and the buzz of high-altitude engines brought the welcoming knowledge that helicopters had been despatched. No doubt to check on the fire. Rick wondered what would happen when they came in sight of the cliffs. If he could hear them, surely they must be close.

Anthony was on his hands and knees, sifting through the dirt. 'Where is it? I need it …'

'Forget it, Anthony. We've got less than a second to come up with a plan of attack.'

'Use the fire,' he mumbled. 'Take them down with the fire.'

Rick couldn't tell if Anthony really knew what he was saying, but the idea was sound anyway. He still had some powder left …

'You looking for this?' Gabriela faced Anthony, one hand outstretched, holding a small black pebble. 'You dropped it after we kicked that Ghoul off you.'

Anthony snatched the pebble and closed his fist around it. 'Fight them with fire,' he said again, and shuffled behind the makeshift altar and across to where fingers of flame reached out for every scrap of bush they could find.

Rick chased after him, following his lead when he saw him breaking off burning branches. He snapped off one for each hand and then passed one of those to Gabriela.

'They're not watching us at all,' he said, yelling now over the roar of the fire. 'I've got enough of the powder left to lay a thin ring of it around the Ghouls. If we let the bushfire do the job of lighting it, we can get into a better position for attacking.'

'We should stay together.' Gabriela's face stiffened, the flickering light made her appear more Ghoulish at that moment than the Ghouls themselves.

'I'll do it while they're fixed on Lael and that head bitch, be quicker and quieter alone. You keep watch from here, maybe get yourself a stack of sticks and branches ready.'

'I don't like it.'

'Gabi, what's not to like?' Rick didn't really like it either, but no better idea was coming to him and Gabriela and Anthony looked equally blank.

'Do it,' Anthony ordered. 'Lael doesn't have much time.'

Rick ran off, shoulders hunched, and set a tattered line of the powder as close to the fire front as he dared go. They had minutes only, he figured. Minutes to kill a thousand Ghouls, rescue one Hunter and dive down into the relative safety of the cave, assuming, that the cave was still the sanctuary they'd be needing.

His back ached, nose and eyes ran from fumes and smoke, but at last he returned to Anthony. Gabriela squatted on the ground filling her now empty pack with as many rocks as she could find. She checked the weight of the bag, added another two rocks and hooked it over one shoulder and under her arm so that the rocks were accessible.

'While they're flesh and blood,' she said. 'They hurt like flesh and blood. Anthony's little boy toy still hasn't woken up.'

'Hopefully, he never will.'

Anthony swivelled his head around, eyes searching for meaning in their words and Gabriela pointed to the far side of the clearing where one Ghoul lay broken and bleeding. He had to shake himself away from staring at the body and remembering what the Ghoul's touch had been like. He paled again, as much as anyone could in the weird light and beneath a thick layer of grime, and looked with relief at Gabriela's rock collection.

'I'm all out of powder,' Rick told them, dropping the empty bag to the ground.

'I have some.' Anthony opened his bag and took out the last small handful he had left. He shared it out between the three of them, dumping small piles of it on their heads and shoulders, smearing the residue left on his hands up and down their arms. He seemed determined to get as much mileage from the stuff as possible.

'Take my hand,' he told Rick, not waiting for Rick to agree, but taking it anyway. 'We need to go into this together. Don't ask me why, trust me. Gabriela, you watch our backs, hit any Ghoul that comes too close, use them for target practice if you have to, just keep them off our backs. I don't know if this'll work …' His voice petered off into indecision.

Faced with torture and certain death, Rick didn't blame him. He entwined his fingers with Anthony's and whipped out a yell so loud the closest Ghouls broke from their daze.

Anthony and Rick charged into their ranks, white fire sparking from their hands and the thrilling song of battle on their lips.

<hr>

Gabriela, less than a stride behind them having taken the fraction of a second she needed to bend down and fill her free hand with burning branches, cursed fluently, the words coming out in a hot stream of defiant menace.

She felt like a berserk warrior, an Amazon warrior plunging her mighty sword into the bodies of the enemy. *What I wouldn't give for a sword right now!*

Rick and Anthony were drawing power from who knew where. Anthony's fist, boosted by whatever power that tiny pebble held, smashed into heads, broke arms and, when enveloped in the vaporised form of the Ghoul, cracked like lightning, turning the vapour into dust. Incoherent words tumbled from his mouth, orders and commands familiar by tone, but otherwise foreign to Gabriela's ears.

Sparks emitted from the two joined hands and Gabriela remembered how flammable the powder was. She threw her sticks into the twirling mass of Ghouls at the same time as the bushfire reached the outer circle Rick had planted. The world exploded into brilliant jewels of white and blue and orange flames. Gabriela's sticks landed on a patch of dried out groundcover and the fire flared up in the centre as well.

A Ghoul hovered over Rick, solid arms protruding from a globulous form. Rick seized its throat and squeezed, somehow forcing it to form into full human shape. Gabriela cracked its head open with a rock.

With a circle formed of fire and centre pyre for dying Ghouls, something new started to occur. Under the sound of Gabriela's wild yells and threaded through Anthony's strange imprecations came a new voice. Lael's song encompassed grief and joy, bitter loss and sweet gain, and in some odd way matched the roaring intonations of the fire at their backs.

In her words came the sound of all things, not in individual description or imitation, but the entire pulse of the world. Rick thought it the most beautiful song he'd ever heard and released the Ghoul he'd been about to smother. Behind him, he heard Gabriela exhale a breath that must surely have lifted a weight from her chest. Anthony let his hand drop, not moving or making a sound, but standing with lips parted, his face, beneath a day's worth of beard and dirt lost in wonder. His shoulders rocked. Rick couldn't tell if with laughter or tears.

Lael's head remained bowed yet her voice grew stronger. The Ghouls too, affected by the song, stood confused. Those who'd remained unformed drifted down and reshaped themselves human with the first touch of their feet on the earth.

Rick moved forward, out of the triangle of safety the three had formed. He had to reach Lael, had to be with her and could feel her need drawing him to the altar. She sang now of love and passion, of coupling and children. Images of their one night together suffused him with remembrance, prickled his body with heat and longing.

He bumped into Ghouls as if they were no more than gawking bystanders, ignored Gabriela's unconvincing warning not to get too close. What else could he do?

The bitch on the altar, he no longer thought of her as Ghoul or woman, stood looming over Lael, her face striped with moving orange-edged shadows, trapped in the same mesmer as the rest of the Gathering.

Rick growled with certain victory. He would walk in, take Lael from under her and leave. The cave offered them all the safety they would need and the fire would take care of everything else.

His hopes collided with reality when the black-haired Ghoul, the bitch's partner stepped forward, kissed her on the cheek and said, in words as dry as sandpaper, 'Don't listen, my love. That's not our song she sings.'

The entranced expression left her face to be replaced with something far more evil; anger, hatred and hunger combined. She put a finger under Lael's chin, forced her head up and slapped her hard enough to knock her sideways. Lael's song faltered, her voice breaking before restarting the song, kneeling again, blood oozing from her mouth.

'No!' Rick's voice sounded distant, pushed through a wadding of cotton wool in his mouth.

A ring of Ghouls closed in around the bitch and Lael. Their arms linked against Rick as they swayed from side to side and started their own song. It matched Lael's in perfect harmony, a haunting melody that sickened Rick with its beauty. How could such ugliness know beauty? How could evil be filled with such love? He shoved against the barrier they formed, kicked and hit, and railed at their backs.

The bitch reached down, took a handful of Lael's hair and pulled her in close. She whispered something to her and hope lightened his heart as he saw Lael struggle in her grip, saw the white fire sizzle in her finger tips, but it wasn't enough. The bitch laughed, forced Lael to stand and threw her up the rocks to the altar. Lael's head hit a ledge, bounced once and she lay as still as dead.

Rick broke through the arms as Lael was picked up like a sack of potatoes and thrown again, this time over the top of the flat rock that formed a natural altar to the sky. Rick couldn't see her face, but the limp hand dangling over the edge of the rock bed, and one loose leg swinging free was enough to tell him that she lay unconscious.

Someone clutched at his foot and tripped him. He kicked them away and scrambled to his feet, arms cart wheeling to find balance. He reached the incline up to the altar as the bitch sat over Lael's body, her boyfriend holding Lael's head. She looked asleep, taking a nap, her face absent of the strain of the last few days.

The Ghoul doubled over, laughed, hot and sultry, and covered Lael's mouth with her own. Rick couldn't scream or cry. Time for any such attempt had vanished in a puff of Ghoulish vapour. He reached the altar, pulled his arm back and blindsided the Ghoul with all the strength he had left in his body. She screamed, a wild banshee call, and reached out with taloned hands to take Rick's throat. Rick locked his hands around her wrist tugging at it, but failed to stop her digging her clawed fingers deep into his flesh. He felt his larynx go, slices of pain shooting into his face and neck, could almost feel his lips turning blue. His vision swam and became a confetti of bright twinkling lights fading to black on the edges. Rick couldn't escape that grip and knew that even if she released him now, he would still go forward, attack her again and again until she lay dead on the ground.

He floundered, as Lael had floundered. The Ghouls reformed the circle he had broken and renewed their chanting song. Lael had failed. He had failed. The Ghouls had Gathered and defeated them all. Surely the time to give up had come. Rick forced his eyes to see and reached out to touch Lael one last time.

Her face was turned toward him, her eyes opened and black, staring at him and then past him as she smiled. An explosion came from somewhere behind, voices yelling. The chanting disintegrated into confusion; someone pushed something into his hand. The bitch Ghoul rocked back on her heels under a shower of rocks and an empty backpack. Burning branches started flying through the air. One hit the black-haired Ghoul across the back and he staggered, still keeping his hold on Lael though his hair ignited.

'Do it now, Moriah! Don't stop!'

'Jedidiah?' She loosened her grip on Rick and he wrenched free, falling into a heap at the base of the rock.

'Now, Moriah!'

Moriah bent down to renew her kiss. 'Hunter,' she whispered. 'May your journey to the void be long and painful.'

Lael's face disappeared under the gaping maw of the Ghoul's mouth. Rick clenched his hands together in a giant fist, Anthony's mysterious black pebble cutting into his palms, and raised up from the ground like an avenging angel, double-fist high above his head. Incapable of speech he still opened his mouth to yell silent obscenities as he brought his fists down in a crashing, hammer-blow to the back of the Ghoul's head, snapping her neck, pushing her down onto Lael.

Her body shimmered beneath Rick's blows, white fire sparked from his bloodied hands. Lael arched her back, raising so high that only her head and one heel touched the ground. A white ball of light ruptured inside her, sent a wave of thrusting light outward in a flat cutting sheet of energy that decimated the Ghouls and dropped them where they stood. Shafts of light shot into the sky, lighting the clouds brighter than the sun. The Ghoul shuddered, pinned to Lael by the light that pierced her body, close to death. Lael bucked again, head hitting the rock with sickening thuds, feet scraping its hard surface and gouging. Teeth clenched together in a death grin, Lael reached out to Rick, taking his hands, still locked together and holding them solemnly.

The light pulsated growing hotter and roaring now with the

release of confined power. The Ghoul, Moriah, died with one helpless shudder then another. Her partner, Jedidiah, lay cut in two, head engulfed in flame.

Lael pushed Rick's hand to the light. 'Do it,' her eyes said.

Rick did.

The hunter's strength is borne of sacrifice and sense of purpose.
Their role is to stop the Bledray and protect the growing race of Rydri.
Yet they too need help
and protection.
The Song of the Alffür sends strength when it is needed most,
on the vibrations in the air,
the first breath of the living,
the last breath of the dying.

— Journal of Malaik

38

Lael could feel the others come to her, hear the murmuring of their voices as they sat in their distant circles and sang words of power; words that gave her strength and vision, words that would see her on her way. She understood now the circle they were all caught in, Alffür and Bledray; Guardians and Ghouls, and the secret knowledge that separated them. Somewhere along the line Guardians had fallen in love with humans, somehow their need to protect had grown until human fate and Guardian mixed. Hunters were born from the sacrosanct melding of the two races, out of the holocaust of a Gathering.

The face of the Ghoul swam in front of her, but had no real meaning. Lael's throat contracted with the instinctive need to gag, but she did not turn from the lunging mouth.

Tonight, her fate was sealed. She would no longer roam the earth; at last, she would find peace and be settled. But it would not be easy; even now the balance teetered between rebirth and destruction. She must find a final modicum of strength within her dying body. Rick, his death tightening around him in a black noose, must also find enough within himself to resist the Ghoul.

The song of the Guardians rang loud in her head and she joined in, feeling the joy of fulfilment course through her. Power banded around her middle, throbbed as the Guardians increased the potency of their song and burst from her in a brilliant blasting release that sent Lael into a rigid spasm. Every muscle locked tight, her teeth snapped together, she tasted blood and fire, felt new life stirring inside her, life destined to free her and become the new Hunter.

She saw Rick hesitate, knew that he too understood what was being asked of him, being offered him. Her heart contracted at the damage done to his body, the pain he suffered for her, but turning back had never been an option. Lael took his hands, fingers mashed and broken, and brought them into the light, pleading with her eyes to make the final sacrifice.

He did it without blinking and they were released together.

*The Alffür will eventually
vanish from this Earthly plane.
Their lives are long:
alternating between
physical and ethereal,
but they are not immortal.
Neither are the Bledray.
Hope lies in the ability of
Guardians to protect
and share knowledge
and Hunters to quell Gatherings.
Yet even in times of trouble,
in the midst of a Gathering,
a new Hunter may arrive.*

All they need is a single light.

— Journal of Malaik

39

Anthony heard and saw, and couldn't react. His legs and arms felt disconnected from the rest of his body. His head buzzed, ears rang; the action in front of him—Rick running, fighting, breaking through—came to him from a narrow tunnel of vision.

Gabriela saved him, woke him from the daze as she ran by throwing every rock she'd collected, brandishing more flaming sticks. Anthony could have sworn that seconds previously Gabriela had been caught in the same hypnotic state. He raced after the reporter with nothing in his hand but the black pebble. Not nearly enough without either Lael or Rick to spark it into life. He leaned down and swooped up one of Gabriela's burning branches and belted it across any non-human body part he could find.

The Ghouls were coming out of their daze with Lael's song broken and voice weakening. Three attacked Gabriela and Anthony set on them with his branch, sending embers flying with each slam of stick against Ghoul. He looked up when Gabriela roared loud enough to pause the Ghoul's attack and Anthony felt like matching the horrible sound with one of his own.

Lael had been dragged up to the altar rock, unconscious, the Ghoul astride her. Rick hung from the Ghoul's grip, arms and legs twitching, dying. Gabriela's ferocity grew as she swept through the back line of Ghouls to reach those in front, singing in an arc between her and Rick. She exploded into them, hacking at linked arms, bashing heads and finally broke through. Anthony slipped through beside her, tripping over the uneven ground, clambering unbalanced up to Rick. He pushed the pebble into Rick's hand, closed limp fingers around it and prayed that it would work for Rick as it had for him.

Fingers locked into Anthony's hair and dragged him backward, throwing him through the air to land flat on his back with a harsh whoosh of air from his lungs. He lay there trying to remember how to breathe, to force his body to move. This was worse than the trance, at least, then he couldn't feel anything. Pain radiated from his back to his front and into his hips. He concentrated on Rick and Lael, and slowly made it up to his knees and no further, trapped now in the last seconds of his friends' lives.

Rick stood with arms raised over the Ghoul. His fists were bloody, shirt sleeves charred and torn. The Ghoul lost shape, reformed and appeared to melt around the edges with a spluttering sparkler-like effect. Her partner, hair on fire and hands holding onto Lael, cried, in pain or loss, Anthony didn't care. Fire spread from the Ghoul's hair to his clothes and flowed down to his legs. It reached out for Lael from arms shrivelled and scarred with the liquefying remains of skin and muscle.

Anthony felt new concern for Lael, unconscious and with fire only a breath away. He stood on shaking legs. A new sound came to him, mingling with the fire and the Ghoul's, and his own wretched breathing. A choir on the wind, deep-voiced and welling with emotion, grief he recognised, and something more than that … abiding love, and then a current of electricity surged up from Lael, balled into a seething mass of power and burst upward, straight through the female Ghoul's body. Gabriela turned and ran to Anthony, crash-tackling him back to the ground as a sheet of that same power pushed outward, killing every Ghoul it touched, shearing heads from necks, torsos from waists and scattering them in a foul graveyard across the cliff.

Anthony groaned and pushed Gabriela from him. She groaned in turn and shook her head. They sat and looked to see the damage done to Rick, in time to watch as he plunged his fists into the light shafting upward to the sky.

The light inhaled on the sighing voices of the choir, sucked back into the bodies on the rock. All sound went with it. The flames of the bushfire battering at the ring of white fire seemed to lean toward the rocks; the whole world concaved on a breath, paused, and then gushed out in a ferocious torrent of spewing light and energy. The Ghoul was turned to dust. Lael and Rick vanished. Anthony threw up his arms to protect his face and was pushed down once more by Gabriela, backhanding and rolling over him so that his back bore the brunt of this new explosion. Gabriela screamed, hollered and cursed God, but the rush of wind and renewed roaring of the bushfire carried the sound away and Anthony couldn't hear, was barely aware, as he watched the world burn.

The bushfire flared over them, the floodgate holding it in check now gone. Anthony knew he should worry, should probably think about getting Gabriela and going back to the cave. He tried not to think about Lael and Rick, immolated surely, as the Ghouls had been. He wondered how long Lael had known that she wouldn't survive this Gathering? If she knew that Rick would sacrifice his life for her …

Only the sparse clumping of bushes kept Anthony and Gabriela from burning up with everybody else on the cliff top. The flames leapt the gaps in vegetation as handily as a child skips over stepping stones, finding new sources of fuel in the grasses along the cliff edge and the bush that stretched for kilometres along the coast. The white rocks were scarred black, the thin layer of sand swirled in rising eddies and covered bodies, trees, and rocks alike with a veneer of ash.

'Rick!' Gabriela called, terrified for her friend. Calling out even though she knew that Rick must be dead.

The column of light shone brilliantly, tinted with surges of orange at its base and pure white as it met the night clouds. Shafts of the light lit the clouds from within, others reflected down in a luminous rendition of divinity over the water. Brown smoke drifted from the cliffs and out over the water, but had no effect on the light.

The Ghouls that remained were dark scabs of charcoal dispersed across the ground in random patterns. Gabriela leaned on Anthony and compelled herself upright. It was entirely possible that she'd fractured a few bones, she could almost feel them grinding against each other. She gritted her teeth and prevented an undignified collapse to the ground by digging fingers into Anthony's shoulder and locking her arm into position. When her balance had returned enough to stand on her own; she let go of Anthony and moved forward.

Rick and Lael were gone, not a mark or sign of their presence left behind. Gabriela approached the rocks on buckling legs, trembling so hard her teeth chattered. On some level Gabriela knew she must be going into shock. *Deal with that later …*

Groaning from behind told her that Anthony too had made it to his feet. She heard the Thwump! Thwump! of helicopter blades and wondered how long it would be before rescue came. The fire had moved on, its red trail cresting over the hills, scouring the southern cliffs and leaving behind a dark, ember-studded stain of destruction.

Except here … The fire had bleached the rock white and brittle, and yet no heat radiated outward. Gabriela reached to touch the light with shaking fingers. *That's about the dumbest thing I ever heard …* Lael's voice sounded clear in her head and she snatched back her hand, looking around for her. Could she have been wrong?

'What is it?' Anthony shuffled up beside her.

'I thought I heard …' Gabriela shook her head. 'No, couldn't have.'

'They're here.' Anthony stared straight into the fiery column. 'In there. But I wouldn't touch.'

'Don't be rid—' Gabriela followed Anthony's gaze. The brightness of the light hurt her eyes, but when she squinted and looked right into the column, two shadowy shapes could be seen. 'Rick?'

The figures moved with each other, making it hard to tell if it was really Rick and Lael or just a trick of light and shadow on over-taxed retinas. No voice came to her, no profound insight. The shapes swirled and separated, one grew larger, appeared to reach out, the faint outline of a hand appeared as if pushing on a window or wall. She knew it was Rick, knew he was okay and this was as close as they'd ever be again.

'What do you figure happened?' Gabriela's voice wasn't much more of a soft growl, her abused throat too raw to emit anything louder. She looked away from the light and at Anthony instead.

Anthony, the detective obsessed with missing people, hard-nosed and obdurate when he had to be, stood there with tears tracking a path through the grime on his face.

'Sshhhh. I think we're about to find out.' Shadows flicked across Anthony's face. His dirty lips pulled back to show white teeth in an awed smile. 'This is it,' he whispered.

The light was going. Fluttering now, drawing in on itself like a candle at the end of its burn time. Gabriela read the coming changes in Anthony's face and turned one last time to watch the single beam of light.

Rick's shadow stood beside Lael and for a fraction of time, Gabriela could see them both outlined, arm in arm, eyes only for each other, then the sharpness faded and their two shadows became one.

And the one stood resolute amid the dying light, and when the light was at last gone, stood there still, strong, black-eyed and with the questing vision of a Hunter.

———◦•◦———

Birth and death cycles do not exist in Alffür philosophy.
The circle rules all, from the Tree to the leaves that fall
from its branches.
The circle is yesterday, today, and tomorrow.
As such, Alffür are not born;
they arrive.
They do not die;
they follow their path.
The forked tree grows
one circle at a time.
We are all leaves on the same tree.

— *Journal of Malaik*

———◦•◦———

40

Sirens echoed below the ridge, red lights flashed from vantage points on the houseline, more dipped and rose in the valleys of the park, following the fire, powerless to do little else.

Choppers with spotlights crowded the sky, gawking at the devastation below. Slashes of light crossed and re-crossed the cliffs, hovered over the group of women and men in a huddle waiting for rescue and dashed off only to return and hover a little more.

Anthony tried not to think about how many times they'd been filmed and commented on, how much speculation they were the focus of. Two paramedics darted from person to person, checking for injuries, chatting casually while asking pointed questions and providing feedback to whoever listened in on their radios.

The younger of the two paramedics treated the women, all in varying stages of shock, for smoke inhalation. They sucked in oxygen and coughed out crap. They stayed together holding hands or just touching, not saying much, their soot-stained and dazed faces telling all that was needed to know. Anthony doubted they'd be walking much further than their own front yards for some time to come.

The second paramedic, older and all business, splinted one of Gabriela's legs, buried the other under a mound of instant ice packs and told her not to move. Looking as done in as a person could get and still be conscious, she didn't argue.

Anthony couldn't tell if the bruised hollows under her eyes and in her cheeks were actual bruises, signs of exhaustion or more of the dirt that camouflaged the rest of her body. Her hair was the most telling of all, Anthony thought. Clumps standing on end tangled with twigs and leaves, and glued together with … Anthony ran a hand through his own hair and grimaced when it came away sticky and damp with blood and some other coagulating mess. He wiped his hand on his trouser leg and promised himself an hour-long scrub when he got home and a shopping trip for new clothes after that.

Any moment now the medic would come to check on Anthony. A full-body cast seemed a good idea at the moment. Head to toe support for head to toe pain. Even his hair hurt.

Only the stranger appeared uninjured, though he had yet to utter a word of who he was or where he'd come from. Anthony and Gabriela had asked—Gabriela full of suspicion and not trusting that the man wasn't a Ghoul. The man didn't seem to comprehend the questions and Anthony doubted if he understood his current state of being either. His gaze was deep, but unfocused. Encompassing, Anthony imagined, of much more than the trivialities presenting themselves on this lonely cliff. The paramedics had skirted around him, sensing perhaps the otherworldness of his stare, more likely though, too busy with those who needed their help.

Anthony knew the stranger was no Ghoul. The light was different. Like Lael, his presence was dimmed and unobtrusive. The only obvious oddness about her had been the whole astral dreamscape thing she'd been able to command at her will. *And the white fire …* The Ghouls had been much more brash, rippling with stolen life and corrupted because of it. Then there'd been the smell that had nearly crippled Rick several times and of which Anthony had merely tasted. That had been more than enough.

The Paramedic, finished with Gabriella for now, tapped him on the shoulder. Anthony lifted his head in pained query.

'Where does it hurt?'

Where does it not? 'Head to toe,' Anthony answered, supplying a grin, which, yes, hurt from ear to ear. 'Just call me one big bruise, give me drugs and we'll be quits. I'll promise to go visit my doctor in the morning or as soon as I get out of bed, whichever comes last.'

The paramedic tugged Anthony's shirt up over his chest and pushed a stethoscope against his skin. 'There's some congestion there …'

'Yes, well I was caught in a fire.'

'… and a lot of bruising around those ribs. How about I strap those ribs for you, stick you on the chopper and send you off to hospital? A nice doctor will give you drugs and a bed, and you don't have to bother your GP.' He stuck his hands inside the shirt and pressed carefully around the ribs.

Anthony nearly bit his tongue trying not to cry. He couldn't help the tell-tale jump though and the paramedic smiled as if getting Anthony to admit he needed him was the highlight of his day.

'Don't be an idiot, Anthony and do as you're told. If I've got to go to hospital, you can bloody well come with me.' Gabriela, Anthony decided, was obviously grumpy when in pain.

He considered complaining and then gave it up when the stranger shifted closer to his side and rested a hand on his back.

'Oh, okay. You win! I'll go.'

The paramedic's smile widened and Anthony considered the possibility that he'd had no choice from the start. *Kind of like this whole experience ...* He lifted his arms as high as he could, hardly at all, and let the man wrap padding and a broad bandage around his chest.

A crunching of bushes came, the straining whine of an engine and red 4WD emerged from the darkness. *Not that dark ...* Anthony looked over his shoulder and saw the brown-grey of dawn. The night had passed into history. *Too bad no one will know it.*

The 4WD stopped at the edge of the clearing, the track it had followed now wider for the experience. A fireman in yellow overalls and a white helmet climbed out, waved to the paramedic and then was drawn back to the cab of his vehicle by the squawking of the radio. He disappeared behind the dash and reappeared holding a receiver in front of his mouth. He answered the squawking with mumbling and muttered something to his partner who had still to exit the vehicle. Anthony watched and listened with numb fascination.

The paramedics, faces showing their concern, helped the women stand and shift over to the truck. One of the group stopped and turned to Gabriela and Anthony. She looked pale and frightened still, strands of long hair pulled free of the rough ponytail she'd secured it in, framed her face. Anthony thought she looked beautiful, a tragic heroine who'd walked through fire, almost literally, and come out the other end tougher because of it.

'You two gonna be okay?'

Anthony, one arm now strapped across his freshly wrapped ribs, struggled to stand. *Oooo, bad idea! Painpainpainpain …* The woman helped him up, though he hadn't seen her move toward him, and steadied him when he would have fallen. He blinked at the dizziness in his head and nodded at whatever she was saying to him though the words were a blur.

'… and we might not see you again, so we just wanted to say thanks for your help.' The static in his head cleared to let the jumble of words string together. He started to nod again and then thought better of it.

'You can't tell,' he blurted out though it hadn't been what he was going to say. 'Not about the … things and not about what happened here. I mean … you can't …' *Shit, someone turn the dial to 'transmit' and let me speak …*

But the woman must have understood. She guided him closer to Gabriela, helped him down. 'We won't. We talked about it in the cave. Who would believe us anyway? Hell, I'm not even sure I believe it and I was right there.'

Another came over, blondish, though it was hard to tell under the dirt. Hair, face, arms and clothes all seemed painted with the same charcoal brush.

'Wendo, we're going,' and then to the men, a hand on each, 'You two look after each other, and your friend …' She nodded her head toward the stranger, but kept her eyes on them. 'Anyone can see he's special. Look after him too.' She stood and left, hugging the woman who'd stayed with the truck and ushering her into the cabin.

Anthony looked after them, wishing suddenly that he was in their circle of caring. A hand tapped his shoulder, cupped it and pressed to get his attention. 'Wendo' had eyes that were deep and dark, and could probe every corner of his mind. He felt laid bare under her regard. She shoved something in his hand, curled his fingers around it. 'Your friend, Jamie, she left this with us in the cave. We only used a little, around the door like magic dust.' Her eyes pooled, she dipped her head and took a steadying breath. 'We didn't see what happened up here. We stayed in the cave the whole time. We saw the fire coming, met up with you and your friends, you guided us to the cave and that's where we stayed. If anyone asks, that's what we're going to say, we didn't see anything.'

'Thanks. We're sorry for what happened.' Gabriela propped herself up on one elbow. 'If your friend needs us …'

'We'll find you if she does. Be seeing you … or not.' She stood then, with a smile that chased the seriousness away, and jogged over to the 4WD, waving as she climbed in beside her friends and slamming the door closed.

Gabriela looked at the pouch still half-full of powder and all but collapsed on the ground, her face wrinkling in pain.

With that powder Jamie and Ben might have survived. But they didn't. They were gone, like Rick and Lael were gone.

They are slowly learning; Miaheyyu is not a single being but a collective wisdom. Miaheyyu is not a god, but a catalyst for life.

— *Journal of Malaik*

41

The fireman stood, hunched and grizzled from a long night's work, at the edge of the cliff that overhung Fisherman's Hut. He'd lived in Bundeena most of his life, fished from The Balconies to his right when he was younger, explored Tumbledowns with his kids and, later, his grandkids. He'd fought fires all through this stretch of the park, driven the fire trails, risked his life every single time, and seen death close up more than once.

Reports were that more people had been on this cliff than were rescued from it. Several were believed perished. Yet no bodies were found. He'd heard the official line come over the radio: hotter than usual fire caused by extreme El Niño drought conditions and wind shifts had destroyed all remains.

Yeah, right … No bushfire burned that hot.

He scratched his chin and remembered the riot of colours that had flared over the entire cliff and the tower of light that came after. He'd been watching through binoculars back at the houses, fire hoses snaking at his feet, his crew bellowing out commands and counter-commands. He hadn't needed the binoculars to see the single light that shone out in the dark, his eyes weren't that bad yet, but they had lent him enough vision to witness the shadow that stepped from its centre and became a man.

He kept that to himself. The fireman was not given to flights of fantasy or denial. A fire was a fire, a man was a man, and he'd seen what he'd seen.

And now, his overalls stiff with dried ash and soot, boots caked with white clay and his helmet hanging loose in his hand, he waited above the cave.

The path down to it was narrow and right on the edge. One wrong step and he'd be wet splatter on the rocks below, yet native grasses lined it, a few hardy and determined scrub bushes formed a guard against the dangers of gravity and humans' inability to fly, and people rarely took that one wrong step. *Lucky as hell, most people, and they didn't even know it.*

A head appeared; dark hair, olive skin, black eyes, followed by the body it was attached to, long and lean. Shoulders strong enough to carry a burden, hands steady and sure as they found holds on the rock wall, legs and feet that didn't falter as they found their way upward.

The fireman watched him come, acknowledged the stranger with a curt nod and reached out to shake the hand being offered him. The touch reassured him that helping this man and keeping it to himself was the right thing to do.

'You need a lift back to town, mate?' He jerked his thumb over his shoulder to the 4WD parked a few metres away.

'Thanks, I would,' the stranger replied, sounding like he hadn't used his voice in awhile. 'Do you know where the two who were flown out of here were taken? I'd like to catch up with them before I move on, tell them a few things they need to hear.'

'I can find out. They friends of yours?'

'We have a mutual friend.' The stranger stared at the pile of rocks behind them. Flat on top, almost level with the rest of the cliff in one spot, they'd been cut out of the sandstone by wind and rain over thousands of years, and turned into a natural altar. The sandstone was ribboned with yellow oxide at its base that faded into pure white crystals about halfway up.

'Strange goin's on here last night, ey?' The fireman slanted a look at the stranger that took in the rock formation central to the light-show he'd witnessed. 'Don't see those auroras around this area much.' Truth was never, but the fireman had learned a certain amount of circumspect stoicism over the last fifty or so years.

'Bad fire,' was all the stranger said, though his face paled and his hands betrayed a tremor that didn't match up with his casual stand.

The fireman nodded his head. *Bad fire, all right.* 'Let's get going then if you're ready, before people start to wonder where I am.' He dumped his helmet back on his head and walked back to his truck.

The truck, like him, was a mess and he'd have to wash it when he eventually got it back to the station, and if that wasn't soon, he'd be up shit creek without a paddle and a whole pile of bullshit to make up. He swung open the driver door and slid into the seat, shoving his key in the ignition, turning it and closing the door in one easy pattern of practiced movement.

The stranger slid into the passenger seat with only slightly less ease.

'So you got a name, pal? Not that I'm gonna go blabbin' it anywhere, but just for m'own peace of mind. I don't get to see fully-grown men materialise in shafts of light right before my eyes too often. Kinda would like to be able to put a name to the first one. Give me some kind of reference point for the next time.'

The stranger laughed and the fireman grinned in response. He liked the sound of it. He checked the rear vision mirror, checked over his shoulder and pushed the gear stick into reverse, planting his foot on the accelerator and ignoring the grunt from the engine and jerk of the truck. When he had the truck turned and pointing back along the fire trail, he shifted it into neutral and stuck out a hand. 'My name's John.'

John's hand was grasped in a firm grip and lifted in a no-nonsense shake. 'John?' the man tested out the name, smiling wide on the last sound, happy with the result. 'My name is David.'

*There are groups of Rydri that are closely connected to
The Way.
Those that live closer
to Earth,
that recognise and acknowledge
Earth's life force.
They remember and
live the Circle
as it is meant to be lived, and remember the stories
and songs from the past.
The Alffür and Miaheyyu live in their songs too.
We are all from the same tree after all.*

— *Journal of Malaik*

42

Rick's funeral had been desolate, or maybe that was the burgeoning guilt she felt for having been unable to save her oldest friend. Gabriela stared up at the stormy sky. Clouds heavy with unreleased rain rolled over each other, parting to show streaks of sunshine and distant blue and then crashing together with ominous yet impotent ferocity. It hadn't rained in months. Soon though, Gabriela knew, by Christmas …

Anthony stood behind her, shoulder rubbing against Gabriela's as if to offer succour, or at least keep her upright. She'd foregone the hospital prescribed crutches in favour of a walking-stick and had yet to perfect the balancing act the change required. Gabriela tried not to lean too much on the shorter man. After all, Anthony too was convalescing.

Annie hovered nearby wanting to help but not knowing how. Something had changed in Gabriella over the last few weeks. She didn't think there'd be any going back.

The women had come, the three that had been trapped by the Gathering and huddled, terrified, in the cave. Eyes red-rimmed, they had passed by with whispered words of condolence and gentle touches of remembering. Anthony murmured something appropriate back. Words couldn't push through the growing ache in Gabriela's throat.

A priest intoned the funeral liturgy. Gabriela had forgotten that Rick was Roman Catholic though this was hardly a traditional ceremony, the formal church rites foregone in favour of simplicity and fresh air. Gabriela reminded herself how much she hated funerals and why, as the first sods of earth were dropped onto the empty coffin. Her eyes burned, filled and overflowed with tears that remained unchecked. She figured she owed Rick that much. If she couldn't save him, at least she could cry for him.

Days came and went, nights loaded with unwanted dreams, before Gabriela ventured back to Rick's house. She wandered from empty room to empty room. All of Rick's belongings had been packed up and sold, or given away to charity. The computer had been emptied of files and dumped at the tip. Rick had lived in this house a long time, memories filled every room, walked paths across the patchy lawns, hammered nails into falling down walls, laughed in the kitchen, told secrets in the bedroom.

She missed him, and had woken in tears more times than she cared to count with the echo of Rick's cynical laugh in her ears. She'd commiserated with Rick's widow several times since the funeral, though the couple had hated each other long before death had separated them with such final permanence. Rick would be laughing, if he knew.

Dr Morell's funeral had been only slightly less painful than Rick's. Confused parents wailing, fellow doctors darting furtive glances in between tears, black-suited detectives watching everyone from behind dark glasses in the rear of the chapel.

She didn't go to Ben's. Heard a memorial service had been held in the Territory somewhere. Maybe she and Anthony would swing by sometime soon.

Gabriela kicked at nothing on the floor, gave the wall an apathetic punch and made her way to the front door.

Harry Stanton hadn't got his front page exclusive. The case of the missing body had eventually been filed away with all the other unsolved cases. No one else took any notice of the whole 'blood thing' or appeared interested in the crime scene that was Bellbird.

And Bellbird? Gabriela closed the front door and locked it. Rick's house had been sold to the government, along with all the other properties in Everline Street, destined to be knocked down and allowed to return to the bush. That or they were planning a highway. Gabriela neither knew nor cared. She and Anthony had been back to Bellbird a few times in the months since Rick's death. It remained a closed town. Coincidentally perhaps, around the same time as the raging cliff top battle, a bushfire had raged through the area and turned all the houses to kindling. Now, the road was so little used that slabs of bitumen had cracked and separated, forming dangerous gullies. The next good rain would wash half the road away and Gabriela thought that couldn't happen soon enough. Bellbird was less than a ghost town and would remain that way. It seemed fitting somehow.

A car horn sounded and Gabriela turned, waved and started jogging down the path. Glad that she was now past the need for walking aids and able to move faster than the limping gamble she'd worked so hard to leave behind. The leg still hurt though and Gabriela winced as she reached the car.

David had visited her in hospital, hung around while broken bones mended, helped out with the physio after, done the same for Anthony and then disappeared. His presence had given her story a more believable air when she'd finally told Annie everything that had happened since her move to the nation's capital.

It had been hard convincing her to return to Canberra. Even harder saying goodbye.

Anthony had gotten wind of people going missing in Far North Queensland. He'd dreamed of lights and strange fires. Gabriela had noticed a certain rotten smell in the air of late. They'd spent the time since their hospital release searching for Guardians and finding none.

Last week, a postcard had come from the Barrier Reef with no message, just a single solid 'D'. The time had come to rejoin the Hunter.

Gabriela opened the car door and folded nearly double into the bucket seat.

'Did you have to get something so small? A woman needs room to stretch a little.'

'This is all that was available, I told you that already. We'll upgrade in Newcastle.' Anthony shook his head and turned the ignition key. He'd had a buzz cut while in hospital and kept it that short ever since.

'Don't see why we can't just fly to Queensland. It's an awful long drive.'

'Some things I want to check out along the way.'

'Well, let's get ourselves gone then.' Gabriela looked back at Rick's house as Anthony pulled the car out into the street. She could see Rick standing there, plain as day, with a wide laughing smile and waving goodbye, like he'd done so many times over the years. Gabriela squinted, let the memory roll on and then grinned when she saw Lael standing beside him. Serious, stern Lael laughing as if all her tomorrows had come at once.

Maybe they had.

Anthony turned the corner and Gabriela's view of the house faded. *On a lonely cliff surrounded by fire and death ... everyone's tomorrows had come.*

Epilogue

'And peace on earth will last for a thousand years or more?'

Lael sent Rick a squint-eyed look that told him not to be a smart-arse, and kept walking.

'We should be so lucky, I suppose?' Rick stopped walking and looked out over the valley that fell in neat folds before him. A river wound through it, black and silver, narrow and rocky in sections, wide and smooth in between. He could hear laughing, children playing, and birds, and music being played. He'd already passed by some kangaroos and some deer, and a wombat with a dignified if somewhat baleful stare.

'I thought, when I saw this place before, that it was someone else standing beside you, not me.'

Lael looked over her shoulder. 'And now?'

'If this is Heaven, bring it on.'

Lael laughed and the sound dropped over him with all the coming home comfort of a mug of hot chocolate on a winter's night. *Bring it on and keep on bringing it on …*

'We'd have to have died to make it to Heaven,' she said. 'And that's a whole other story. This is Home, just another place, a shift in time if you like. Earth, but not.' Lael waited for him to catch up and laced her fingers between his. 'The world as you don't know it.'

'There are more things in Heaven and Hell, Horatio?' Rick asked, squeezing her hand in his.

'Infinitely more, Hamlet. Infinite and full of possibilities.'

Sydney Morning Herald, 23ʳᵈ November 2015

BREAKING!
Tragedy as bushfires bypass one town, but razes the next!

The town of Bellbird this week was completely destroyed by out of control bushfires raging down the coastal bush areas south of Sydney. It is not known yet how many residents have lost their lives, but hopes dim as reports filter out of a village wiped off the map …

Acknowledgements

I would like to take this opportunity to thank fellow Odyssey author, Tracy Joyce, who is always available to offer practical advice and pushed my first novel at markets all over Victoria. Thanks also to Michelle Lovi, editor and publisher at Odyssey Books, without whose support and enthusiasm for new authors, I would not be writing these acknowledgements in the first place. Finally, I would also like to thank my sister Kathy, my extended collection of parents—John and Sue, Sandra and Phil, Tom and Shirley—and close friends Michele, Karen, Lyn and Lynne for lifetimes of support, interest and love.

About the Author

Patricia Leslie is a Sydney author with a passion for combining history, fantasy, and action into stories that nudge at the boundaries of reality. Urban fantasy is the ideal genre for exploring alternative history and Patricia does just this in her debut novel, *The Ouroboros Key*; a contemporary quest story set in the Rocky Mountains of Colorado. Her second novel, *A Single Light*, leaves known history behind, and joins fantasy with beach and bush south of Sydney where the mild seeming landscape becomes the setting for a potential world-altering event. Walks through the bush will never be the same again!

Patricia is a visual writer and dedicates time to exploring locations and allowing snapshot scenes to run through her head before combining them together into one story. She is also a dedicated, some say compulsive, reader and collector of books.

www.patricialeslie.net

www.ingramcontent.com/pod-product-compliance
Lightning Source LLC
Chambersburg PA
CBHW051258210726

48287CB00002B/563